THE BLACK OWLS

An Oxford Nightmare

by

ALAN THOMPSON

THE BLACK OWLS An Oxford Nightmare © 2013

All rights reserved by Patrick Thompson

A-Argus Better Book Publishers, LLC

For information:
A-Argus Better Book Publishers, LLC
9001 Ridge Hill Street
Kernersville, North Carolina 27285
www.a-argusbooks.com

ISBN: 978-0-6158638-7-0
ISBN: 0-6158638-7-6

Book Cover designed by Dubya

Printed in the United States of America

For my bride who, having twice shouldered the burden, still smiles

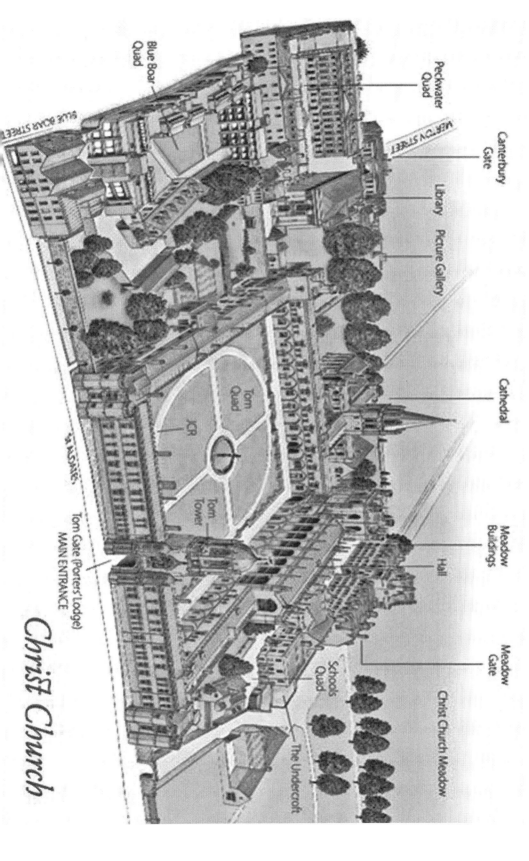

Christ Church

BOOK ONE

There they lay, those multitudinous and disparate quadrangles . . . negligible beneath infinity. And new, too, quite new, in eternity; transient upstarts – Sir Max Beerbohm

Aylesbury

A GREAT roar rent the silence of the cold Buckingham night, and timbers and stones and remnants of furniture in place for centuries rained down from the sky. Moments later, the Duke of Aylesbury – Tony Markham to his intimates – met the servants on the path. His clothes were torn and dirty, and his right arm hung limp at his side. "They've blown up the church," he said. "And they nearly had me." He approached the manor house where his sister, a long cloak wrapped around her body, stood in the doorway. He brushed past her and entered the Great Hall.

Inside, he let his eyes rest first on one object and then another, icons of the family who had resided there for more than four hundred years. How much longer would they last? When would the Markhams of Aylesbury Abbey, and the country that they had served for so long, submit? He smiled. The rest of Britain might be resigned to its fate, but he would go down with colors flying. The destruction of the ancient church and the chapel where he and the twelve dukes before him had been baptized was regrettable, but it was just the most recent salvo.

She followed him into the room. "What happened? What's wrong with your arm?" She reached for him, but he turned away.

"They've bombed the church and the chapel. I was just outside the door." He walked down a passageway to the telephone. When he returned, she had removed her cloak. Despite the hour, she was still fully dressed. "Where've you been?" he said.

"I was walking in the garden." He stared at her. She gazed back, her face without expression.

"And Cromwell?"

"Asleep, I suppose."

"He slept through that blast?"

She ignored the question. "What are you going to do?"

"Just what I've been doing. They'll have to kill me to shut me up." He paused. "But I believe I'll call in some reinforcements."

Annapolis

I DESCENDED the steps of the big white house on Captain's Row, turned right and walked to the corner of Blake and Buchanan Roads. I was five minutes early. Loitering, I wandered through the Superintendent's garden, its hedges and beds and walkways overlooked by verandahs and dormers with blue and white awnings. The sudden cold had erased the color – only the near-blackness of the hollies and boxwoods remained. Three minutes later, I turned into the circular driveway and approached the gleaming Beaux Arts mansion. A marine wearing a white cap, khaki shirt, and blue trousers with a red stripe down the side was posted behind a wooden podium next to the doorway. The marine saluted. I returned his salute and identified myself: "Commander St. Cyr. I have an appointment with the Admiral at 0900 hours."

The marine, who had admitted me to this house dozens of times over the past year, remained expressionless. "Yes, sir. He just called. He's expecting you."

I passed through the door, climbed a short flight of stairs and emerged into a wide two-story foyer lighted by an elaborate crystal chandelier. I crossed the hall to the Admiral's office and knocked on the door. A gruff voice responded: "Come in, Commander."

I entered the room, closed the door and advanced to the desk. Three feet away, I stopped and drew my body to rigid attention. Raising my hand to salute, I said, in a clipped military voice so unlike my own, "Commander St. Cyr reporting as ordered, sir." The pungent aroma of the Admiral's pipe aggravated my nose.

The slight, balding man behind the desk looked up at me, a smile playing on his lips. "Stand easy, Fitz," he said. "This isn't about last night."

"Thank you, sir." I allowed my body to return to its normal posture, relaxed but alert.

The Admiral gestured toward a leather armchair in front of his desk. "Have a seat." I pulled the chair back to make room for my legs and lowered myself onto the cushion, shoulders and arms and elbows spilling over the sides. "I had a call from the Chief this morning," the Admiral said. "He wants to see you today at 1400 hours." He paused. "Here – not the Pentagon."

"Did he say why?"

He shook his head. "The Chief of Naval Operations doesn't have time to explain himself to me, Fitz, even if we *were* roommates forty years ago. I guess I should be flattered that he called me himself."

I frowned. "I'm an English teacher. What does he want with me?"

"You and I may think you're an English teacher now, but the Navy doesn't see it that way. They look at all that training and education, which cost hundreds of thousands of dollars –"

"Shoved up my ass a nickel at a time."

He smiled. "Yes, just like the rest of us. They see all that – talent, and they want to make use of it." He paused. "I told you when you came here that it might not last."

"I'll resign my commission. I don't need the Navy."

"Fitz, you don't even know what he wants. Hear what the man has to say before you resign."

"I have a class at two o'clock."

"Get somebody to cover it. Or cancel it. You have to be in this office at two o'clock."

We sat quietly. "Is there anything else, sir?"

"No. I believe that's it." I rose and saluted, and turned for the door. "Oh, Fitz, there *is* one more thing."

"Sir?"

"My daughter tells me that she proposed to you last night. Thanks for turning her down."

I departed Buchanan House by way of the front door, and walked past the chapel and the administration building to Maryland Avenue. The trees were red and yellow, and the first leaves were beginning to fall. I raised a half-hearted hand to the marines standing guard at Gate Number Three and passed from the jurisdiction of the United States Naval Academy into that of the City of Annapolis, Maryland. I made my way along the narrow sidewalk to State Circle, turned south, and entered the morning silence of Harry Browne's. A bouquet of beer and tobacco reached my nose. Seated in one of the high chairs at the bar, I said, "I'd like a Bloody Mary, please."

The man behind the bar turned around, eyebrows raised in mock surprise. "Are you still here?"

"Very funny. Just make the damn drink."

Harry Browne's was a refuge. The house on Captain's Row was far more than I wanted or needed – I occupied about ten per cent of its porches, bedrooms and baths. In typical Navy fashion, it had been assigned to me not out of necessity but because it was suddenly vacant and I was the highest-ranking officer looking for a place to live. It was not a home — like many things in my life, it was only temporary. Accustomed to a lack of permanence, I was not reconciled to it, and Harry Browne's had afforded an irregular sanctuary ever since I graduated from the Naval Academy.

The first Georges St. Cyr came with Lafayette in 1777. They landed in South Carolina at Georgetown, a hundred miles north of Port Royal, and joined the American forces two months later. In the interim they had enjoyed the lavish hospitality of Georgetown, Charleston and Port Royal. St. Cyr fought bravely at Brandywine and Monmouth, and participated in the siege of Yorktown, and he stood by Lafayette's side at the British surrender.

When Lafayette returned to France, his friend stayed behind. The fledgling United States of America, short of cash but long on real estate, offered him his choice of the vast acreage up and down the Atlantic coast. Recalling the pleasant days in South Carolina before the fighting started, he chose land at the southernmost tip of that state – several of the sea islands clustered between St. Helena Sound and the Broad River, and twenty-five acres in the heart of Port Royal, a town that had lived under Spanish, French and British rule since its founding in 1562. When his father died, Georges renounced his right to the property in Brittany – and the title that accompanied it – in favor of his younger brother who, in turn, furnished him with a substantial income and the funds necessary to build the chateau in Port Royal.

Ladies of sufficient beauty and charm being in short supply in Port Royal, he spent most of his time in Charleston. His refusal to at least pretend to propriety exasperated his relations on the other side of the Atlantic, especially his mother. In the face of her threat to cut off his allowance, he finally agreed to marry the girl that she had selected for him before he left France. A very lapsed Catholic himself, he had joined Lafayette in part to escape her oppressive piety, but the possibility that the money might stop caused him to recall her in a more favorable light. Thus was sown the seed of the conflict that had destroyed my family almost two centuries later.

Harry Browne looked at his watch. "Starting the day a little early, aren't we?" I didn't bother to respond.

I gazed into the mirror over the bar. There was a mirror behind me, too, and the images reflected in the glass – the bottles and clocks and Harry and me – were replicated endlessly, ever smaller and less significant until they disappeared. The dwindling reflection pleased me, and I was loath to alter it.

Harry slid the Bloody Mary across the scarred wooden bar. We had entered the Academy together twenty years earlier – in July, 1959 – but Harry had bilged out before the end of the first summer. A local boy, he had applied on a whim, he said, because he wanted to test himself, and when he quit – just before the Brigade returned for fall classes – it wasn't because he had failed. "I can't think here, Fitz," he said the day he left. "And even if I could, it wouldn't matter." He had walked a few blocks up the street and sought admission to St. John's College, whose culture was the direct antithesis of that of the Academy. He flourished there but when he graduated he discovered that the ethos outside his cloister was closer to that of the Naval Academy than St. John's, and he had wandered for a time. When an uncle died and left him the little bar on State Circle, he found his true calling.

Our friendship had been forged in the crucible of plebe summer, the miserable combination of mental and physical abuse that serves as everyone's introduction to the Academy, and it was sustained by our love of books, especially those that had defined Western civilization before it became unfashionable. Only the evening before, we had had a spirited debate over the purported symbolism not discovered in the works of Herman Melville until twenty years after his death. Harry sided with the revisionists while I, whose appreciation for *Moby Dick* had been irrevocably sabotaged at prep school, believed that they were charlatans more interested in their careers than Melville's book.

I pushed the empty glass back across the bar. Harry hesitated, then slipped it into the soapy water in front of him and reached for a clean one. "You're still teaching over at the boat school, aren't you?" I glared at him. "Seriously, they'll jump your ass if you show up drunk."

"I appreciate your concern. Thanks."

"You're welcome." He filled the new glass with ice. "That was a good-looking woman with you last night."

"She's a baby, Harry. And she wasn't with me." He stared at me for a moment, then turned his back and finished making my drink.

Gillian French was the Admiral's daughter. Only a couple of years out of college, she had come to Annapolis to serve as his hostess after her mother died. Small and fine-boned like her father, she had not inherited his demeanor – a fiery temper that lurked just beneath the surface required little to become manifest. The only child in a Navy family that had been stationed around the world, she seemed to relish the relative permanence of her father's last tour of duty. A widower myself, I was a useful man at Buchanan House, always available to escort ladies without men and, since Gill's arrival, I often found myself escorting her. It was pleasant duty that had become more complicated of late.

I had just paid my always understated tab when she appeared at the door accompanied by one of the Academy's most notorious libertines, a marine captain attached to the Commandant's office. It was apparent that Harry Browne's was not their first stop. Gill had insisted that they join me at the bar despite the captain's efforts to seat her at a small table in the window. I ordered another drink and prepared to wait him out. Neither of us was in uniform but our hierarchy remained and, after several fruitless attempts to re-direct her elsewhere, he had conceded the field to me.

As soon as the door closed behind him, I rose and said, "Let's go home." Without waiting for a reply, I called for my new check and pulled the wallet from my hip pocket.

"No."

"What?"

"I said no. I don't want to go home."

"Gill, it's almost midnight. I –"

"I don't care. I'm not ready to go home. You can't just run the man off, God knows why –" She stopped. "Why did you?" I didn't answer. "Anyway, I'm staying." She turned her glass up. "Barkeep," she called, "another Brandy Alexander."

Harry shifted his eyes to me without moving his head. I hesitated, then resumed my seat. He picked up a bottle of brandy and turned to the blender. "I didn't run him off," I said.

"Yes, you did. He was intimidated like everyone else."

"Why didn't you go with him?"

"Because I wanted to stay here with you. And drink," she added as Harry set the glass before her.

Approaching Buchanan House an hour later, I could see the lights still on in the Admiral's office. When we reached the top step, the door opened. "Good evening, Commander."

"Good evening, sir."

The Admiral turned to his daughter. "Gill?" She looked up, her head tilted slightly. "I'll take it from here, Fitz." He took her arm. She released her grip on my elbow and crossed the threshold. The door closed.

"AT EASE, Commander." The Chief of Naval Operations rose and moved from behind the Admiral's desk. He stopped in front of me and held out his hand. "It's good to see you, Fitz. It's been a long time."

I tilted my head and looked into the other man's eyes. The Chief was one of the few men in my experience that I had to look up to. "Yes, sir," I said. "Not since the funeral."

He looked down. "Yes," he said softly, "I guess that's right." He remained in his bowed posture for a moment, still gripping my hand, then turned to the other man in the room. "This is Sir Geoffrey North, the British Ambassador. Mr. Ambassador, Commander Georges St. Cyr."

North approached, hand extended. "I'm happy to meet you, Commander."

"Thank you, sir."

The Chief walked to the door. "I'll be going now. Take care of yourself, Fitz." After nodding to Geoffrey North, he passed through the door and closed it behind him.

Surprised, I turned back to North. "Let's sit down, shall we?" he said, moving toward a round work table surrounded by low club chairs. "Why did he call you Fitz?"

"My middle name is Fitzpatrick, sir." The man's scent, some kind of wood or leather, was almost overpowering.

"Of course. The American penchant for fraternity and informality." He managed a thin smile in an effort to moderate his distaste. I remained silent. The Ambassador cleared his throat, obviously unenthusiastic about his errand. "I've come to ask for your help, Commander."

I was surprised again. Requests for "help," especially from another country, came down through the chain of command. I glanced toward the door, wondering if perhaps the Chief, or even the Admiral, might still join us. North followed my eyes and smiled again. "This is not a formal request from my country, Commander, nor is it yet a matter of military concern. The President knows about it, and your Chief knows about it, and now you will know." He paused. "And that's all." He stopped again. "I should tell you that I personally disagree with the decision to – to appeal to you in this way. If our government requires that a task be performed, there are no quibbles. It's done. It seems that you are to be given a choice."

"You're not very good at asking for help, are you, Mr. Ambassador?" He flushed. "I'm a professor of English Literature. I suspect that your request has nothing to do with my academic expertise. I have no idea what the President thinks, but I imagine that the Chief was reluctant to *order* me to do something that's no longer in my job description." I rose. "And the fact is, I wouldn't do it anyway." I turned for the door.

"Wait." North stood and walked toward me. "I'm sorry." He looked down at the floor. "You're right. I don't want you involved. It's our affair and we should handle it, but I've been overruled. And I'm aware of your – credentials. It *does* require your expertise, though God knows we've more than enough English professors." He smiled wearily. "Please. Hear me out. I believe you'll want to help us." He returned to the table and sat down. After a moment, I joined him. "Thank you." He withdrew a handkerchief from his breast pocket and wiped his brow. "A bomb exploded two days ago. We believe that it's the same organization that blew up *Victoria.*"

"*Victoria?*"

"Yes. And a friend of yours was nearly killed in this latest attack." I had stopped listening. The image that I had created because I couldn't bear the reality moved from its privileged location on the edge of my consciousness and displayed itself right before my eyes. I saw the horrific explosion and the great ship disintegrating, and I saw her, composed in death, slipping beneath the waves. I closed my eyes. I knew that the truth was far worse, but I had never permitted myself to imagine that. I heard North's voice again. "I say, a friend of yours was almost killed."

"Who?"

"The Duke of Aylesbury. It was he who demand – requested that you be involved. Under all the circumstances, the Prime Minister decided that we could do worse – I mean, that you would be welcome to help with the investigation."

I smiled to myself. The Duke of Aylesbury had been an important part of the best years of my life. "Is he okay?"

"He's alive and largely intact, but he has lost the use of his right hand."

We sat without speaking. Tony Markham's right hand was very important to him. I recalled the only time we fought, in the Long Gallery at Aylesbury Abbey. We were alone when we started, but by the time the final touch was acknowledged all of the other guests and several of the servants were there to applaud. "What happened?"

"The church at the Abbey has been destroyed. His Grace was there at the time." North paused. "There is evidence that it was the work of the *Victoria* bombers. And we have reason to believe that they have plans for more."

The ruined buildings at Aylesbury Abbey were more than eight hundred years old. The Abbey had been built by exiled monks, stolen by Henry VIII during his purge of the monasteries, and given – along with thousands of acres of rich farmland – to one of Markham's ancestors. Despite their wealth, his quietly Catholic family chose not to maintain the church and other monastery buildings – the politics of religion in England was dicey for centuries – except for the chapel west of the nave. We had stood together one evening, looking at the red ball of the sun framed by a lancet arch over the remnants of the church.

Other arches supported by massive columns, and windows in thick stone walls stood on either side of us. The floor was carefully trimmed green grass, and the ceiling was the open purple sky. "We were never kings," Markham said, a wistful smile on his face. "We should have been." The chapel had been preserved for over four hundred years. The family's most precious heirlooms were displayed on its walls and floor.

"Was the chapel destroyed, too?" The Ambassador nodded. "Why would a group of terrorists bomb a ruined church?"

North shook his head. "We don't know. The Duke thinks they were trying to get him."

"Why?"

"He's been quite outspoken on the subject of Muslim immigration recently – foolishly so, in my opinion. He gave a speech in the Lords last month that seemed to stir things up. It looks a bit of overkill to me, but that's what he thinks."

"What about *Victoria*?"

"Whoever bombed the church is now taking credit for *Victoria* as well."

We were quiet. The only sound was the swinging pendulum of the Admiral's clock followed, after a time, by chimes announcing the hour. "What do you want me to do?"

I GAZED at the cobalt Tiffany window over the altar. Its depiction of Christ, face radiant, walking atop the waves of the Sea of Galilee had once brought me peace. Now its imagery disturbed me and, in the agony it aroused, I saw another face, the face of a girl with raven hair and eyes as blue as the water in the window. She would not approve. She would grant me the purity of my motive – she had always done that – but she would deny the righteousness of the retribution that I sought. Violence was evil and revenge was worse, regardless of the reason for it. I sat back in the pew. A few minutes later, I stood and turned for the door.

Another girl was seated at the back of the chapel. She was young and fresh, and her vermillion hair framed features that were nearly flawless. The mouth was perhaps a little too wide, and the dark brows against the pale skin a trifle overbearing or – maybe not. She scorned the mannequin's tricks. The barest makeup touched her eyes and lips, and the brows were not plucked. I reached the last pew and stood looking down at her, silent.

She turned her head. "You are the rudest man I've ever known."

I smiled. "How come?"

"I've called you five times. You never answer the telephone."

"Maybe I was out."

Gillian French shook her head. "I can see your house from my window. You were there." She paused. "You knew it was me."

I reached for her arm. "Let's go outside." She rose and we passed through the chapel's heavy bronze doors. At the bottom of the steps I said, "How about a cup of coffee?" She nodded. We turned right and walked the few paces to Dahlgren Hall, once the Academy's armory, now its only cafe. Inside the door, I pointed to the staircase. "Let's sit upstairs. You find a table and I'll get the coffee."

I joined her a moment later. The balcony overlooking the hardwood floor was deserted. "I didn't have any trouble finding this table," Gill said. "Does anybody else ever come up here?"

I laughed. "No. That's why I like it." I looked over the railing. "They used to hold the fencing matches here, and the finals of the boxing tournament." I sat down across the table from her and sipped my coffee.

"I didn't mean to interrupt your – prayer," she said. "I'm sorry."

"I wasn't praying, exactly." I stopped. "It's a good place to think. The chapel was a refuge when I was a plebe, and I guess it still is."

"But I found you anyway."

I laughed again. "I wasn't hiding from you, Gill. Honest."

She reached across the table and touched my hand. "Dad told me that you had resigned. I thought you liked what you were doing here."

"I do, but – there's something else I have to do."

"What?"

I hesitated. "It's really too complicated."

She frowned. "When are you leaving?"

"Tonight."

"Where are you going?"

"England."

"England? Why?"

"I can't really say. It's – it's an opportunity I can't turn down."

Gill frowned again. "I don't understand this. It's not like you to just abandon your students and your work." She stopped. "Something's wrong. What is it?" I shook my head but didn't respond. "You know I want you to stay." I remained silent. "Say something, damn it."

I laughed. "Thanks. It's nice that someone cares about my comings and goings."

"Nice for you maybe." She stood up and I rose as well. "I know what I want, St. Cyr, and so do you." She put her arms around my neck and kissed me hard on the mouth – her scent, roses, reached my nostrils. Surprised, I embraced her awkwardly and she took the opportunity to press her body against mine. Then she stepped back. "But I'm not a patient woman. Don't stay away too long."

London

MARKHAM BUCKLED the soft body armor around his torso and pulled a black sweater over his head. A black leather jacket, purchased specifically for this occasion, completed the ensemble. He looked in the mirror. The effect was bulky, top-heavy, not unlike the muscular body of his youth. He made sure that each chamber of the revolver had a bullet, and slipped it into his pocket with the rest of the tools. He considered his preparations. The man he would meet in a few minutes was a coward who didn't hesitate to hide behind women and children, but he had grown careless in the bosom of a culture that refused to call him what he was. The guards would be only in the obvious places, though precautions were still necessary. He had much to do, and he would not permit it to go undone because of his own carelessness. He left the house in Belgrave Square and turned north.

It was a moonless October night in the great city, and the fog that lay thick on the ground added to the anonymity of the evening. Entering Hyde Park at the southeastern corner, he continued north and emerged at Cumberland Gate. From there he proceeded along North Row to Audley Street where he paused before the seedy grandeur of the old church. It was just past 2 a.m., and the Mayfair night life was reaching its crescendo. As the herds of people passed by, he caught snatches of conversation in a number of dialects, none of them English. The cancer was spreading, even to the toniest parts of town, and the genesis of the affliction lay inside St. Mark's Church.

St. Mark's was a Greek Revival structure built during the short reign of George IV when the pews of the Anglican Church were spilling over. Squeezed between newer buildings, its portico, columns and tower seemed forlorn and empty among the Mayfair bustle, but looks were deceiving. It had served the parish well for a century and a half but five years earlier, in 1974, the London Diocese – in vernacular that only a cleric could love – had declared it "redundant." The real word was "abandoned," and St. Mark's wasn't alone. The Church itself had been abandoned and it was the clergy – Archbishops, bishops, vicars and curates – who led the way. The great religions of the West were all in retreat, and the vacuum was filling up with another, one whose dogma permitted none of the quaint, mannered debates that marked what was left of modern-day Christianity. His own sect had once been possessed of the same mindset, and its adherents had fought the Muslims for centuries. The Prophet's followers had been held at bay and then diminished, but they bided their time and now it appeared that their time had come.

St. Mark's Church was a metaphor for the weary capitulation of England's so-called elite. The Black Sheik and his acolytes, sensing that no one would stop them, had simply seized and occupied the old building. After much dithering by the City and hand-wringing by the Church, they had been "permitted" to remain, though everyone understood that the imprimatur of Church and State merely confirmed a reality that neither was prepared to contest. The church had been stripped of everything Christian. The pews, the lectern, the chancel were gone. Only the pulpit, from which the sheik exhorted the faithful every Friday, remained. Another quarter of London, this one perhaps more symbolic than others, had been ceded to the enemy.

Because the church was enclosed by buildings on three sides, there seemed to be but one way in and one way out, and that path was heavily guarded. The thugs who protected the sheik were where they had been on Markham's earlier visit – lounging on the broad steps leading to the portico from Audley Street, and undoubtedly stationed again in the long, narrow narthex and galleries overlooking the nave. Markham, however, after a visit to the offices of the Mayfair Conservation Area, had found another way. A closed, gated passage from Balderton Street, a block east of Audley, led to the crypt beneath the church's stone floor. The entrance to the crypt had been sealed with lath and sheetrock when the parish deserted St. Mark's, but it was shoddy work open to the elements, and would be no barrier to entry. The vestry, which the sheik had claimed for his cell, was directly over the crypt, and access was by way of a winding stone staircase.

He walked to Balderton Street. He had opened the simple padlock earlier that day, so the iron gate was easily breached. Switching on his light, he made the short journey to the wall of the crypt without incident. He carried a plasterer's tool in his pocket, but it proved unnecessary. Standing on his toes, he grasped the top of the wallboard and peeled it away. The board on the other side took a little more time, but within minutes he had an opening sufficient to squeeze through. He wouldn't chance the light again, so he waited for his eyes to adjust to the blackness, wondering if the chamber was an actual catacomb or merely an architectural detail.

He moved to the wall on his left and advanced cautiously, feeling for the steps with his feet. When he found them, he paused, considering again this final stage of his quest. He had no idea what he would encounter at the top of the stairs. Would there be a door? Was it locked? Would he have to disturb the sleeping occupant to gain admittance? It didn't matter. He had a gun and six bullets, and he would use them if he had to.

The door was unlocked. He moved noiselessly into the small room. The heavy breathing of the man asleep on a pallet continued unbroken. Markham went to the other door – it was bolted from the inside. Turning back, he surveyed the room. Besides the sheik and his modest bed, there were only books, props used by the mullah to give credibility to his message of hatred. They were written in many languages, most of them obviously seldom used. He swiftly scanned the titles and selected one that would never be opened – *The Book of Common Prayer*. Drawing an envelope from his pocket, he buried it in the pages of the slim volume and returned it to its place.

Turning to the sheik, he took the revolver from his pocket and carefully slipped the barrel between the man's lips. He pulled back the hammer. The sheik's body stiffened as he opened his eyes and stared. Markham hesitated. The finger on the trigger began to tighten and the sheik's eyes bulged from their sockets. A foul odor filled the room. Markham laughed. "If you raise your voice, you're a dead man. Understand?" The sheik barely nodded his head, the movement restricted by the gun in his mouth.

Markham lifted the revolver and stepped back. "You know who I am?" Another nod. "I'm not going to kill you. I'd like to, but it would serve your ends, not mine."

"Very wise, Your Grace," said the Black Sheik in a smooth English voice that bespoke his education at one of England's finest public schools and the London School of Economics.

Markham raised the gun again. "Don't tempt me." He paused. "I came to tell you that we are not all eunuchs. Some of us will fight, more than you think. Many of you will die."

The sheik smiled. "Does that matter?" There was no response. He laughed. "Only to you. That's why we will win."

"Maybe, but you won't be here to enjoy it. I found you this time, and I'll find you again." He paused. "Turn around."

Fear showed again in the old man's eyes. "But – you said –"

"Turn around!" Seconds later the sheik lay unconscious across his bed. Markham retraced his steps to Balderton Street, aware again of the terrible fatigue that dogged him. He ignored the mortality it seemed to promise. His country needed him, and the pace was picking up.

Lahore

ABRAM KHAN stood behind the bowling crease and squeezed the red leather ball in his powerful hands. He turned his back to the English batsman and let his eyes sweep the great circular stadium. The sixty-five thousand people were on their feet, hushed. His teammates, dressed in white trousers and shirts like his, were motionless, figurines against emerald grass burnished by the yellow Asian sun. The result was already determined. By the end of the third day the English knew that they were beaten, but even they were solemn and still as he prepared to deliver the last ball. A moment before he had bowled out their ninth batsman, breaking his wicket with a ball that struck the hard pitch and shot past his bat at just over a hundred miles an hour. Before that, the eighth batsman had endured a similar fate, a slower ball curving around the bat and knocking the crosspieces from the stumps. Never before, in all the Test Matches that they had played for a hundred years, had England suffered broken wickets on three consecutive balls.

He spoke to the umpire, then called to the striker some seventy feet away: "Changing sides!" England's tenth and last batsman, surprised, nodded as Khan moved to his right and prepared to bowl the ball around the wicket. He took a few quick steps forward, planted his right foot parallel to the crease and, as his left foot came down on the line, wound his fully-extended right arm in a whirling vertical arc and released the ball. The batsman, ready for a low, bouncing ball, tried frantically to deflect it but it sailed past his knees and struck the wicket, tearing two of the three stumps from the ground. Gaddafi Stadium erupted. The English captain, who was standing beside him, shook his head. "Well done, A.K.," he said, extending his hand. "Did you learn that last one at Oxford?"

Khan smiled. "You know better than that, Cobb," he said in the crisp English accent typical of his caste and his creed. "Full tosses weren't permitted at the Oxford Cricket Club. Not even by mistake." He stood on the pitch for a long moment, savoring his final cricket match, then turned for the dressing room.

BREATHING HEAVILY, Khan slumped on a bench outside the glass-enclosed squash court and reached for his watch. After a minute's reflection, he decided to go home and clean up – he had an hour before his meeting with the General. He walked to the car park and climbed into the bright red Jaguar. The monsoons were over, but the light rain that had been falling since the day before continued. He left the Royal Palm Golf and Country Club, turned onto Canal Bank Road and drove past the old neighborhood where he had learned to play cricket. At the Mall he turned right, then veered right again onto Davis Road where he stopped in front of the Senior Staff flats at Aitchison College.

He sat for a moment contemplating the drab brick apartment building where he lived. His was the largest of the twelve flats and the farthest from the road, and it was far more than most of the citizens of Lahore enjoyed, but it was much less than a man of his wealth and stature might have had. He was an aesthete – fabulously rich by Pakistani standards and extremely well-off by any other, he chose to live in relatively spartan quarters on the edge of the Aitchison campus. A master of languages at the college, he saw no reason to go elsewhere. The Pakistani people, especially the upwardly mobile Punjabis of Lahore, did not understand why their idol would choose to live so simply, and he had grown tired of explaining it. The Jaguar was his only pretension.

Thirty minutes later, he entered the long narrow drive to Governor House, a sprawling white structure situated in the center of acres of lawns and gardens. He passed the main entrance, a massive three-story portico supported by six pairs of tall columns, and parked near the entrance to the Darbal Hall. It had no columns, just two curved stairways leading to a gallery and a relatively modest door. Inside, he stated his business to the functionary at the desk and was led through the Sword Room – its walls bristling with antique weapons and trophy heads – to a small, elegantly-furnished room on the third floor. General Zhev was waiting.

Zhev rose and hugged him. "Abram," he said. "What a wonderful exhibition yesterday. I was so proud."

"Thank you, my father. It all begins with you."

"Nonsense. I didn't teach you to play cricket."

"You provided the opportunity and Allah did the rest."

Zhev looked at him closely. "Don't be too humble, my son. People will underestimate you."

"Isn't that best?"

"Only to a degree, Abram. They should fear you as well." Khan nodded. Zhev sat down in a tall leather chair and gestured to the sofa beside him. After Khan was seated, Zhev said, "Your country needs you again, and it's far more urgent than a cricket match."

One of the many problematic legacies left by the British when they partitioned the Indian sub-continent was Pakistan's Directorate of Inter-Services Intelligence. To be sure, the British had no hand in the creation of the hydra-headed monster that ISI was thirty years later – that was the work of Pakistan's own generals and politicians. ISI was an alternative state, one more dedicated to the suppression and destruction of "enemies" within Pakistan than without. The continuation of the country's ruling regime or, when necessary, the creation of a new one, had become its paramount purpose. Its activities within the country and outside it, in places like Kashmir, Afghanistan and Bangladesh, were all conceived in support of that mission. On the surface, power was exercised by the great political families or the Army, but it was ISI that determined who that would be.

Ahmad Zhev was ISI's Director General. A native of the Punjab, he was a third- generation military officer who had entered the Pakistani Army a few years before Ayub Rham, Pakistan's first modern autocrat, graduated from England's Royal Military Academy at Sandhurst. They had become friends while Zhev served as attaché at the embassy in London, and Rham had recruited him to ISI after he seized power. Punjab was Pakistan's richest and most populous province and Rham's plan, and that of most of his successors, was to preserve the power and perquisites of the Punjabi aristocracy as well as those of a military grown fat since the 1947 Partition. ISI exploited outside "threats," most particularly the various quarrels with India, to justify the continued existence of their privileged status quo. Zhev was fully committed to that program, but he had other issues to deal with, too.

"Four years ago, a bomb exploded aboard a British ocean liner," Zhev said. "The ship was called *Victoria*. There were no survivors and no clues as to who was responsible. We had reason to believe that certain – elements within Pakistan were involved, but when the British turned up nothing we closed our file." He stopped. "New information has come to our attention."

"Another bomb?"

Zhev shook his head. "There *was* another bomb, but not the one that we're concerned with." He went to the credenza on the other side of the room and lifted a porcelain teapot. "Tea?"

"No, thank you."

Zhev poured a cup and carried it back to his chair. "Our man at Whitehall says that someone is threatening to blow up parts of England. There are indications that they plan to use the same bomb that destroyed the cruise ship. That could be a problem for us." He paused. "We have re-opened our file, but we need someone watching it from the other end."

"Do you want me to stop it?"

Zhev smiled. "No. We don't care about that. The more chaos the better. But Pakistan must not be involved. The current government, even the country, might not survive if it's discovered that our people are implicated."

Khan leaned back on the sofa. When he was four years old, his father had been murdered in an attack on his barracks by fundamentalists encouraged but not quite controlled by ISI. Zhev, a colonel at the time, had taken an interest in him though, in truth, he was more interested in Khan's widowed mother in the beginning. Nevertheless, he had encouraged the boy to join one of the cricket teams that played on the grounds near his home in Zaman Park and, when it came time for school, he made sure that Khan was accepted as a scholarship student at Aitchison College. One of the best boys' schools in southeast Asia, Aitchison was located only a few steps from Zaman Park.

Khan had thrived at Aitchison. At sixteen, he was considered the finest bowler in Lahore, and when he graduated he was among the best in the entire country. His prowess as a cricketer, combined with an outstanding academic record, had made it possible for Zhev to pull the strings necessary to send his protégé to Oxford. Khan had matriculated at Exeter College and helped ensure four consecutive cricket victories over Cambridge. His summers were spent at home where, in between cricket matches, he was indoctrinated into the ways of the Directorate of Inter-Services Intelligence.

Zhev had become chief at ISI just before Khan left Oxford with a first in Romance Languages. By then Khan was an international cricket star and potent source of pride for the Pakistani people, and Zhev knew that he would be wasted as an ordinary ISI operative. Aitchison was happy to take him on as a languages master and cricket coach, and Zhev used him sparingly on assignments that capitalized on his prominence and access to powerful people. Khan was never asked to perform the dirty, mundane tasks of the average ISI agent – the killing and blackmail were left to others. His function was to acquire sensitive intelligence or to spread false information from and among the government and business leaders he encountered during his international travels. Each journey by the Pakistani national team, or by Khan alone as a world-wide celebrity, led to a small but significant victory for ISI.

"How are we going about this?" said Khan.

"You shall return to the scene of your undergraduate glory. One of the places threatened is Oxford. We've arranged for you to assist the cricket coach at the new Muslim college." He stopped. "It's been built since you were there, I believe – Saudi money. Its name is the College of the Prophet Muhammad, but they call it 'the Mosque.'" He paused again. "The Chancellor of the University is a man named Cromwell. He's very political. Get close to him. Check in with your friends in London."

"Is that – John Cromwell?"

"Yes. Do you know him?"

"No. I – I've heard the name."

As Khan prepared to leave, Zhev produced a small parcel wrapped in brown paper. "I want you to deliver this for me while you're in London," he said.

Back in his flat, Khan examined the travel documents that Zhev had given him. They were written in English, another marker left by the British that continued to shape Pakistani society. Pakistan's official language was English. Its laws and Constitution were written in English, its colleges and universities taught in English, its government officials and military officers spoke in English. The "national" language was Urdu, a hybrid of several tongues universally viewed as inferior to English. This duality of language performed a significant function for ISI and its clients. It perpetuated the divisions in Pakistani society – it was impossible to advance to another social class without knowing the language – and the government provided English educations only for the children of the military and the elite. The people remained where they were, barely aware of anything else.

He pushed the parcel and papers into a narrow leather briefcase and looked at the clock. He must see his mother before he left. He considered the car, then decided to walk. After crossing the wide lawn in front of the Headmaster's House he turned right past the Sikh gurdwara and the Hindu mandir, architectural relics from the late 19th century when Hindus and Sikhs still lived in the West Punjab. Both were shaded by huge banyan trees with aerial roots that writhed like serpents escaping from the nether world. Further on was the masjid of the Muslims, only slightly better attended in this heedless secular enclave.

On the far side of the football fields he turned north, passed between the library and the tennis complex and crossed the road to Zaman Park. He followed a cracked sidewalk to the circular cricket grounds and turned into a small walled garden. She was working in her flowers. He called from the gate. "Mother."

She looked around, smiling. "Abram." She opened her arms and they embraced. "I'll make some tea," she said, taking his hand.

He watched her as she moved about the kitchen. She was a Kalash from the valleys of the Hindu Kush.

Descended from Alexander's troops, she was taller than other Pakistani women, her skin was fair and her eyes were blue. Although the women of her village never cut their hair, she had acceded to Zhev's request that she cut hers, and she now wore it in a single thick braid. The customs of the Kalash people were very different from those of the other tribes, and their women enjoyed unheard of freedom. This blasphemy naturally enraged the Muslim mullahs who lived in the surrounding provinces, leading to periodic raids against Kalash settlements and the abduction of their women and girls. Khan's father had rescued his mother from one such encounter and taken her to Lahore. When she turned fifteen, he married her.

"Did you see me on television yesterday?" he said. She looked at him, a question in her eyes. "I played in a match on television yesterday. Did you watch it?" She shook her head. Cricket, and the money and fame it brought him, didn't interest her. She loved her son and she cared for Zhev and, other than her house and garden, there was really nothing else.

He looked around the kitchen. She had loved her daughter, too – photographs of his beautiful, troubled sister were everywhere. The barely slanted blue eyes under dark brows and honey-colored hair gazed at them from all directions. They might have been twins except for the hair. Barely a toddler when their father died, Aden had clung to Abram, and he had done what a four-year-old could do to protect and comfort her. As she grew older, though, she clashed with Zhev, and Khan – unwilling to take her part against his patron – had watched as she turned inward, relying only on herself and charting a course that would end in disaster.

Her death a few years earlier had aged his mother. Not yet fifty, her luxurious black hair was turning gray, the eyes dull and puffy from weeping. He had kept the degree of Aden's shame from her, though bits and pieces filtered through the barriers that he erected. Zhev had washed his hands of Aden completely and declared her dead years before she actually died. Nothing in her life, however, excused the manner of her death, and now he was in a position to punish the people responsible for it. He would do what Zhev had asked if he could, but that was secondary. And there was another thing to perhaps do something about: John Cromwell. "I'm leaving for England tomorrow, Mother," he said. "I don't know when I'll be back."

Oxford

THE LIMOUSINE slowed to a stop in front of St. Giles' House. Three men emerged from the back seat, each dressed in long, flowing robes and turbans – white for the first two who climbed from the car, solid black for the last. The man in black carried a small green suitcase. Stationed on the other side of the street, Tony Markham checked the date setting on his camera, then raised it and snapped a picture, taking care to see that the man and the suitcase, and the façade of the house, were prominent in the photograph. After conferring among themselves for a moment, the men passed through the gate and entered the house.

Markham stepped from the shadows and surveyed the road in both directions. The new term started in a few days and activity was picking up. He walked to the corner at Keble Road and took up a new position in the courtyard of the Church of St. Giles. From that vantage he could still see the limousine and, looking past the short stretch of Keble Road and across University Parks, its next probable destination. He sat down on a carved stone bench to wait.

An hour later, the Muslim clerics returned to the car. The man in black still carried a suitcase but this one was brown. The limousine pulled away from the curb and moved toward him. After it turned onto Keble Road, Markham crossed St. Giles' and watched as it entered the Parks and disappeared behind the walls of the Muslim college. He cursed the treachery of the man inside St. Giles' House – the home of the Chancellor of the University of Oxford – and returned to his original post. Within minutes, John Cromwell emerged and turned south. The small suitcase in his hand was green. Markham climbed the steps, unlocked the door and stepped inside.

The office of Chancellor had been purely ceremonial for centuries, but when the new government installed its man in the post the ancient powers he once exercised were revived. In a matter of months, John Cromwell – backed by the uncompromising authority of Whitehall – had seized control of all facets of the University, and begun to insinuate himself into the affairs of the colleges and the town. His disdain for Oxford's history and tradition was well-known, and shared by many of those, careless of the freedoms they were eschewing, at the University itself.

The government's appeasement of the alien culture that infected the country had reached Oxford, and John Cromwell was the chief enabler. Cromwell himself was no more tolerant of the Muslims than his friends in London, but it was easier to placate the mullahs than oppose them. While the College of the Prophet Muhammad had been built under a previous government, all the special privileges and exemptions – the never-ending accommodations – had been established by Cromwell. None of the rules that had governed the University and the colleges for centuries applied to the Prophet's college. At the end of each term, the Caliph merely submitted a list, and an Oxford degree was summarily conferred. An institution that had withstood religious zealots, monarchs and war for almost a millennium was nearing its useful end.

Minutes later, Markham passed out of the house and turned south on St. Giles'. He paused at Beaumont Street and watched a gaggle of tourists crowd their way through the doors of the Randolph Hotel. He smiled. He had once been a regular patron of the Randolph, but those days were gone forever. Things were different now.

Las Vegas

PAMELA SMYTHE-KING smoothly stepped from the glittering blue pool and accepted a towel from the man who greeted her. She dried her naked body, slipped on a robe and crossed the deck to the parapet that encircled it. She looked north to a boarded-up ghost town surrounded by desert, then south to the Potemkin facade of the Las Vegas Strip. It rose from the sand like a narrow range of plastic mountains looming over the concrete ravine that was Las Vegas Boulevard. From her aerie atop the Flamingo Hotel she watched the tiny creatures move up and down the sidewalks and escalators and staircases, searching for another life that they would never find.

Sin was the commodity on offer, and sin could be purchased anywhere. The only innovation here was the blessing of the state. The state regulated, advertised and taxed the sin in Las Vegas. That arrangement provided a patina of redemption for its patrons – the sex and the gambling and the gluttony couldn't be *too* bad if the mayor encouraged you to participate. Ordinary people, who would never dream of buying a five hundred dollar hooker or betting a grand on the turn of a wheel, did so without trepidation, secure in the knowledge that it was sanctioned by the government. When first conceived and implemented, the collaboration between government and sin had given Vegas an advantage in the traffic in corruption, but the benefit was eroding. The state was expanding its franchise and as authorized sin became ubiquitous it became commonplace. Activities that had titillated and enticed mankind since the discovery of fire were now banal. What would all these little people do when they realized that their sin, co-opted by the Leviathan, was as meaningless as their lives?

She had been Eliza Booksund for the first eighteen years of her life. Born at the Royal London Hospital in Whitechapel, her mother, a sixteen-year-old prostitute, had promptly abandoned her. She passed through various social agencies for orphans and deserted children until she was old enough to be enrolled at St. Luke's School, the successor to the London Orphan Asylum. One of only forty girls in a school of five hundred adolescents, she was much in demand, and her willingness to oblige the appetites of her male classmates had led to her expulsion at seventeen, just before sixth form year. She drifted into the frenzy of the "arts and anarchy" scene in Whitechapel, and quickly took up her mother's profession on a more genteel, and more lucrative, basis.

Tall and lissome, Pamela – as she was known by then – was not strictly beautiful. Her brown eyes were larger than they should have been and the lashes were too long. Her small nose tilted upward and the cupid's bow mouth seemed contrived with paint though it was not. Pale skin contrasted with dark hair that, parted on the side, cascaded in curls over her forehead. Her hands and feet were far from dainty, and she had no hips. Nevertheless, by the time she was twenty Pamela was reckoned one of the great beauties of the metropolis and her favors were highly prized no matter the price. She still encountered prejudice in certain circles, like an actress or a dancer in more modest times, but most of her countrymen had long since shed the arbitrary restraints of those primitive days.

Pamela Smythe-King was in the business of sin and she was just about to cash out. Tomorrow her conglomerate of whores, film studios and pornographers would be sold to a faceless enterprise whose masters believed that sin was still worth a few bucks. She would use her real name when she signed the papers, but the world would continue to know her as Pamela Smythe-King – courtesan, porn star, adult movie mogul. And those few who still scorned her would soon understand that business was, after all, just business. She felt a tap on her shoulder. "Drink?" he said.

She turned and accepted the V-8 and tonic water. She had stopped abusing her body years ago. She still took whisky, but only during business hours. "Thank you, Geoffrey."

He was drinking vodka. His casual clothing looked odd on a man seemingly born in a Savile Row suit and, unlike his regular apparel, it failed to conceal the evidence of his life-long decay. Weak, narrow shoulders, a belly that hung over ungirded Bermuda shorts and scrawny, hairless legs all combined to give the impression of an insect standing suddenly erect. Open sandals and black socks, thankfully without the garters that he usually wore, completed the picture of the modern English aristocrat that he actually was. She didn't like men much anymore, and this particular specimen was especially disappointing, but he was a necessary part of the current campaign. The cost to her – the satisfaction of infantile fantasies that only required a few minutes of her time – was minimal. "I just got off the phone with Cromwell," he said. "They have formally rejected your offer."

She nodded. "What did he tell them?"

"He suggested that a compulsory purchase might be necessary. That got their attention."

"How does that work again?"

"The government seizes the property. If no value is agreed, it's submitted to the Lands Tribunal." Geoffrey North smiled. "Two surveyors and a barrister. All appointed by us." He smiled again. "We sell or lease it to you. Cromwell gets his cut."

"But I'm willing to pay them what the property's worth."

"I know, but they don't want to sell." He stopped. "Cromwell has set up a meeting for next Tuesday. I think they'll come around."

"Did you tell him my plans?"

"Yes. He's booked a suite at the Randolph. Let him know what train you'll take. He'll meet you at the station."

She walked to the sliding glass door that led to her bedroom and pushed it open. Inside in the frigid air, she paused before the portrait that hung over the mantel. Blue eyes under heavy brows looked down at her. She knew that they were blue even though she had finally commissioned this portrait in black and white and shades of gray. The real colors – the blue eyes, the fawn skin, the golden hair – were inadequate to depict the face of the woman she had loved so completely. Pamela smiled. Aden was an angel and a demon, and the sly expression in the painting – the brows slightly lifted, the grin at the corners of her mouth barely suppressed – gave no clue as to which it was at the time.

Later, after dinner, North poured himself another glass of brandy. "There may be a bit of excitement in Oxford next week," he said.

"What do you mean?"

"We have received at least a hint that someone wants to blow it up."

"Why?"

"God knows. There are some in the government who think it's a joke, but I'm not so sure. We have people looking into it."

"Do you know who's behind it?"

North shook his head. "The evidence so far suggests that it may be the same crowd that bombed one of our ships at Southampton a few years ago."

Pamela stared at him. "What ship?"

"One of the White Star passenger line – *Victoria.*"

London

I CROSSED The Lawn, actually a wide expanse of pavement between the Great Western Hotel and Paddington Station, and entered the controlled bedlam of the vast railway station. After checking my watch, I turned left and walked to the ticket windows. Outside the train shed, the old station struggled to adapt to the new age – shops, kiosks, money machines – but inside, beneath the glass roof braced by iron girders, wrought-iron arches and steel columns, it had changed little in 140 years. The trains made less noise, and the air was a little cleaner, but Paddington still served as the London terminus of the Great Western Railway, though it was called something else now. A map of its routes looked like the left ventricle of England's heart. The main arteries stretched to the sea – to the north, to Manchester and Liverpool – to the west, to Bristol and the coast of Wales – and south, to Devon and Falmouth. Hundreds of branch lines served smaller places, and the hamlets and villages and towns with a Great Western station numbered in the thousands. My brief journey, to a destination only fifty miles northwest of London, was on one of the first lines built.

The few hours in town had proved fruitless. The man I really wanted to see was out of the country and wouldn't return for several days. The inspector at Scotland Yard had been called away, and his second-in-command knew nothing beyond what North had already told me. No one at the Home Office knew who I was and none was interested in finding out. I hoped that Markham, at least, could tell me something.

I found an unoccupied car and sat down. As the train left the station I looked out the window, first at the crowded Victorian terraces of Bayswater, then the slightly less dense streets of the outer boroughs, and finally at the Middlesex countryside, what was left of it. Centuries earlier, this trip might have been made along the Thames, or on it, but there wasn't time for that now. I re-read the notes that I had made, and considered what lay before me.

"The Duke has a great deal of faith in you," Geoffrey North had said, "and I must say that the people who worked with you in London share it." I nodded. "There were reservations. Some worried about your – withdrawal, so to speak but, all things considered, we believe that you can help."

"You mentioned evidence?"

"A few hours before the church was bombed, the Home Office received a map. No letter, no explanation, just a map."

"A map of what?"

"England. It had a black circle around Aylesbury, and there were other circles as well – London, Portsmouth and Oxford."

I frowned. "Oxford? I can understand Portsmouth. I guess the Royal Navy is still there. And London, obviously. But why Oxford?"

He shook his head. "We don't know. We want you to find out and stop it. And you must work quietly. We don't want a panic, and we certainly don't want the press to know." He stopped. "As you might imagine, the bulk of our resources will be directed toward the other two targets." He paused again. "Your former association with the University suggested the means of introducing you into the situation discreetly. The Michaelmas term begins next week. We want you to take another degree."

"What am I going to study?"

He reached inside his coat and handed me an envelope. "You've been admitted to the Master's program in creative writing. It's part-time. You can actually be a student without doing much. The Duke – did you know that he's now Master of Balliol?" I shook my head. "He's spoken to the Dean of your old college. They will find a place for you."

I rose and looked out the window. "You haven't really told me how *Victoria* is connected to all this."

"There was one more black circle. Around Southampton. It was over the Water, actually." North paused. "It had a red X crossed through it."

We were silent. "Who else knows about me?"

"Aside from a small group within the government, only two. The Duke of Aylesbury, of course, and the Chancellor of the University, John Cromwell. And *he* doesn't really know why you're coming yet."

"Another Cromwell is Chancellor?"

North smiled. "Yes, and he, too, is a Cambridge man. As am I."

A few minutes later the Ambassador took his leave. I stayed behind, gazing out the window past the monuments and the gazebo to the grotesque buildings, dedicated to science and technology, on the horizon. North was one of the new aristocrats, one never permitted to call the Duke of Aylesbury by his Christian name, even when Markham wasn't present. The Duke had introduced himself to me as Tony Markham and I never called him anything else, but I was not unaware of the formalities usually associated with the English aristocracy. When I asked him about it, he smiled. "We use titles in England to maintain distinctions that vanished decades ago. The nobility once deserved the deference. That's no longer the case. The arrogation of those titles by men who shouldn't have them disgusts me." He paused. "Anything I can do to subvert the ceremony undermines whatever legitimacy they still have." He stopped again. "Don't misunderstand me, St. Cyr. I appreciate the money and the place, and the title, my father left me. I just believe that I can behave like a duke without placing a coronet on my head every morning."

The door opened and the Admiral entered the room. I started to rise. "Don't get up, Fitz," he said as he took the chair vacated by the British ambassador. "What's the poop?"

"I'm afraid I'm leaving you in the lurch, Admiral. I'm resigning from the faculty."

"Don't worry about it. We'll find another English teacher." He removed the pipe from his pocket and began cleaning the bowl.

"I'm also resigning from the Navy."

He looked up. "That's a different matter. Is it really necessary?"

"I don't know. I just think it would be better if I'm a civilian. And – it's something I've been thinking about for a while." I smiled. "Can I use you as a reference if I change my mind?"

"I doubt that will be necessary."

PAMELA OPENED her eyes and stared at the tray ceiling over the bed. It took her a moment to realize that he was gone. She rose and crossed to the bathroom where she examined her face in the mirror – not bad for a thirty-four-year-old whore. She ran her fingers through the chestnut hair and reached for a brush. Fifteen minutes later she passed back into the bedroom, dressed and walked down the stairs.

In the kitchen, she poured a glass of grapefruit juice and gazed out the window at the back garden. She decided to walk – it would do her good. The sun was shining, and her flat in Cadogan Square was less than a mile away. She drew a pair of low-heeled shoes from her purse, slipped the pumps into the bag and went to the door where she paused before returning to the kitchen. There was a pad of blank paper next to the telephone. She sat down at the table to compose her goodbye.

> *9:30 AM*
>
> *Tony,*
>
> *Thanks for a wonderful evening. I'll see you next week.*
>
> *P*

She had worked her way through several telephone numbers and overseas operators before he finally came on the line. "Pamela," Anthony Markham said, "is everything all right?"

She laughed. "Yes, everything's fine."

"Good. It's just – it's been a long time."

"I know. I'm sorry for that but you were going to be married, and – well, I didn't think that my business ventures were compatible with the Duke of Aylesbury." There was silence on the end of the line. "Tony?"

"I'm still here. Thanks for the concern but it's really my call, don't you think?"

She had encountered him early in her career before she was as savvy as she needed to be. She had been beaten by one of his "friends" and cheated by another, and on both occasions the men responsible made it good under threat of bodily harm from Tony Markham. Another time she found herself being escorted from a hotel by two burly policemen when Markham intervened. She became one of his favorite playthings, and the grace and style that had helped make her such a success had been absorbed in his company. "I'll be in London next Wednesday," she said. "I'd like to see you."

Silence again. She waited. "All right," he said finally. "I'll be at Belgrave Square on Wednesday. Come by at seven. I'll give you supper."

He had opened the door himself. She hugged him, and he smiled at her surprised expression. "Servants are hard to come by these days, Pamela. No one wants to work, even those who say they do." He paused. "The dignity of work has been replaced with the chimera of equality. Why should someone cook my meals or answer my door when they're just as good as me and the government pays them not to." He took her hand. "I'm actually a very good cook."

They caught up with each other over a veal chop, salad and white wine. When the meal was finished, he stacked the dishes in the sink and said, "Let's have brandy in the study." A moment later they sat before a blazing fire, snifters in hand. Markham looked at her. "All right then. Let's have it."

She grinned. "Does there have to be an *it?*"

"Of course. And believe me, I don't mind. I'm very glad to see you. What's up?"

"I've sold everything, Tony, and – and it's a great deal of money. I've told you before what I think about *class* in this country and I'd like to finally do something about it." She stopped. "I know you don't agree with me."

"You might be wrong about that, Pamela. I'm under no illusion about the so-called aristocracy here. I don't mind *people* trying to level things up. It's government picking and choosing that I object to." He poured more brandy. "So what are you planning to do?"

"I'm going to build a new college at Oxford."

The expression on his face was hard to read for a second and then he laughed out loud. "A college at Oxford?"

"Yes. Please don't laugh."

"I'm sorry. It's just – the irony is so delicious. A college founded on the wages of sin amongst all the others created to suppress it. It's really too perfect."

"You're not angry?"

"Not at all. We have colleges built on automobiles and beer. Why not pornography?"

"Well, I don't intend to make that a big selling point. I'm a wealthy woman who wants others to have a chance." He nodded. "You won't stand in the way?"

He shook his head. "I couldn't if I wanted to. They stopped hearing me on these things years ago. You'll be welcomed with open arms."

"I'm trying to buy the land from Christ Church. *They* aren't very friendly."

"That's economics and tradition, my dear. They still care about that." He paused. "The only people who will oppose the *notion* of your college are the Muslims."

"Who?"

"The College of the Prophet Muhammad. Their view of sin is far different from ours." Markham smiled. "When are you going up?"

"Sunday."

"What about coming over to Aylesbury toward the end of the week?"

"That would be fun. Thank you."

"Have you ever been there by train? From Oxford?" She shook her head. He found a pen and paper and wrote out the directions. "That will get you to Aylesbury Station by five o'clock, assuming the trains are still running. Someone will be there to meet you."

"Why wouldn't the trains be running?"

"There's been a bomb threat."

"Oh, yes. A friend mentioned that a few days ago."

"A friend?"

She smiled. "You're not the only big shot I know. What's it about?"

A few minutes later they climbed the stairs to his bedroom. Sex had not been mentioned and she knew that he'd be just as happy if she went home, but she wanted to do something for him, to share what she could. They had slept together many times, usually with another woman. She had learned long ago that sex was played on the pitch between your ears and, whatever Anthony Markham had in his head, it didn't allow him to play the game. That didn't keep him from trying. His stamina was profound, but the women were not as strong so they took turns, resting between the forceful, sometimes violent, couplings but the result was always the same. If he achieved any satisfaction at all it was finally induced by a hand or a mouth. Last night, though, he had turned her aside, a first in their relationship.

Aylesbury

MARKHAM BACKED away from the stone, the freshest in the ancient cemetery, and walked down the hill. He climbed once more into a low-slung automobile, turned around on the narrow road, and began the last leg of his journey. A chill shook his body despite the warmth of the day. A few minutes later he ascended the steps to the platform at Aylesbury Station and approached the Maid of Morven, an antique observation car purchased from the London, Midland and Scottish Railway. He had donated the car to the state-owned rail company on condition that it be always attached to one of the three trains used on the route between Aylesbury and Oxford. Although it was his responsibility to maintain its brown and cream paint, its wide curved windows and plush leather seats, the car was open to the public, and he smiled at the delight of the passengers who encountered it after the grimy, modern utility of the rest of the train.

Today, however, he was alone. He took the telegram from his pocket and read it again: "ARRIVE OXFORD 6 PM. ST. CYR." Concise and to the point, just like the man himself. He leaned back and closed his eyes. Georges St. Cyr was descended from French aristocrats, but he had nothing of the Frenchman's *laissez-faire,* his *je ne sais quoi* style. Similarly, though born and raised in the American South, the romance and languor often attributed to natives of that part of the world were nowhere to be found. St.

Cyr's demeanor was puritan and his outlook warlike unless there was a woman involved, in which case he affected a more indulgent attitude. And, of course, he was a stone cold killer, though death was only a by-product of his profession.

He had not seen St. Cyr in more than four years. Their last meeting, and the sequence of events leading up to it, was burned into his brain, and a sense of unfinished business remained with him always. St. Cyr was in England now, would be in Oxford in a few hours. Perhaps, together, they would end it this time.

Markham found his new spectacles, opened the briefcase beside him and withdrew a large blue envelope bearing the seal of the oldest firm of solicitors in London. He sorted through the documents again. The absurd complexity, and corresponding outrageous fee, for such a simple undertaking irritated him, but it had finally been done. These papers embodied the fulfillment of the great ambition of his life and, yet, he would now do all he could to ensure that the outcome they contemplated was never achieved. He smiled at the conundrum.

When the last train came to a halt he stepped down from the platform at Oxford Station and, burdened by his baggage, hailed a cab. He was well-known to the drivers. "Balliol, Your Grace?" Markham glanced at the identification tag clipped to the visor. "No, Reggie, I need to make a couple of stops first. Take me to Carfax."

Carfax Tower, built on the highest point of old Oxford, was in the center of the ancient city. The roads leading from each of Oxford's four medieval gates met at Carfax. The Town Church, built in the 1300's, had once occupied the site but now only the tower remained, mangled by a stair-turret and Gothic buttresses added at the turn of the century. There was a clock as well, and two bells flanked by garish mechanical Romans who struck the bells with hammers every fifteen minutes.

Markham climbed the steps to the roof. Looking east, he could see the town and the University spread out before him. The walls and the towers and the spires reflected the golden light of the late afternoon sun but, as he watched, angry black clouds gathered to block the light and erase the pleasing aspect of shadow and stone. From that perspective, Oxford appeared two-dimensional, as if imprisoned in a photographer's lens – a facade without nuance or life. He sighed, and turned away.

Back in the cab, he said, "Drive me to the Cricket Pavilion, Reggie. Take the long way around." He paused. "And stop at the next post box."

An hour later he sat behind his desk pondering again the visit from Georges St. Cyr. Could he convince St. Cyr that the threat was real? Between them, the invaders and the government were about to achieve something – neutering the British people – that had evaded Hitler and the Kaiser, and the people themselves, reduced to drones by the bankrupt largesse of that same government, were difficult to stir. Nevertheless, the battle had begun. Speeches and rallies were reaching more and more people, especially in the shires. The rally in London tomorrow would say much about his efforts and the bombs, and threats of more, would surely help. St. Cyr's motive might be questionable – he had come to England for revenge – but his cooperation was essential.

Oxford

I STOOD outside the Master's Lodgings on Broad Street. The exterior of gray Bath stone joined by dark mortar matched that of the buildings on either side of it. Despite their relative youth in a village that dated its birth from the 10th century, they had darkened over the decades, presenting a grim, brooding aspect to the street. Autumn was further along here – the few elms that remained, the willows and oaks, were almost bare. The only color was provided by the ever-present yew hedges pressed against the walls. I knocked on the door. A tall man dressed completely in black, his long white hair swept back over his head, opened it. "My name is St. Cyr. Is the Duke in?"

He opened the door wider and stood aside to let me pass. The small foyer led to a larger hallway. Indicating a room to the right, he said, "If you will wait here, sir, I will see if His Grace is available." The room – appointed with hard wooden furniture, drab ornithological prints with Latin labels, and a worn woolen rug – was uninviting. It smelled like moth balls. I imagined the legion of undergraduates who had stood there, afraid, awaiting the judgment of the Master of Balliol.

A man of medium height appeared in the doorway. Just past forty, Tony Markham called to mind a fully drawn longbow, arrow nocked, waiting impatiently to be loosed. His yellow hair was parted in the middle, and the large black eyes contrasted with fair brows and pale skin. The scar on his left cheek, usually almost invisible, had reddened and seemed to pulse.

The thirteenth Duke of Aylesbury was no duke at all at the time of his birth. A second son, he was only a "Lord" until his brother James plunged into a Roman aqueduct on the property and drowned. His father, whose wife had died giving birth to their only daughter, mourned the loss of his eldest son but could not conceal his conviction that Providence had chosen wisely. James Markham was frail, sickly and withdrawn, a combination unlikely to succeed in the high-powered political world that the Duke of Aylesbury was expected to occupy. The younger brother, on the other hand, dominated every occasion. He intimidated the older boys at school, beat them at their games and refused to lose in any competition. By the time I met him the intensity had been reined in, but the compulsion to prevail at any cost remained.

Markham leaped into the room. "St. Cyr," he said, "it's been too long. How are you?" He started to raise his right hand, encased in tape and plaster, then extended his left instead. I took it, smiling at the iron clasp that refused to be enveloped by my own much larger hand.

"I'm fine, Tony, thanks. What about you?" I had not seen him since Gabrielle's funeral. There had been a few notes back and forth across the Atlantic, mostly about the sport that had brought us together, but I had forgotten the vitality, the sheer *aliveness* of the man. Still, he was thinner now, and the dark circles around his eyes hinted at a weariness I'd never seen before.

Markham looked down as if he, too, were recalling the occasion of our last meeting. "I'm well," he said finally.

"How's the hand?"

Markham held up his right hand and looked at it. "Useless at the moment, I'm afraid."

"What happened?"

"Tendons and muscles in the hand and wrist. Torn. I tried to dig my way through the wreckage."

"Were you – buried?"

"Oh, no. I ended up several yards from the blast. I was trying to get at my books and tried too hard."

I nodded. "Was anything salvaged?" He shook his head. "I'm sorry."

"They were just things." Markham looked down again, perhaps reflecting on the centuries-old "things" – the product of intricate, painstaking labor and a love of learning – that could never be replicated.

"So the bomb was nothing like the one they used on *Victoria?*"

He shook his head again. "The stones are still there. They've just been rearranged." He smiled suddenly. "The scotch is in the library." He turned and passed through the door. I followed.

A moment later we sat comfortably in a more cheerful place, surrounded by books and warmed by fire in a gray stone fireplace. "Have you been by the House yet?" Markham said. I shook my head. "Dean West has invited us to dine at the high table this evening."

"Really?"

"Yes. He claims to remember you. He was a Senior Fellow in those days, at Merton I believe. Greek. You didn't study Greek, did you?"

"No. I studied *English*. Most unsatisfactory, as I recall. There were no English dons at Christ Church. I had to go across the street to Pembroke."

He laughed. "I believe that English is still frowned upon at the House. Still lots of Greek and Latin, though." He stopped. "Probably other languages, too, as long as they're at least two thousand years old and nobody speaks them." We both laughed. "In any event," he said, "you'd better enjoy the delicacies of the high table tonight. Tomorrow you're just another student with a lower case s."

We spoke of old times and old friends for a few minutes. When Markham rose to refresh the drinks – awkwardly, using only his left hand – I said, "I want to tell you what I learned from the Ambassador, and then I want you to tell me what else there is." He nodded. Twenty minutes later I said, "That's all I know. Is there anything else?"

He thought for a moment. "Did he really say that all of the government's attention would go to London and Portsmouth?"

"I believe he said 'the bulk of.'"

"The bastards. I think that if North and his friend Cromwell and the rest of those smug *scientists* in the government had their way, Oxford would be vaporized tomorrow. They might warn us, but I'm not even certain of that."

"Cambridge ascendant?"

"It's not Cambridge itself. It's the attitude, and we have plenty of it here." He stopped. "Sorry. One of my hobby horses." He paused again. "To answer your question: The basic outline is as you stated it. The church at Aylesbury was destroyed four days ago. I had just left the chapel when the bomb exploded. The Home Secretary received the map the same day. It had the black circles and the red X you described."

"Do they know anything more about it?"

"No. The intelligence people analyzed it and found nothing. It was a road map, available virtually everywhere. The circles and X were made with ordinary marking pencils."

"North said something about a speech you gave."

Markham nodded. "Speeches, actually. We've been hell-bent on creating a welfare state in this country since the '30's and we're almost there. Others have noticed, and we now have a large Muslim diaspora that accepts the largesse of the British people without bothering to become British. It's like the Romans opening the gates for the Visigoths. They're mostly in London now but it's spreading." He paused. "The government seems not to care. I said something about it in the Lords five weeks ago. The yawns were barely suppressed." He stood and poked the fire. "However, there were reports of restlessness in the mosques. Letters full of bile in the newspapers." He smiled. "We have systematically degraded the religious beliefs of our own people for centuries and, yet, the ranting of some Muslim cleric is perfectly suitable for the *Times.*" He stared into the fire. "It's a war, and we're losing."

"Were you threatened?"

"Oh, yes. Hellfire and brimstone of the worst sort. But nothing of the immediate variety."

"Do you think they're behind these bombs?"

"I do."

I hesitated. "The Ambassador told me that it was you who insisted that I be involved in this." He nodded. "Why?"

"When I saw that red X over Southampton Water, I thought you might be interested."

"I'm not really trained in police work, you know."

"Yes, I know. You were actually on the other end. Still – it takes a thief to catch a thief."

I laughed. "Why would the group that bombed *Victoria* do something like this?"

"Why should *anyone* wish to blow up the ruins of the church at Aylesbury? Maybe they don't like churches. Maybe it was a trial run to show that they're serious about the rest of it. And if they managed to kill me, so much the better."

We sat in silence. "Is there anything more you can tell me?" I said.

My friend looked at me steadily for a moment. "North didn't mention the diagram?" I shook my head. "There was a diagram with the map, sort of like very detailed building plans. The paper was blue and the lines and letters were white."

"Do you know what it was?"

"No. It was gibberish."

"What language was it in?"

Markham laughed. "English." He paused. "I understood only two things on that sheet of paper. In the bottom right-hand corner was a box with the letters 'AEA,' and under that a date: September 1, 1967."

"Does that mean anything to you?"

"Not the date, but I believe that the letters are the acronym for the Atomic Energy Authority."

"Never heard of it."

"It was the original custodian of our nuclear weapons. It's been reworked many times, but back in the '50's and '60's the AEA was in charge of the design and manufacture of Britain's nuclear warheads."

"What did your friends in the government say about it?"

"Nothing. I don't believe that they intended for me to see it at all, and based on my last inquiry I think they may soon deny its existence altogether."

We were quiet again. I broke the silence. "This doesn't make sense. Both of the bombs we're talking about were conventional weapons, and very different ones, too. It sounds like your diagram might deal with a nuclear device." I stopped. "I don't think we're getting the whole story."

"It wouldn't be the first time." Markham hesitated. "I'll tell you something else. It's possible that the *Victoria* bomb was one of ours."

"What?"

He nodded. "I can't say any more now, but I suspect you'll learn all about it soon enough."

I hesitated. "So we have a map and a diagram. Anything else? Anything we can actually work on?" He shook his head. "What's the government done?"

"Nothing, as far as I can tell. It's possible that they're going through the usual procedures – spies, informants, that sort of thing – but they seem to be waiting for the next shoe to drop." He paused. "There are certain circles in London that would probably yield a great deal of information, but the government is completely unprepared to discover it."

"Can we?"

"It's not the sort of thing you can just barge in on. The groundwork should've been laid years ago. And – I'm not sure that they're really interested."

"What are you talking about?"

"This government goes out of its way to overlook every outrage committed by these people. They could care less about the church at the Abbey. The threat to London and Portsmouth is the only reason they're engaged now." He looked at his watch. "We're due at Christ Church Hall in an hour. You might want to see your rooms before dinner." He smiled. "West has found you a place in Tom Quad. Some undergraduate elected not to appear this term." He moved behind his desk, opened a drawer and withdrew a manila folder containing a few inches of paper. "This is the government's dossier on *Victoria,*" he said, handing it to me. "I know it may be difficult reading, but I thought you should have it. I'll see you at dinner." As we walked to the door, he said, "By the way, I want you to come down to Aylesbury tomorrow."

Aylesbury's altitude was considerably higher than the low-lying swamp from which Oxford rose, but in England every direction from Oxford was down. "Thanks. That'll give me a chance to look at the church."

Outside on Broad Street again, it was almost dark and strangely deserted. Chilled, I walked up Turl to the High and turned right. Pausing for a moment at Carfax, I watched the two centurions hammer out the quarter hour. At St. Aldate's I turned left and, after a few more paces, stood before the Gothic splendor of Tom Tower. Its octagonal lantern and square campanile, and the great bell inside, soared above the gate of my old college. Red Virginia creeper climbed the walls. The porter, Yates, scrutinized me carefully as I searched my pockets for the paperwork. "Why, it's Mr. St. Cyr, ain't it?" I nodded. "Couldn't forget one as big as you, could I? Welcome back, sir." Heartened, I passed through the gate and crossed the quad in search of my staircase and my rooms.

A HALF hour later, I climbed the stone steps and entered the great hall at Christ Church. Markham was standing just inside the door, talking to a small man wearing a black gown and mortarboard. "St. Cyr," he said, "this is the fellow who's providing your lodging. Ian, this is Georges St. Cyr."

I took the proffered hand. Ian West was a legend at the University. A kindly, forgetful man of the sort routinely lampooned in the London papers, he had been at Oxford as student, tutor and don for more than forty years. Known to talk to himself at great length – sometimes taking several parts – he often got his words twisted when speaking to others, but he was a widely respected scholar of the first rank. He was also an Anglican clergyman – one of the few unmarried dons left at Oxford – hence his selection by the Queen to be Dean of the Cathedral Church of Christ in Oxford, a post that made him head of the House as well. He introduced me to the Students in our vicinity and took up his place at the center of the table.

The talk was all about the latest assault on the colleges. Theoretically independent of the University, most of them had been created by elements of the Catholic or Anglican Churches to provide food, lodging and instruction for boys intended for the clergy. Nearly all of them were endowed, and some of those endowments were substantial. The University itself, on the other hand, relied on the government for funding. As long ago as the 15th century, the autonomy of the colleges had been challenged by the Crown, and later by Parliament, but not until four hundred years later did interference from the government become systematic.

The first Royal Commission had objected to Oxford's failure to teach the sciences and its refusal to admit non-Anglican students. Subsequent acts of Parliament forced changes to the rules by which each of the supposedly private colleges were governed, altered the methods of examinations, required the colleges to fund University programs, and removed Greek and Latin as admission requirements. The most recent criticism from the politicians in London and the bureaucrats within Oxford itself had led to a proposal for two new colleges funded entirely by the five wealthiest existing colleges, of which Christ Church was the richest. All five had been founded by bishops, and it was the celibacy of the priests – a curious convention no longer observed in Oxford – that had ensured the strength of the endowments.

"I understand they are teaching automobile mechanics and carpet manufacturing," said one of the dons seated across the table from me.

"And they won't be required to take examinations," said another.

"There's talk that the government plans to change admissions standards again," added a third.

"Why not?" said Markham. "If they're coming here to learn how to fix a car or make carpets, why have any standards at all? Why not create a college for every group that Parliament deems worthy?" He looked around the table. "This 'New Jerusalem' we've created is destroying the country and the University." He gestured to the students sitting a few feet from us. "Those kids will never be able to fight a war or manage a country. All they can do is pass examinations written by other people who don't know how to do those things."

There was an embarrassed silence. The dons at the table, who certainly bore some responsibility for the changes in Oxford's student body that Markham complained of, were too timid or too polite to take up his challenge, so I did it for them. "You think Oxford was better off with wealthy amateurs who played cricket and didn't bother to take a degree?"

He smiled. "Yes, because they weren't all like that as you well know. In my grandfather's time, this place produced men who guided monarchs and presided over an empire. All this crowd can do is shuffle paper and feather their nests." He paused. "The bureaucrats and politicians are today's gentry. They claim that it's all equal now, that it's based on merit, but it's not."

"Why not?"

"Because *they* say what merit is."

"What do you mean?"

"If you can pass a test devised by the current elite, you can go to Oxford. That requires that you know and believe what they know and believe. Nothing else matters. It's self-perpetuating, just like the nobility used to be. They've manipulated the system so that it is *they*, rather than the priests and dukes, who enjoy the pleasure and profit of an Oxford education, and they don't pay a shilling for it." He stopped. "They are cleverer than the old aristocrats, too. Who can argue against merit?"

"But surely," said the Student across the table, "it's still better. The middle class and the blue collar people deserve a chance."

"Yes, they do," said Markham. "But that's not what's happening here."

"But –"

"Only those with sufficient money to prepare for these infernal exams get in. Poor people can't afford that sort of thing." He paused. "In the old days, the wealthy amateur paid his way here and the worthy scholar who couldn't afford it received a stipend. Now the state – the ratepayer – pays for everything." He laughed. "The poor are *subsidizing* everyone else."

"But that's how it's always been," I said.

"How do you mean?"

"None of these colleges could have been built without the poor. The priests wrote the checks, but the money was extracted from the people a farthing at a time."

The remainder of the meal was concluded in silence.

MARKHAM, HEAD bowed, grasped the iron railing and pulled himself up the steps to his lodgings. It had been a very long day. He had left London at sunrise and it was now almost midnight, but the time was well-spent. St. Cyr seemed firmly on board. All they lacked was the next clue.

He let himself into the house – his man, furnished by the college, had gone hours ago. In the library, he stirred the fire and added some wood, and poured a glass of brandy. The afternoon post was stacked on his desk. He stared at the square brown envelope on top, his knell and his redemption. The first one had arrived – in breach of the deal that had been struck – four years earlier. The perfunctory anger had dissipated immediately and the emotions expressed in subsequent notes – defiance, hope, resignation – had corresponded to his own. His weakness, though, was no excuse. The rubric by which he had lived his life was affirmed, and he would destroy those who failed to observe it.

The town's afternoon paper, the *Oxford Mail*, lay unopened before him. He spread the pages on his desk and searched for news of the campaign. It was there, but it had to be unearthed and assembled: an MP stepping down in Leicester, a man that Markham had approved eager to take his place – rallies in Bristol and Coventry and Liverpool, all well-attended despite efforts by the press to minimize them – confrontations in places large and small where, a year earlier, the natives would have given way to the invaders without a word. The country was not yet at the tipping point – that required inroads into the boroughs of the great metropolis – but the struggle to regain a way of life was gaining a foothold. The next few days would be critical.

Over the years he had become cynical. As Duke, don and Lord he had an unobstructed view of the evolution of Britain and Oxford but, even as his opinions grew marginal, he never lost the certainty that things had been better before and might still be again. And, though usually able to conceal it, the overarching obligation to his family consumed him to such a degree that it was hard to apply himself elsewhere. The recent resolution of *that* problem, though far from perfect, had allowed him at last to turn to other things.

I WOKE the next morning feeling a little queasy. Five or six courses of rich food and unending claret followed by several glasses of port, standard fare for high tables at Oxford, were still with me. I threw my legs over the side of the bed and stood up, frowning at the *Victoria* file on the dresser opposite. The bundle of firewood and kindling was on the landing, just as I had asked. I picked it up and carried it to the fireplace where a few burning coals remained. A moment later, a small fire and the scent of oak cheered the spartan room. I had decided not to bring personal tokens across the Atlantic. As a consequence, there were no books or photographs, no ornaments on the mantel and only a single rug, a small one furnished by the college, on the dark wooden floor. The other furnishings provided by Christ Church were a narrow bed with low posts, a mahogany dresser and nightstand, two lamps, two worn leather chairs and a desk. The walls and ceiling were painted white, and a mirror with a gilt frame hung over the fireplace.

Someone knocked on the door. "Yes?"

"It's me, sir. Andrews."

"Come in."

The scout, who looked after the needs of everyone on my staircase, stepped into the room. "Good morning, sir."

"Good morning, Andrews."

"Will you be having breakfast this morning?"

"No."

"Can I bring you something? Toast? Marmalade? Tea?"

"I can't face food at the moment, Andrews. Some tea would be nice."

"Do you require anything else?" I shook my head. "Very good, sir. I'll bring your tea." He turned to leave. "Oh, wait, I almost forgot." He reached into his pocket and withdrew an envelope. "This was left for you at the gatehouse." He handed it to me, his curiosity obvious. The front of the envelope had only my name in a flowing script. The flap on the back was embossed in gold: "Chancellor, University of Oxford." I opened the envelope and looked at the stiff, heavy card with the arms of the University – a blue and gold escutcheon with three crowns and an open book – at the top:

Mr. St. Cyr:

I should like to speak with you this afternoon. Please call on me at St. Giles' House at 2 P.M.

Cromwell

I looked up. "I am without appropriate writing materials, Andrews. Can you advise the Chancellor's Office that I'll be happy to see him today at two o'clock?"

"Yes, sir."

When Andrews was gone I walked to the window and gazed across the quad at the hall where I had dined the night before. The largest and most elaborate of all the dining halls at Oxford, the pinnacles atop its buttresses were bristling arrowheads aimed at the sky. Shifting my eyes to the left, I could see the spire of Christ Church Cathedral towering over the Dean's residence. I considered the Chancellor's "invitation." He knew I was an impostor of sorts, but he didn't know why. And Markham didn't like him. He was a *scientist,* which was Oxford shorthand for those who insisted that the University leave the 16th century and join the 20th. And, of course, the scientists had largely prevailed.

I sighed. Having put it off for as long as I could, I picked up the manila folder from the dresser, dragged one of the chairs to the window and sat down. *Victoria* had been the pride of the White Star Line. Along with her counterpart *Alexandra,* she plied the Atlantic on a weekly basis from Southampton to New York and back again, with an occasional interim stop on the coast of France. More than eighty thousand tons, the ship had just fewer than two thousand cabins, only half of which were occupied when she left England that day four years ago. I shuffled through the shockingly vague report and felt the helpless rage again. Nothing, absolutely nothing, had ever been done. The British government, embarrassed and defensive and apparently without a clue, had declared it "terrorism" and filed it away. I wondered about that now. Did they know more than they were letting on? Had one of their own weapons fallen into the wrong hands?

Terrorism was crime with an ideology. Though not as old as war, acts of terrorism had been committed before the birth of Christ. The modern incarnation had received its impetus from the French Revolution. Isolated acts in the 1920's – the bombing of a palace in Bessarabia and a cathedral in Bulgaria – had been called terrorism and, more recently, the destruction of airplanes over Siberia and Malaysia and government buildings in Turkey and Greece had been added to the list. But terrorism was pointless, even to terrorists, if the ideology was not revealed somehow and held up as superior to the culture attacked. No one had ever claimed responsibility for the bombing of *Victoria* and the murder of a thousand unsuspecting examples of the Western bourgeoisie. Because Muslim clerics in the Middle East – and their counterparts in London – had gloated openly, suspicion had been cast in that direction, but nothing was ever proved and the effort to do so was feeble. A few people had suggested that the force of the blast made it an unlikely weapon for terrorists, and they were ignored.

I ran my finger down the passenger list and stopped when I reached her name. I saw again the great ship, its three red and black stacks distinct against the sky, moving slowly down the Southampton Water to the Channel. I had remained on the dock – having finally decided to do what she desired, I needed another day in London. *Victoria* was still in plain view, just past Netley Abbey, when I turned to walk back to the car. Suddenly, a great burst of light seemed to engulf me, followed by the ear-splitting ferocity of an explosion and a succession of shock waves. I turned back to the Water. *Victoria* had disappeared, replaced by a brilliant eruption of fire that hovered over the horizon for a few seconds before becoming a black plume of dust and smoke rising into the sky. A fearsome weapon of incredible intensity, it had pulverized the ship and everyone on it. There was no need for lifeboats because there were no lifeboats and no one to launch them.

I stared out the window, and smelled again the stink of oil over Southampton Water. It was raining. Students and dons crisscrossed the quadrangle on this first day of the Michaelmas term, the newest arrivals marked by the college scarves that they wore. I looked back at the passenger list, shocked for a second to see my name directly under hers, and then I remembered: I would join the ship, and her, in Cherbourg, a thirty-minute flight across the Channel. I had changed my itinerary to accommodate the errand that would make us whole at last.

London

ABRAM KHAN leaned back in his chair and looked out the bow window at St. James's Street. He had been an honorary member at White's since his graduation from Oxford. He didn't fit the profile for membership at the time – wealth, privilege, nobility – but he *was* Oxford's greatest bowler and that counted for a lot, especially among the members who had wagered so spectacularly on his strong right arm. Many of his most successful commissions for ISI had been achieved at White's.

Khan closed his eyes and recalled his time at Oxford. He had never been so alone. The sole foreigner at Exeter College and the only student with tinted skin, he had been an exhibit at Oxford, pointed at and discussed surreptitiously, rarely addressed in the normal way. He was used to the attitudes – self-conscious contempt from those too busy or too awkward to play games, fawning deference from those who did or wanted to – but he had never experienced the *separation* that he encountered at Oxford. The dons were no better than the students. When his tutor finally realized that Khan was bright and serious about his studies he helped and encouraged him, but always in the manner of a circus trainer surprised at the achievements of his charge. Even his teammates treated him like a novelty off the cricket pitch.

Life had improved his second year when Anthony Markham returned to Oxford. Markham's snobbery was of a different sort – he reserved his disdain for those unable or unwilling to achieve. One of the old elite by birth, he pushed himself relentlessly to justify his place, and mocked the new aristocrats for their endless rent-seeking disguised as even-handedness. A world-class athlete himself, Markham was relaxed in Khan's presence and treated him as the Duke of Aylesbury would treat any other man in full. He was completely free of Oxford's paternalism, and the frequent invitations to Aylesbury Abbey enabled Khan to spend much-needed time away from the contrived atmosphere at the University.

The man he was watching for came into view. Charles Wellbourne had been the Cambridge cricket captain the first time that Khan had bowled for Oxford. Cambridge's innings at Lord's that year were the briefest in the history of the match, but Wellbourne never held it against him. During his early days in the House of Commons, he had been a crucial source of information – not in a treasonous sort of way but only in an effort to impress – and Khan hoped that with his new leadership role in the government he might prove more useful still.

He rose as Wellbourne approached the table. "A.K.," said Wellbourne, a broad smile on his face. "It's good to see you again."

"Thank you, Charles. And thanks for coming by."

"Are you joking? Whitehall's pretty dull stuff when the great Khan is in town." Khan smiled. "I watched the last few minutes of the Test Match. They say you're retiring. Is that right?"

Khan nodded. "I decided to go out on top. Your boys have had their last shot at me." Both men laughed.

"What brings you to England?" Wellbourne said.

"I've agreed to help the new college at Oxford with its cricket team."

Wellbourne frowned. "You're going to Oxford?"

"Yes. Religious solidarity and all that, you know."

"I'm not sure that –" Wellbourne stopped.

"What's the matter?"

"Nothing." He paused again and smiled. "You're going to need more than religion. I understand that only Muslims are admitted to the Mosque." Khan nodded again. "I also hear that most of the students are Saudis and Turks. Not much cricket there. You'll need to recruit a few of your own people." They laughed again.

A waiter appeared beside the table. "I'll have a gin and –" Wellbourne looked at Khan. "I'm sorry A.K., I –"

"No, no," said Khan. "Have your gin and tonic. I'm far too jaded to be offended." He looked at the waiter. "I'll have quinine with a slice of lime, please."

They talked about the past for a few minutes. When the drinks arrived, Khan began to steer the conversation into the necessary channels. "I plan to look up the new Chancellor while I'm in Oxford. His name is Cromwell, I believe. Do you know him?"

"Yes. He's one of our people. I'll call him as soon as I get back to the office."

"No, no, that's not necessary. I'll find him. Tell me what he's like."

"He's a grumpy old Cambridge man. Never played a game in his life. What do you want with him?"

"I'm not playing games anymore either, Charles. I have to make my way in your world now."

As they prepared to leave, Wellbourne seemed to come to a decision. "A.K., I'm not sure you should go to Oxford just now."

"Why not?"

"There may be some trouble up there."

"Trouble?"

Wellbourne nodded. "We've had a bomb threat."

"Terrorists?"

"Possibly. There's also the chance of, shall we say, more conventional criminality."

"Such as?"

"Money. Extortion."

"Have there been any demands?"

"Not yet. But many of the usual elements associated with terrorists are absent. If it's not terrorism, it's crime or – war."

"You think a foreign country is involved?"

"We're looking into it. The weapons involved are extremely sophisticated." Wellbourne paused. "Beyond the capability of most criminals, for instance."

That was pretty close to the bone. Khan pushed a little further. "Have you narrowed it down at all?"

Wellbourne smiled and shook his head. "Not really. There are a number of possibilities. And it may be a hoax." He stopped. "Aylesbury's a friend of yours, isn't he?"

"Yes. Why?"

"He believes that the Muslim community is responsible for all our ills, including this bomb threat. He's given dozens of speeches about it. Did you know that the ruined church at the Abbey was destroyed a few days ago?"

"No."

Wellbourne nodded. "He blames the Muslims. He has no evidence, of course, but there it is." He stood up. "Are you staying in town for a few days?"

"Yes."

"He's speaking at a rally at Trafalgar Square tomorrow night. You might take it in. I'm told it's quite a show."

Outside, Khan watched his friend turn the corner, then hailed a taxicab. He looked at the package in his hand. "Audley Street," he said. "St. Mark's Church."

"YES, JOHN, thank you. I'll see you in a few days." Pamela hung up the telephone and sighed. John Cromwell was an odious man who had imposed on her life for years, first because of Aden, now because he was the Chancellor at Oxford. He had no right to stick his nose in her business, but her friends at Whitehall had insisted that she work through him and she had, of course, agreed. The wellspring of his influence – accounting for his appointment as Chancellor and his continuing hold over North and the others – was a form of extortion that Pamela laughed at but Geoffrey, burdened by the hypocrisy of his politics, took it very seriously indeed.

She looked out the window to the street. A limousine stopped at the curb and a man emerged. He spoke to his driver for a moment, then started up the walk. She opened the door before he could knock. He smiled. "Hello, Pamela." She stood aside and he crossed the threshold.

They had met when she was just getting started and her success in the London beau monde was by no means assured. He was short and heavy, and smelled of the pomade he wore on his hair, but in those days her ability to pick and choose her clients was minimal. Although he spoke perfect English, he was clearly a foreigner. He came and went unexpectedly, and they always met in out-of-the-way hotels in Whitechapel or Chelsea.

She had quickly moved beyond his unappealing appearance. He was kind and free with his money and, unlike her English clientele, he didn't treat her like a whore. Food and champagne, and the drugs of her choice, were always available, and she had come to regard him as a generous friend who just happened to leave a hundred pounds on the bedside table when he left her. Their friendship had ended abruptly fifteen years earlier, and she had neither seen nor heard from him since. "What do you want?" she said.

He smiled again. "No small talk? Remembering old times?"

"No. I'm sure you want something. What is it?"

He nodded. "I want you to steal something for me in Oxford."

"How did you know I'm going to Oxford?" He didn't answer. "Why would I do that?"

"Because if you don't, I'll show your government friends the tape. The original. I don't believe they'll be amused."

She hesitated, then led him to the little parlor at the end of the hall. "Would you like a drink?" He nodded. "Vodka and water?"

"Yes."

She made his drink and poured herself a glass of wine. Even now, all these years later, the memory sickened her. There was a man that he wanted her to meet, he had said, a very important man with very unusual needs. He would consider it a great favor if she helped this man, and he would pay her a bit more than usual – say, five hundred pounds. The acts that he described were truly disgusting but, even at the tender age of nineteen, Pamela knew that something more was involved. Badly in need of money, though, and buoyed by the knowledge that she would be doped to the gills, she agreed. The following evening, she had spent an hour with the important man, collected her five hundred pounds and made herself insensible with vodka and drugs before passing out in her own bed.

Three days later she saw the important man's photograph, and those of his wife and children, in the newspapers. He had just resigned his post as the country's Ambassador to Pakistan, and rumors of further, worse trouble for the government and his party were swirling about London. There was a film, it seemed, that confirmed the Ambassador as the worst sort of pervert. It was far too vile to show the public, but sniggering policemen and members of the opposition assured everyone that it was thoroughly nasty. When the Ambassador put the barrel of a loaded revolver into his mouth and pulled the trigger, the Prime Minister resigned.

Bad copies of the film had circulated amongst the smart set in London for weeks. Pamela had seen it several times but watched it only once. The scenery – the tile, the porcelain, the chrome fixtures – was easily discernible in the glaring white light but the faces, hers and his, were grainy and blurred. No one cared about the woman on the tape. She had satisfied herself that she was impossible to identify and pushed it to the back of her mind where it festered like a suppurating wound. The Prime Minister's party, Geoffrey North's party, had wandered in the political wilderness for years.

KHAN LEANED uneasily against the balustrade that bounded the terrace at the northern edge of Trafalgar Square. The staircase leading down to the plaza, and the granite deck of the Square itself, were packed with people. The fountains and statues, and the four recumbent bronze lions, were all draped with human forms. Behind him, the broad steps of the National Gallery – its pediment, columns and cupola brilliantly lighted – were likewise crowded with men and women listening solemnly to the cultured English voices coming from the loudspeakers. Even the children were still, their faces unsmiling.

Light from the streetlamps around the Square, pale aureoles atop slender black stems, merged with the deep yellow of powerful spotlights aimed at the sky like flaming torches. A gentler illumination was thrown on the speakers who stood on the scaffolding that surrounded Nelson's column. British flags fluttered here and there, and massive banners bearing the red and white Cross of St. George swept over the audience, sails unfurled on a turbulent sea.

It was an unusual gathering for London. All the faces were white, all the tongues Anglo-Saxon. Khan was vaguely ashamed of his discomfort, the old feeling that his brown face was unliked and unwanted. No one had said a word to him, but the antipathy, the unwillingness to accept him as one of them, was evident. The speeches from the platform halfway up the great column, however, had been rational rather than incendiary – foreigners, rising taxes, Muslims, welfare, aliens, government, were all addressed as problems to be resolved. It was only when the Duke of Aylesbury stepped to the microphone that the crowd began to stir and respond, silently at first and then out loud, a single voice in complete agreement with his own.

The other speakers were dressed in dark business suits, but Tony Markham wore the blue dress uniform of the Royal Marines. Rows of medals, to which he was well-entitled, lay on his chest. Unmarried and childless, he was the last of a long and distinguished line. Educated at Eton and Oxford, he had taken a first with honors in Greats – classic literature taught in the original Latin and Greek – at Balliol, and been a Fellow at All Souls for five years. Britain's fencing champion four years running, he had won the silver medal in foil at the Mexico City Olympics.

The scion of a family who had somehow retained its wealth and property despite the onset of Britain's welfare state, he was frequently the target of vicious attacks in the newspapers and the House of Commons. Most of them were anonymous. Markham was known to have a very long memory, and it was rumored that the scar on his cheek was the product of a real quarrel that had not turned out well for the other fellow.

He was not the dilettante depicted in the papers. There were no undergraduates at All Souls, one of Oxford's richest colleges, a circumstance that gave rise to the plausible notion that its Fellows had little to do save play croquet and swill port. Markham, however, took on more than his share of graduate students and gave weekly lectures at various venues within the University. He was also largely responsible for preserving All Souls from the "reforms" imposed, bit by incremental bit, on the other colleges. His success had spurred Oxford's critics to greater oversight of the rest of the University.

He did other things as well. Rather than start his academic career immediately, he had served three years as a commando in the Royal Marines. He managed Aylesbury Abbey, its gardens, crops and livestock, and employed several hundred people in Buckingham who might otherwise be on the dole. He sat on boards and gave to charities and took his seat in the House of Lords seriously, although the creed he preached from his pulpit there had been dealt a mortal blow on the banks of the Somme and finally interred on the beaches at Dunkirk.

Easily the most exalted aristocrat among them, they didn't care. He was "Tony," and what did it matter that the life he lived was far different from theirs? He knew their fears and shared them, and he would restore the people, the backbone of England since before the Romans, to their rightful place.

Markham had begun like the others, but as the words poured out they became louder and more urgent. Questions were asked. "Is it right that these people, who pay no taxes, be pampered by the government at our expense?"

"NO," roared the crowd.

"Is it right for them to disobey our laws and expect us to submit to theirs?"

"NO," louder still.

"Is it right that this government has permitted large swathes of our country to be occupied by people who hate England and refuse to learn our language?"

"NO."

He lowered his voice. "Will you help me take our country back?"

"YES."

The faces were no longer sober. Eyes bulged, and spittle splashed from open mouths as they howled their full-throated approval. Heads turned toward Khan, but Markham raised his arms and they were quiet again. He gestured to the space around them. "This place was created to commemorate a great victory over a tyrant who sought to dominate the world." He pointed to the statue on top of the column. "But even Lord Nelson would never claim that he won at Trafalgar alone. It was the resources and resolve of the British people that made his victory possible." He paused. "We have a new tyranny to defeat. Desperate times require desperate measures. Every man must do his duty." The tumult started again. He raised his voice to speak over it. "The great lions that guard this place have been asleep too long. It's time for the lions to rise and roar again."

Khan moved to the edge of the crowd as the noise rose to a crescendo. Markham remained still, watching, as they called his name and their rapture played out. Finally, he lifted his arms again. "Remember – this is not about me. It's about a great people and a great country." He smiled. "Together, God willing, we will make it ours again."

Aylesbury

AYLESBURY WAS only twenty miles east of Oxford, but travel by train was complicated. The initial leg was south on the main line to the first stop – a platform without a name – then east on a branch line to Princes Risborough, then north to Aylesbury, the last station on another branch line. Considering the time between trains, and the stops, it took more than an hour. As the train pulled into Aylesbury Station, I caught a glimpse of Markham leaning against an old E-Type convertible in the car park. A moment later, I tossed my bag into the boot and squeezed into the left-hand seat. "Is there a servant problem at the Abbey these days?" I said.

Markham grinned. "I'm an egalitarian now. Equal everything for everybody. And I like to drive." He switched on the ignition and turned right out of the lot. "We still have a chauffeur and a Bentley – two of them, actually. My sister requires them."

"Is she here?"

"Yes." His forehead wrinkled. "You've never met Guin, have you?"

"No. She was living in France when I was here last. Is her husband with her?"

"There is no husband." I turned my head toward him but said nothing. "She's very modern, you see. Lavish church wedding – bishops and cardinals in all their splendor – quiet divorce." He stopped. "For no particular reason. Incompatibility, I believe she said." He laughed. "The idea that a man and his wife must be 'compatible' is very modern, too, isn't it?" I didn't respond. "Her current man arrived earlier today. He says you've met, by the way."

"Who's that?"

"John Cromwell."

I nodded. "Yes. He summoned me to his office this afternoon."

"Prying?"

I nodded again. "Not very effectively, I'm afraid. He took the position that as Chancellor he should know all there is to know. I agreed, and suggested that he get in touch with North or the Prime Minister. He was unable to say that they've refused to tell him, so the inquiry sort of petered out."

"His father was once the Marmalade King. Sold out, like all those fellows do, and used his capital to move up in the ranks. House in Grosvenor Square, country place in Hampshire, low-level bauble on Honors Day." He paused. "Couldn't buy Oxford for his boy, though." He stopped again. "Of course, that was thirty years ago."

"So he went to Cambridge."

"Yes. He carried on Chadwell's work there."

"Chadwell?"

Markham nodded. "He discovered the neutron. Our contribution to the bomb. Worked on the Manhattan Project and the rest."

"Then Cromwell really is a scientist?"

He nodded again. "He is. Or was. He was involved with the nuclear program for years." He paused. "Rumor is that Cromwell's lost everything his old man had."

"How did he end up at Oxford?"

"Kissing up, like his father." I laughed. "Now I think about it, he must have worked at the AEA part of the time."

"Would he talk about it?"

"Probably not – voluntarily. Perhaps a few drinks and a careful question or two would draw him out."

"Do you think he knows anything about the diagram?"

"If it has something to do with a nuclear weapon, he does. What did you think of him?"

"I was only with him for fifteen minutes." We had reached the East Lodge gate at Aylesbury Abbey. Built when Henry VIII was on the throne, the twin structures that flanked the gate had abbreviated battlements, sloping tile roofs and chimneys topped by chimney pots. Markham turned into the drive and slowed, dropping his left hand from the steering wheel to a button on the dash. The gate opened. I continued: "He's ambitious, I think, but unsure what he's ambitious for." I glanced at him.

"You may be right long term. Short term, though, I believe he knows what he wants."

"What's that?"

"My sister. Aylesbury Abbey."

"What's in it for her?"

"Well, Guin's ambitious, too." He paused. "Her politics are also very modern. He *is* the bloody Chancellor of the University of Oxford, and he has very well-placed friends. I believe she thinks he's going somewhere."

"Is he?"

"Anything's possible now." He paused. "He's really too *English* for that crowd at Whitehall. Not in the inner circle – not cosmopolitan enough." Markham smiled. "He still believes in the white man's burden. He's just unhappy with his place in the pecking order."

We were quiet as we drove beneath the avenue of limes. Almost bare, the trees were as old as the house. Their short, thick trunks lined up on either side of the roadway, the massive lower limbs bent to the ground while the upper branches joined overhead, and the few remaining leaves were yellow. Then, suddenly, the manor house at Aylesbury Abbey rose before us.

The first time I came here I had expected the usual Tudor stronghold – towers and turrets and battlements – but this was a home, not a castle. The house and grounds had been laid out according to precise specifications. The square wall that surrounded it was a quarter mile from the house on all sides. When it was first built, the enclosed quadrangle was also a perfect square eighty feet and three inches per side. Three wings of the original house survived. The facade was red brick excavated and made only a few miles away and the decorative features – the parapets, cornices and finials, and the flourishes around the doors and windows – were all of molded terracotta in the Italian Renaissance style. The narrow, crenellated parapet at the roofline over the Great Hall was a remnant of the old and the twelve Cupids over the doorway were harbingers of the new, but the arms, emblems and devices – some older than the house – painted on the windows ensured that the past would not be forgotten.

Markham climbed out of the car without bothering to open the door and pulled my bag from the rear. "Welcome back," he said.

I smiled. "Thanks. I'm glad to be here."

IN THE spring of my first class year at the Academy, I had been awarded a scholarship to Oxford. The scholarship, endowed by a man who had reveled in the now-vanished Empire, was usually redeemed immediately after the bachelor's degree, but I had prior commitments that had to be kept. It was not until eight years later that I finally found myself walking down the High in a black gown with streamers that hung to my knees. I was still in the Navy and still working for the Office, but during my two years at Oxford my professional activities were limited to small affairs in and around London.

Oxford was different from American universities. A student's first loyalty was to his college – where he slept, ate and studied – rather than to the University itself. Communal meals were taken in dining halls, the "dormitories" were usually fashioned into quadrangles where the rooms were organized vertically on staircases rather than along horizontal hallways, and different groups had different rooms or buildings dedicated to their use. There was always a chapel and a library, and each college had its own rules and traditions. Those charged with instructing, tutoring and otherwise overseeing the undergraduates might be called dons or professors, but their formal designation was "Fellow," except at my college where they were called "Students." The men at the top might carry any one of several titles – "Warden" at All

Souls, for instance, "Dean" at Christ Church and "Master" at Balliol. The academic year began in October and was divided into three terms – Michaelmas, Hilary and Trinity – of three months each.

I had elected to read for a Master's degree in English Literature and, despite its antipathy for my chosen discipline, I was awarded a place at Christ Church, known familiarly as "the House of Christ" or just "the House." As a consequence of my delayed arrival, I was among the oldest students there. The four hundred undergraduates seemed like children, and the graduate students – half that number – not much further along. And they were all men, or boys. Women had been admitted to the University in small numbers for years, and women's colleges had been in place for almost a century, but the male colleges had yet to open their doors to females. My days were spent at lectures and seminars, and once a week I met with my tutor – a crusty old don who preferred sherry to tea – to judge the progress of my thesis. I dined in the hall every evening and sometimes had a drink in town afterward, most often at The Bear on Alfred Street just a few steps away from Christ Church.

My solitude ended when I met Tony Markham. Returning to my rooms one evening I encountered my scout on the staircase. "You had a visitor today, sir," he said.

"Really? Who?"

"The Duke of Aylesbury."

"The *Duke* of Aylesbury?"

"Yes, sir. His card's on the mantel." The little man followed me inside. I picked up the thick ivory card. It was engraved "Anthony Gerald Markham" and, underneath in smaller letters, "The College of All Souls of the Faithfully Departed." I looked at the scout. "Markham's his Christian name, sir. His title is Duke of Aylesbury."

"What does he want with me?"

"Look on the back."

I turned the card over and read out loud: "I understand that you fence. There are now two of us. If you're available, meet me at the Eagle and Child tomorrow after dinner. Markham."

I looked at the scout again. "It's on St. Giles', sir. Up from St. John's."

The next evening I walked up St. Aldate's to Cornmarket. As I passed the unadorned Saxon tower of St. Michael's Church, the oldest building in the ancient village, I slowed my pace and studied the landscape ahead of me. This rendezvous had been suggested by someone else, and it was never wise to simply show up without taking precautions. I stood in the shadow of another old church and surveyed my surroundings. Balliol was to the right, and beyond that I could see – past the plane trees and the streetlamps – the gables of St. John's College. The Randolph Hotel, Oxford's finest, was just ahead, and the Eagle and Child was a few blocks further on. I remained still for several minutes and then, satisfied, continued up St. Giles'. I smiled to myself. The truth was that it was impossible to be sure in Oxford. A dozen assassins, a hundred abductors, could be concealed in any one of its streets. A moment later I stepped inside the pub.

The room was full of people with cameras and nametags, but my attention was drawn immediately to a man standing at the bar with two elegantly-dressed women. Slender, just under six feet tall, he created the space about him. The other people at the bar, and in the rest of the room, were shoved together like chess pieces in a too-small packing case while he and his companions stood and smiled and gestured without intrusion, as if they were alone. My eyes shifted to the women. They were beautiful – one a full-breasted blonde, the other dark and slight – and I detected a hint of the professional in the carefully tended bodies and disinterested eyes. They probably traded in trinkets like those on their fingers and wrists, rather than cash.

The man turned his head and saw me. He said a few words to the women, then crossed the room. "St. Cyr?" he said, extending his hand. I nodded, grasping it. "Tony Markham. Glad you could come."

"Thanks."

"Join us, won't you?"

We returned to the bar. Introduced as "Susan" and "Alice," the women were ignored for half an hour while Markham and I talked about fencing. "You're quite – large for a fencer, aren't you?" he said. I nodded again. "What's your favorite blade?"

"Saber."

"Mine's the foil."

"I know. I looked you up in Debrett's."

He smiled. "I thought Americans liked team games."

"We do. But my father insisted that I learn to take care of myself. There would always be a time, he said, when you were alone."

"Did he teach you to fence?"

I shook my head. "He sent me to a school in Virginia. My fencing master was an Italian and my boxing coach was a Brit."

"We'll have to have a go some time. Maybe a small wager."

"It would have to be a *very* small wager."

Markham laughed and the conversation turned to other things. Susan and Alice spoke occasionally, but only when a question or comment was directed their way. Finally, he looked at his watch. "We must be going. Would you –" He stopped. "What about lunch on Saturday? My rooms?"

"Yes. I'd like that."

"Right. I'll see you then." After the door closed behind them, I waited a minute, then stepped outside. Following discreetly, I watched as he and the two women entered the Randolph Hotel. I had nothing against working girls, but it seemed remarkable that a man as prominent as the Duke of Aylesbury would dally with two of them in Oxford's most obvious hotel. Still, with his money and blood perhaps it was deemed merely eccentric.

We had become friends. The lavish luncheon at All Souls was followed by one less opulent at Christ Church. He had insisted that we ignore the small, messy metropolis that Oxford was becoming, and we did – we consciously confined ourselves to old Oxford and the activities associated with it. We punted on the Cherwell, watched football on Iffley Road and bicycled, precariously, on the High. I visited the house in Belgrave Square, the clubs on Northumberland Avenue and St. James's Street and, finally, on the day after Christmas, I passed through the gate at Aylesbury Abbey where I was subsequently welcomed many times. I became proficient in the history of Aylesbury and the Markham family while Markham was oddly circumspect. He listened to whatever I chose to reveal but never initiated the conversation, leading me to conclude that he knew exactly who I was.

His only serious idiosyncrasy, as far as I could tell, was his lack of interest in ordinary women. He was rarely accompanied by the same girl twice, and all of them looked like Susan or Alice. He was obviously no prude, but the subject of sex and its adjuncts – love, marriage, children – were scrupulously avoided. He smiled at my occasional romance but never sought any particulars. For my part, after being firmly turned away several times from any such query, I stopped asking.

Fencing was often a topic of conversation, but we had fought only once. It happened during one of my early visits to the Abbey in the midst of an extended weekend when the house was full of guests. The four women had already gone to bed and the men – the parish priest, a florid colonel long retired from the Coldstream Guards, and two of Markham's friends from London – had begun to go one by one. After gently shaking Colonel Ross-Throckmorton and urging him off to bed, Markham had turned to me and said, "What about a little exercise tomorrow, St. Cyr? Epee. Fifteen minutes, four minutes rest."

I smiled at my friend. "All right. Are we going to keep score?"

"Of course. We shall call it ourselves and reconcile it every five minutes."

"Fencing rigs?"

"I don't think so. I don't have anything that would fit you. Let's just go with masks."

I considered that. "All right. Where?"

"The Long Gallery, I think. The other rooms are too crowded."

I nodded. "What time?"

"Before everyone else is up. Say, seven o'clock."

The Long Gallery at Aylesbury was just that – a wide second-floor hallway that ran half the length of the east wing of the house. It had paneled walls and tall windows and, except for a few chairs around the perimeter, no furniture. Dozens of portraits and tapestries hung from the walls and a huge woven rug, itself centuries old, covered the floor.

Markham was waiting when I arrived. Each of us wore tight-fitting trousers and snug long-sleeved sweaters. Sunlight poured into the room through the uncovered windows. We pulled on the masks and faced each other for a moment, epees raised, and then he attacked.

Epee fencing is as close to a real sword-fight as modern sensibilities permit. Heavier and less flexible than either the saber or the foil, an epee is really a small sword without the sharp point. The rules of epee are less restrictive than the other two, and points are scored when the blunt end of the blade touches any part of an opponent's body.

It was immediately apparent to me, and certainly to Markham, that he was the better fencer. I had been a champion at the Naval Academy, and won a number of outside competitions, but he had once been among the best fencers in the world. His footwork was effortless, his thrusts and parries instinctive, and when the first five minutes were over his blade had touched me ten times while I had scored only once.

As we began the second period, I noticed that the other guests and a few of the servants, probably drawn by the clash of the heavy blades, had gathered at one end of the gallery to watch. This time he invited me to attack, content to turn my blade without countering, and when we rested again we agreed that the score was fourteen to five. I had detected a slight flaw by then but was unable to take advantage of it. Whenever he parried a thrust to his left his blade dipped for an instant, leaving him open to a high slashing blow. In saber competition, slashing touches counted as points – in epee only the point of the blade scored. The final five minutes were the most spirited – we moved up and down the great room and passed each other repeatedly – but at the end the margin was unchanged.

"HOW'S YOUR drink, John," I said as I crossed the room to the ebony cabinet that served as Tony Markham's bar.

"I'll have another brandy and soda, if you don't mind," said John Cromwell.

The public rooms of the house at Aylesbury Abbey were very large – the Great Hall, for instance, was more than fifty feet long and twenty-five feet wide, and the ceiling was over thirty feet high – so intimacy was created by the arrangement of screens, furniture and rugs. The room in which we were seated, called the Little Hall, had a billiard table at one end and a grand piano at the other. In between, an enormous Persian rug covered the stone floor, and leather sofas and chairs and low mahogany tables were placed around the arched terracotta fireplace. A large portrait of Markham's brother James hung over the mantel.

Markham stood by the fire, warming his left hand behind his back. I handed the glass to Cromwell and resumed my seat. Markham looked at me. "I see where you Yanks have invented a new bomb in case all those nukes don't get the job done. 'The mother of all bombs,' I think it's called. Know anything about it?"

"No more than you, I guess. I understand that it's very powerful but not a nuclear weapon."

Markham turned his head. "What about you, Cromwell? You used to be in the bomb business."

John Cromwell was a tall, pear-shaped man whose coat would not button over his considerable stomach. His lank dark hair was unruly and had to be constantly swept from his forehead. He pursed his lips. "I was *not* in the bomb business as you call it. Most of my work had nothing to do with weapons."

Markham grinned. "Most of it?" There was no response. "Well, give the Americans credit. If anyone can move us a step closer to annihilation, it's them."

"The Americans didn't invent it," Cromwell said, "though it's just like them to pretend that they did." He took a long swallow of his drink.

"Who did?"

"The theory's been around a long time. Any reasonably sophisticated country could make one."

"So we could build one?" said Markham. Again there was no reply. "How does it work?"

"It's a conventional weapon that's designed to yield far more explosive force than is usual for the materials used to make it. It generates tremendous temperatures and shock waves and everything in range is simply obliterated."

"Like *Victoria,*" I said softly.

Cromwell looked at me as if surprised to find me still there. "No – no. It's not like the *Victoria* explosion." He paused. "Nothing like it."

Markham and I looked at each other. "You said the theory's been around for a long while," said Markham. "How long?" Cromwell didn't answer. "Well, no matter. You scientists will kill us all anyway."

Cromwell's face turned pink. "Science isn't all about bombs, Markham," he said angrily. "We've increased lifetimes by decades, for example."

"Yes," said Markham, "but you're not content with that. Preservation of human life isn't enough. Now you want to create it." He paused. "And where will that lead? There's always something else, isn't there? Something that must be done in the name of *science.*"

"Tell me one thing that your precious Greats or – or any of that old stuff at Oxford has done to advance civilization," said Cromwell.

Markham smiled. "I believe that would require an agreement between us as to what 'advance' means, and I think that's doubtful." He looked over his glass. "I'll answer you this way: What harm has it done?"

"It's useless. It has no value."

"I disagree with you, Cromwell, but I won't argue the point. Answer my question. How has a group of silly old dons wearing caps and gowns and disputing in Greek and

Latin for a thousand years *harmed* civilization?" Cromwell didn't answer. Markham nodded. "And yet, it's inarguable that in just a few decades your science has brought us to the brink of total destruction." He stopped. "You call that advancing civilization?"

"Would you have us simply submit to our enemies?"

"Don't confuse the issue, Cromwell. We're not talking about the ambitions of kings. We're speaking of the science that enables them." Markham stopped. "Cain and Abel fought with their hands. When Oxford was young, when the priests called to one another in Latin, men fought with sticks. Hastings was the fiercest of all the medieval battles – there were only six thousand casualties, all of them combatants. No villages were razed, no women and children slaughtered. Three hundred years later, when they began to speak Greek at Oxford, the deaths at Agincourt were fewer and they still used sticks. Only with the advent of the great god Science have we been able to destroy entire cities and kill hundreds of thousands of people with a single weapon dropped from the sky." Markham paused for breath.

"Casualties in the Pacific would have been far greater had the Yanks not used the bomb," said Cromwell.

"Yes, as a consequence of yesterday's science, of weapons only slightly less destructive than an atomic bomb." Markham closed his eyes. "And now, God help us, there's a bomb that destroys so utterly you can't even count the bodies. At least they could bury the dead at Hiroshima."

"Look, Markham," said Cromwell, "warfare's not the only –" He stopped and turned his head toward the arched doorway.

The woman who entered the room had the same vitality, the same glow, as her brother. An inch or two shorter than him, and several years younger, her hair was a pale polished bronze swept away from her face in a heavy, thick mane. The narrow brows over large black eyes were just darker than her hair, and her skin was the shade and texture of heavy cream. Her nose was a perfect ridge against her face and the mouth was slightly open, the full lips unpainted – the only makeup was a faint lavender around her eyes. The bodice of the long black dress tied behind her neck, barely containing the loose breasts, and the only ornamentation was a strand of pink pearls. She reached Markham and kissed him, then turned, eyes glittering.

"Guin, this is Georges St. Cyr," Markham said. "St. Cyr, my sister Guin."

Her eyes locked onto mine as she extended her hand. Rather than accept the brief pressure my fingers offered, she gripped my hand like a man and pressed back. "Tony says that your family is French," she said. "Some of our people came from France."

I smiled. "So we might be cousins?"

She looked into my eyes again. "Perhaps. But not close enough to matter." She turned to Cromwell. "John, be a dear and make me a martini, please." Cromwell stared at her but didn't move. "John?" Cromwell seemed to shake himself, then crossed to the bar. Markham laughed.

As we left the room for dinner, a boy about eight years old approached Guin and spoke to her in a low voice. She nodded and turned back to me, her hands on the boy's shoulders. "Georges, this is my son, Gerry." She bent and spoke in the child's ear. "This is Mr. St. Cyr, Gerry, a friend of your uncle's." The boy lifted his eyes and smiled at me. The resemblance was startling – he looked exactly like Guin, or a younger version of her brother. We murmured words of greeting to each other, and the boy looked again at his mother. She slipped something from her pocket and handed it to him. He turned toward the staircase, holding the object to the side of his head.

At dinner, the men around the table were silent but she didn't seem to notice. She asked us questions and replied to our brief answers while devouring the whole of each course placed before her. I wanted to talk to Markham about the bomb and the problem I had been asked to solve, but Cromwell's presence made that impossible. Near the end of the meal, Markham engaged Guin in a discussion of the events planned for the following day, but Cromwell and I remained quiet. When she left us, after announcing her intention to retire early, it was as if a great storm had passed, but the conversation was still fitful.

Port was served. After tossing off a couple of glasses, Cromwell said that he, too, was going to bed. As he stood up, one of the servants appeared in the doorway. "You have a telephone call, Doctor Cromwell," he said.

Cromwell looked at his watch. "Who in bloody hell would be calling at this hour?"

"It's the Home Secretary, sir." Startled, Cromwell hesitated, then left the room.

Markham and I sat without speaking. "Something must have happened," Markham said finally.

I nodded. "Maybe another bomb. Not like *Victoria*, of course."

Markham smiled. "I'm afraid friend Cromwell got a little jolt this evening." I raised my brows. "I was watching him. When Guin turned those big black eyes on you, he shivered." I laughed. "Don't laugh. And be careful." He paused. "Be careful of both of them."

Cromwell re-entered the room. "There's been some sort of threat against the University," he said. He looked at me. "He wants to speak to you."

WE SAT around a circular table situated beside one of the large gabled windows in the roof. Cups, saucers, coffee and tea had been left on the sideboard next to the table. Charles Wellbourne poured himself some tea and looked around. "This is very – delicate, Cromwell," he said. "We've decided to take you into our confidence because St. Cyr may need your help. It goes no further unless you hear from me directly. Understood?" Cromwell nodded. "This is all covered by the Official Secrets Act," the Home Secretary said. "Is *that* understood?" Everyone nodded. Wellbourne opened his briefcase and withdrew three white envelopes. "These were received yesterday afternoon. One posted from London, another from Portsmouth and the third from Oxford." He drew a folded sheet of paper from one of the envelopes. "We've analyzed the paper, glue, envelopes and stamps. They're all quite ordinary. No fingerprints or other indicators." He unfolded the paper. "This is the one from Oxford."

THE SEED IS PLANTED. IT WILL
BLOOM IN SEVEN DAYS, AT THE
END OF THE GREAT BELL'S CHIME.

"What's the 'great bell?'" said Cromwell.

I smiled at the Cambridge man. "There are lots of bells in Oxford, John, but the 'great bell' 'is Great Tom at Christ Church. He chimes a hundred and one times every evening at five minutes past nine. I'm sure you've heard him."

Wellbourne passed the paper to me. "The intelligence people believe these messages are related to the attack on the church here."

"Why?"

"The marker used on the map and letters is the same. It, too, is quite commonplace, but there are dozens of them out there, and the coincidence seems a bit far-fetched." He looked at me. "What do you think?"

"About what?"

"About these – communications."

"I don't think anything about them and probably never will unless you tell me what you're afraid of."

"I don't understand."

I shook my head. "You *know* what these letters mean. You and your friends have lied to me, or withheld the truth, from the beginning. In fact, you've been lying for four years." I stopped. "There was a diagram with the map that was apparently produced by your nuclear agency. North didn't mention it and neither have you." I paused again. "I believe that you believe that bombs, probably of the *Victoria* variety, have been planted in London, Portsmouth and Oxford. I think you know more about *Victoria* than you've said. If you tell me the truth, I'll try to help you. Otherwise, I'll be gone well before the bombs explode."

The Home Secretary had listened to the charges attentively. Now he smiled. "I'll correct only one minor point. *This* government was not in power when *Victoria* exploded. Technically, then, *we* have not been lying for four years, but I was fully briefed when we came in. Until now, there's been no reason to reconsider the secrecy imposed by the previous government." He rose and walked to the window. "Eight years ago we began to work seriously on a highly explosive thermobaric bomb. Our nuclear arsenal was aging, it was expensive to maintain, and we hadn't the will to use it anyway. The thermobaric weapon, on the other hand, is relatively cheap, and the consensus was that it *would* be used if necessary."

"But it's a completely different bomb," I said. "It has nowhere near the range of a nuclear weapon. Its use in warfare would be very limited."

Wellbourne turned back to the table. "Yes, but we didn't intend to use it that way."

I leaned forward. "Meaning what?"

"We planned to use it as a bit of insurance," said the Secretary. "Planted in the appropriate places in, say, Moscow or Beijing or –" he smiled again "– Washington, detonated remotely, we thought we could protect ourselves without the expense and folly of nuclear weapons, that the threat of *personal* destruction would deter our enemies."

"You planted a bomb in Moscow?" said Cromwell.

Wellbourne shook his head and sat down. "We didn't get that far. The basic bomb was simple but it was far too large for our purposes. Portability was the problem." He leaned back in his chair. "Eventually, the scientists solved that problem. Something about seeding the chemicals to increase the yield. Four test bombs, each the size of a small suitcase, were produced. They were never tested."

"Why not?" I said.

"The trouble with portability is – portability. They disappeared without a trace." He stopped. "We looked for them, of course, to no avail. Whoever it was, they didn't get the detonators, very complex devices themselves, and it was hoped that would prevent them from being used."

"But it didn't?" said Markham.

"We can't be sure. Other countries – the Soviets, for example – were working on these things. However, the bomb that destroyed *Victoria* performed exactly as anticipated, so the government has been operating on the assumption that it was one of ours."

"And you think the other three are now planted in Oxford, London and Portsmouth," I said.

"Yes."

"But why?" said Cromwell. "Have there been demands for money or – or something?" The Home Secretary shook his head. "Are you still looking for them?"

"Yes, but it's – they are very small, and could be hidden anywhere, especially in a place like Oxford. We don't want to create a panic. And if it turns out to be a hoax, we'd be a laughingstock."

"Better than lots of dead people, surely," said Markham.

"Of course. But the cost of a panic or an evacuation would be astronomical. If nothing happens –" He lifted his shoulders.

"Do you suspect anyone in particular?" said Cromwell.

"We're looking into *Victoria* again. But so far – nothing."

"What was the range of the test bombs?" I said.

"Estimated at half a million square meters. Just less than one-fifth of a square mile."

"So it would kill hundreds of thousands of people in London and maybe none in Oxford, depending on where it's placed," said Markham. Wellbourne nodded. "But Oxford could be evacuated easily, couldn't it? I mean, it's less than a hundred thousand people altogether. And you wouldn't have to move them very far."

"Yes, but what would be our reason? What would we tell the rest of the country?"

"Make something up, Mr. Secretary," I said. "That's how you've handled it so far." We sat quietly. After a few seconds, I said, "You haven't said anything about the diagram."

"It was taken from plans for a project that was abandoned over ten years ago. We have no idea what it means – it has nothing to do with these bombs." He reached into his briefcase again, produced a larger envelope and handed it to me. "The map and diagram are in there. I'll leave you the Oxford letter."

"Is there anything else?" I said. Wellbourne shook his head. "You realize that if what you believe is true we're searching for the proverbial needle in a haystack?"

"Yes."

I hesitated. "I'm not sure what I can do, Mr. Secretary, but I'll try to help you if you will see that certain things are done."

"Yes?"

"I'll concentrate on who the bombers are. You search for the bomb as thoroughly as possible in the time that remains."

"All right. What else?"

"Oxford must be evacuated within the next five days."

Later, we stood in the courtyard and watched the Secretary's car disappear into the trees. "You should be pleased, Cromwell," said Markham.

"How do you mean?"

"We're all terrorists now – even the Queen." He looked at me. "What should we do first?"

I smiled. "Are you sure you want to be involved in this?"

"Certainly. They blew up my church, didn't they?"

I examined my friend carefully. "All right. I think we'll start with the ruins of the ruins then." I looked at Cromwell. "You'll see about the other?"

Cromwell nodded. "I'm going back to Oxford this afternoon and –"

Markham interrupted, smiling. "Is that wise?"

Cromwell looked puzzled for an instant, then a slow flush crept up his neck and face. He turned back to me. "I'll alert the Town and the colleges that something's up. When the Secretary has decided upon his strategy, we'll meet and decide how and where everyone is to go."

"Don't let time get away from you, John," I said. "Wellbourne's not too keen on the evacuation idea." I turned onto the path to the church and Markham joined me. Cromwell went into the house.

"Maybe you should ease up on Cromwell," I said. "He could be very useful."

"It's him and his ilk who have brought us here, St. Cyr, men without honor interested only in what's good for them." He paused. "They have dragged this country down to their level, and the rest of us are paying for it. We'll have to deal with them after –" He stopped again.

"After what?"

He shook his head. "Can you imagine a Britain reduced to planting bombs like – like some lunatic Guy Fawkes? It's pathetic."

"Still –"

"Still – I'll bear it in mind."

We had reached the site of the old church. The stones and arches and beams lay scattered everywhere – no portion of the structure remained though the family cemetery on the far side of the path had been spared. Most of the great trees – oaks, cedars, beeches – had survived. There was a wide depression a few feet deep where the chapel had stood. Its doors and pews and altar now intermingled with the remnants of the rest of the church. I stared into the pit. "I guess we can draw a red X through Aylesbury," I said. "Is this how it was?"

"Yes."

"Anything moved or taken?"

"Just the remains of the things inside the chapel."

I wandered among the rubble. "There's something I don't understand."

"What's that?"

"What is Aylesbury's connection to the rest of this mess? Why destroy the chapel? Why not use one of the big bombs?"

Markham looked around at the destruction. "This church was a powerful symbol of Christianity in a culture that becomes less Christian, less religious, every day. We now live cheek to jowl with another culture for which religion is both a mania and a weapon. And I speak up about it." He stopped. "They didn't use one of their fancy bombs because they didn't need to. The old science was more than adequate."

"You really believe these people are after you?"

He nodded. "I'm certain of it. I'm all that stands in the way of total capitulation."

"Setting aside the Muslim clerics in London, is there anyone else who wants you out of the way?"

"Cromwell." I laughed. "I'm serious. Guin and – and Aylesbury would probably just fall into his lap if I were dead."

"You don't really think he wants to blow up Oxford, do you?"

"I put nothing past him."

Back in my room, I pondered Markham's words. The worst barbarism in the history of mankind had been committed in the name of religion. The English had savaged one another for more than a hundred years though some would say it was power and politics, not religion, that was at the root of the quarrel. Three men had been burned at the stake only a few steps away from the Master's Lodgings at Balliol. Continents, countries and even families had been riven by doctrine for as long as history had been recorded, and probably longer, and I was personally acquainted with the pain that it caused.

◇◇◇

I RUBBED my eyes. Reduced to dummy for the final hand, I had left the bridge table a few minutes earlier and returned to my room. The company had been jovial in a hale but shallow way and it seemed as if I had met them all before, but no one acknowledged a prior meeting and I couldn't recall one either. Only the Markhams, brother and sister, were vivid, he attired in the traditional evening clothes that his fathers had worn for generations, she in a blazing blue gown that covered less than it revealed. I smiled at the thought of her. It was unlikely that any of the previous chatelaines at Aylesbury Abbey had ever worn such a costume.

I switched on a lamp that arced over the writing desk and examined the map. It raised as many questions as it answered. Why had it been sent? Why would those engaged in this very deadly game reveal, even in a general way, where the next attacks would come? I shook my head – that wasn't all that the map represented. The circle with the red X was a target *already* struck, more than four years before. Why? To take credit? To establish *bona fides?* I briefly considered whether or not it was all a hoax as the Home Secretary feared. It seemed doubtful – the attacks on *Victoria* and the church at Aylesbury were certainly real enough.

I grimaced. An enlightened citizen of the West, my professional training had included a philosophical explanation for why all the killing was necessary. War is the state of man unless he is at peace, and he is not at peace unless another man has subdued him. There's no law in war, no right or wrong, no justice or injustice. Force and fraud are all that matter, and the ends justify the means. The cowardly slaying of a thousand innocents was no better or worse than the courtly duel of opposing princes. All the efforts to "civilize" war had failed. I closed my eyes.

I awoke an hour later, instantly alert. The light over the desk was just enough to see the doorknob turn. I leaned forward, bent at the waist, shifting my weight to the balls of my feet. As the door opened, I tensed, then relaxed as a figure clad in gold swept silently into the room. The black eyes found me immediately, now seated again and turned toward her. A hand went to her waist as she walked toward me, and the long silk robe fell open. She wore nothing under it except a string of pearls, white this time, around her graceful neck. When she stood before me, she shrugged her shoulders and the golden robe slid to the floor. She reached across the desk and turned off the light. I inhaled her scent, fresh and sweet but unidentified. "It's past your bedtime," she said, and reached for my hand.

MARKHAM STOOD in the shadows of the loggia and watched his sister cross the quadrangle in the moonlight. He waited to see if St. Cyr would refuse her and when, as expected, he did not, he pushed his way back through the narrow French doors and re-entered his bedroom.

He and St. Cyr had met eight years earlier. The Warden at All Souls had pointed him out on the High one day, noting that St. Cyr was a fencing champion. Because of the military background and unusual delay in coming to Oxford, Markham had made inquiries at Whitehall and learned that St. Cyr was one of America's premier saboteurs, perhaps the most dangerous of all its intelligence agents. Markham's source had described successful operations in India and Africa, and added that St. Cyr was known to be his agency's foremost assassin. Intrigued by this background, and because men who could use a foil or epee well were few in Oxford, he had sought the younger man out and nurtured their friendship.

He poured a glass of brandy and looked into the fire. He had expected something like this from Guin, and St. Cyr was soft when it came to women. Somewhere along the way Guin had decided that, despite the laws of England and the terms of their father's will, Aylesbury Abbey was really hers. When he announced his engagement and the prospect of a new mistress at the Abbey, reality set in. As the wedding approached, rancor turned to obsession and defiance. His engagement had been broken and their lives tragically altered. The nightmares that had visited him since his brother's death grew worse. He was weak, and he was ashamed of his weakness, and he lived in terror that his depravity would be discovered. He had finally confronted Guin with some of the truth, certain that she would do something about it. The midnight tryst with Georges St. Cyr was undoubtedly part of the plan, but the rest of the truth would render her scheming meaningless.

BOOK TWO

Sweat started from the brows of the Emperors. They, at least, foresaw the peril, and they gave such warning as they could . . . Surely, it is a sign of some grace in them that they rejoiced not in the evil that was to befall the city of their penance – Sir Max Beerbohm

CHAPTER ONE

I LOOKED at my watch as the train pulled into Oxford Station. One of the infrequent meetings of students and dons in my creative writing program would be held at noon and I had decided to attend, despite the possibility that my actual task here would be done or not in seven – now six – days. It would only take a few minutes, and there was no reason to jettison my cover story yet.

A light rain was falling as I left the station and turned onto New Road, passing Nuffield College on the left and the remains of Oxford Castle on the right. I continued east on the single block of Queen and passed Carfax to the High. At St. Mary's Church, once the administrative heart of the University, I turned left on Catte Street and walked to Radcliffe Square. Ignoring the circular splendor of Radcliffe Camera, I entered the Schools Quadrangle and – on the other side of the quad – climbed the steps to Arts End, part of the Bodleian Library adjacent to the Divinity School. With its floor-to-ceiling bookcases, galleries and smell of old leather and books, it had always been a favorite place to study and to think.

The only occupant of my part of the long narrow building, I chose a table in front of one of the tall windows and sat down. Light cast arcading shadows over the table and onto the floor. I arranged the thoughts in my head.

The obvious starting point in the hunt for the bombers was the government's investigation of the missing bombs. Sensing the Secretary's reluctance, I had suggested that Markham be given that task and Wellbourne had grudgingly agreed. I had assigned myself a more creative task – to attempt to divine the *reason* for the threatened attack on Oxford. The Home Secretary had never answered that question, and I hoped it was because he didn't know. I was convinced that the answer to the *why* would lead to the *who*. *Where* was another issue. I had agreed to provide Wellbourne a list of potential targets for the battalion of troops who would arrive tomorrow. It was doubtful that the bomb he had described could be found, but the effort had to be made.

What were the apparent facts? The British had developed a powerful weapon that was stolen before it could be tested. The detonators for the bombs had not been taken. Nevertheless, a weapon that the Brits believed was one of the stolen bombs subsequently destroyed *Victoria.* After that, four years of silence. Why? Ideologues were seldom so patient in promoting their agendas and they reveled in the spectacular. The current targets were equally available four years ago. Why wait?

When the silence *was* broken, it wasn't a sensational attack on an iconic location. Instead, a historic but nearly forgotten pile of rocks had been reorganized by a low-yield conventional weapon. The church at Aylesbury was truly significant only to the Duke and his family. Hundreds of similar ruins dotted the English countryside. Why choose Aylesbury Abbey? I was not inclined to credit Markham's theory. There were far more significant symbols of

Christianity in the country – St. Paul's Cathedral, for example – to attack. And if they really wanted to kill Markham, why not use the bomb now intended for Oxford and ensure his death? Or cut his throat instead of providing clues? Still, he was sure that his Muslim enemies were responsible, and it had to be considered.

Guin's image interrupted me. I smiled at the thought of her. She had remained with me the entire night. Fully erect when I rose from the chair, had it been left to me our time together would have been measured in minutes instead of hours. But Guin had a repertoire that she wished to perform and she had done so, with charming variations, repeatedly. She made every part of her body available and insisted that I make use of them in the same way, I imagined, that Markham's women did. And like them, I was certain, her favors did not come free of charge. She had no need of money or jewels – her payment would be something more personal. Sooner or later, the *quid pro quo* would be demanded. I wondered what it was.

I looked at the map again. It implied that whoever blew up the church had also destroyed *Victoria,* and it conveyed the threat that further attacks were planned. What kind of attacks? The British government had leaped to the conclusion that the high-explosive bombs would be used, but there was no evidence that the people they were seeking even had the three bombs. Or the four bombs, for that matter – the Brits had *assumed* that the *Victoria* bomb was one of theirs. None of those assumptions was unreasonable, but they were assumptions nonetheless.

I turned to the diagram. The Home Secretary had been reluctant to even discuss it. Next to the box that Markham had mentioned was a logo, a rhomboid in the shape of the state of Nevada with a red star in the southwestern corner. It had an odd frame around it – after studying it for a moment, I decided that it was a stylized rendering of the rack of an elk or a moose. What was the significance of that? Did it have anything to do with either of the weapons in this case? I stood up.

An hour later, I had a partial answer regarding the blue and white diagram. The logo certainly resembled the outline of Nevada, but it looked like something else, too. From 1945 to 1969, the British government had used the Maralinga site in South Australia as its testing ground for nuclear weapons. The outline of South Australia was similar to that of Nevada, and the red star coincided exactly with the location of Maralinga in the Woomera Prohibited Area. Hundreds of tests had been conducted there, but there was no record of conventional weapons testing and, according to Charles Wellbourne, the British had not begun to develop the new bomb until three years after Maralinga was shut down. That seemed to make the diagram irrelevant to our inquiry. So why was it sent with the map?

I picked up the letter postmarked at Oxford three days earlier. The letter and its companions seemed to confirm the threats implicit in the map. The bombs were in place and would be detonated in six days unless . . . There was no *unless,* which argued for terrorism. Terrorists destroyed for glory and revealed themselves after the fact. But no one had come forward after *Victoria.* And why provide the map and the letters, giving the government time to do something to decrease the effectiveness of the attacks?

I had some decisions to make and there wasn't much time. Where should we concentrate our attention? It was almost an intellectual puzzle now. I had secured Wellbourne's promise to evacuate the town, so only a half million square meters of Oxford itself were at stake. A new idea occurred to me – the bombers must know that as well. Whatever might be done in London or Portsmouth, surely they understood that the citizens of Oxford would be gone when their bomb exploded. That made terrorism even less likely. Terrorists sowed fear by killing human beings. The destruction of the town then, or some part of it, would be the goal. But why? And where? I rose from the chair again.

A few minutes later I resumed my seat, a detailed map of the City of Oxford before me. I found a sheet of paper in one of the drawers and made a few calculations. If the maximum range of the bomb was a half million square meters, and the force spread evenly from its locus, it would destroy everything within four hundred meters, meaning a circle of destruction eight hundred meters wide. I looked at the map.

The distance from the railway station to the easternmost college, St. Catherine's, was two thousand meters. From the University Science Area to Christ Church Meadow was fifteen hundred meters. Lady Margaret Hall and a few of the new colleges, plus Jericho and all of North Oxford, were outside those boundaries but, assuming the bombers wanted to maximize the damage to *Oxford,* they could be ignored. Somewhere within slightly more than one square mile the "seed" was probably "planted."

I leaned back and closed my eyes. Where would they get the most bang for the buck? If the bomb were placed beneath the table at which I was sitting, or behind the books on the shelves a few feet away, or in a similar location at any one of the fabulous old buildings within a hundred yards of where I was, it would destroy knowledge, books and artifacts gathered over more than seven hundred years, not to mention the unique structures that contained them. But why would anyone want to do that?

I looked at the map again. The Science Area north of South Parks Road was now the dynamic center of Oxford, and the colleges that surrounded it were modern in both the chronological and attitudinal sense. Why blow up ancient structures full of things deemed less relevant every day when you could pulverize the laboratories and the experiments and the scholarship that really mattered? If these were rational people, the bomb was planted somewhere in the Science Area. There was another thing, too – the Mosque had been built in the center of the new Oxford. If Markham's Muslims were indeed responsible for the bomb, they could locate it there with impunity. I put it at the top of the list and spent the next hour selecting various institutes, laboratories and libraries that should be scrutinized first.

I checked my watch a third time. My meeting, in the Luncheon Room at the Examinations School on High Street, was fifteen minutes away. As I stepped out onto Catte Street and re-traced my steps to the High, I pictured Guin Markham once more, naked and inviting, her mouth open and her eyes almost closed, the pearls snug around her neck. I smiled – perhaps a cold shower would help, or maybe it would require another visit to Aylesbury Abbey.

AFTER LUNCH, I returned to Arts End and completed my list. As the bells of Oxford were tolling three o'clock, I walked down Merton Street and entered Christ Church through Canterbury Gate. I emerged into the small quadrangle and saw Dean West approaching. I spoke as we passed and, as expected, received no greeting in return. I smiled and continued across the quad when I heard my name. "St. Cyr! I say, St. Cyr!" I looked back and saw West hurrying toward me.

"Yes, sir?"

The Dean stopped and caught his breath. "I say – you *are* St. Cyr, aren't you?"

I smiled again. "Yes, sir."

"May I speak to you for a moment?"

"Certainly."

He looked around. "Let's sit in the library," he said, turning toward the white and gold columns of the north facade of Christ Church Library. I followed. Inside, we ignored the undergraduates hanging over the balustrade of the gallery and found two leather chairs underneath the window at the east end of the room. "The Chancellor talked to – I mean, I've just been speaking with the Chancellor on the telephone. It was most distressing. Your name was mentioned."

"Mine, sir?"

"Yes. I didn't really understand all that he said, but it seems that some lunatic has threatened the University again. Bombs or some such. He said something about your, ah, military background."

Why would Cromwell do that? Was the man stupid or – malicious? "What else did he say, Dean West?"

"He asked me to canvas the Students about a voluntary evacuation. He's speaking to the other heads as well."

"Voluntary?"

"Yes." He paused. "Of course, no one will go. We get loopy threats here all the time. But –" he rose "– my colleagues I – I shall have to consult my colleagues all the same. Some of them may speak to you."

I frowned. A *voluntary* evacuation would never work and Wellbourne and Cromwell knew it. I stood up. "Dean West, I don't believe this is an empty threat. It's very serious. It would only be for a few days and –"

The old man smiled. "Yes, yes, I'm sure you're right. I'll certainly mention that." He turned for the door.

I sat back down. The Dean was correct, of course. None of them would leave unless they were forced to. They had been here for a thousand years and they would be here for a thousand more. I checked the impulse to go to Cromwell, and I knew that I would never get through to Wellbourne. They had made a political calculation – they would do the bare minimum and hope for the best. If the worst came, they would say that they had done what they could and try to ride it out and, if the bombs exploded in Portsmouth and London, the reckoning over Oxford would be a long time coming.

What could I do? I could speak of some of it – the map, for instance, and whatever I had learned from Markham and the Ambassador – without running afoul of the law, but it probably wasn't enough. And who would listen? Without the evacuation, though, the stakes were infinitely higher.

◇◇◇

KHAN WATCHED as the tall slender woman climbed the steps and disappeared through the doorway at Cadogan Place. Now what? He had spent an hour or two outside this building each time he came to London, but this was the first time that she had ever appeared. His sporadic vigil had begun after Aden died. He had a vague idea of confronting her, blaming her for his sister's degradation and death, but time had muddled the mission. *He* was more responsible for Aden than Pamela. His determination to succeed had left no room for Aden and, when she understood that he wouldn't help her, she went her own way. A selfish, headstrong child, she did exactly what she wanted to do, and it was unlikely that Pamela Smythe-King had any control over her at all. In fact, he had heard rumors that it was the other way around. So, what to do now that Pamela was here at last?

He knocked on her door. It opened almost immediately. She stared at him, the large brown eyes growing larger, then stood aside. He stepped over the threshold into a foyer of harlequin tiles. She closed the door and leaned against it for a second, then crossed the hall to a room furnished with overstuffed white sofas and chairs and a large oriental rug. He followed her. The gas logs in the fireplace were lit. She smiled. "I don't believe we've met, Mr. Khan. I'm Pamela Smythe-King." He remained silent. "You're very much like your sister."

Having broached the subject of their mutual affection, Pamela seated herself in one of the armchairs and waited. Khan sat down on the edge of the sofa. "I came to blame you for her life and her death," he said, "but I've changed my mind. She left a lot of victims behind, and I suspect that you're one of them."

She shook her head. "No. I was a willing participant. I loved her very much." She paused. "She was coming to me when she was killed." Tears trickled down her face.

He rose. "I'm sorry," he said, turning toward the door. "I shouldn't have bothered you."

"No. Please. Please stay." He paused, then resumed his seat. She produced a handkerchief and wiped her eyes. Trying to smile, she said, "Did you come all the way from Lahore to scold me?"

"No. I'm actually on my way to Oxford."

"Oxford?" He nodded. "Is it about the bomb?"

He looked at her sharply. "What do you know about that?"

"That – that they think it's the same people who blew up the boat that Aden was on."

"How do you know?"

The smile came easier this time. "I have friends in high places. You'd be surprised."

"What else have you heard?"

She told him about the map and the diagram and the attack on the church at Aylesbury. He considered the possibilities. "I'm going up to Oxford to coach a cricket team, but I'm interested in these threats."

"So am I, Mr. Khan. I'm going to Oxford, too."

"My given name is Abram."

She grinned. "Mine's Eliza, but you can call me Pamela."

"Where are you staying?"

"The Randolph Hotel."

"Do you mind if I call on you – Pamela?"

"Not at all, Abram." She hesitated. "Your new cricket team – does it have anything to do with the Muslim college?"

"Yes, it does."

PAMELA WALKED him to the door. "I'll see you next week," she said. Khan nodded and smiled. She went to the window and watched until he was out of sight. He *was* like his sister, but he was different, too.

She had met Aden at the zenith of her London notoriety. Abram, then at Oxford, was the star of the school's cricket team and Aden had come to London to see his final match against Cambridge. Pamela had accompanied the Duke of Dorset to Lord's that day, and she could still remember the stir in the Pavilion when Abram Khan and his sister walked down the steps of the center aisle and sat behind the rail in the first row of seats. The toffs in the Pavilion didn't quite know what to do. They wanted to engage the young man, already in his whites, but what remained of their dignity restrained them. The presence of Oxford's already legendary cricketer had diverted their attention from his sister, but Pamela's eyes never left the younger woman. When Khan rose to go down to the pitch, Pamela immediately took her leave of the Duke and claimed the empty seat beside her. "I'm Pamela Smythe-King," she said. "You're very lovely."

The wide mouth smiled. "I'm Aden Khan. Thank you."

"Khan? Are you his sister?" The girl nodded. "You're Pakistani then, aren't you?" She nodded again. "Do you live here?"

Aden smiled again. "Not yet."

She had been less interested in the cricket than Pamela. "I've seen him play a thousand times," she said after their conversation was interrupted by cheers for something her brother had done.

As Cambridge's final batsman advanced to his wicket, Pamela said, "Are you staying in town?"

"No. We're going back to Oxford or – not Oxford, really. We've been invited to some place near there. Alyes – Aylesbury something."

"Aylesbury Abbey?"

"Yes."

Pamela nodded. "You'll enjoy yourself. The Duke is a charming man." She paused. "When are you going home?"

"I'm supposed to leave next Tuesday."

Pamela took Dorset's card from her purse and wrote her name, address and telephone number on the reverse side. She handed it to Aden. "I live only a few blocks from here," she said, allowing her fingers to brush the girl's bare knee. She stared into the ice-blue eyes. They gazed back without blinking. "Call me if you need anything. Or just drop by."

On the following Tuesday, Pamela was sitting up in bed reading the morning post when she heard the bell. A moment later, her maid appeared in the doorway. "It's a Miss Khan, ma'am."

Pamela rose and sat down at her dressing table. She quickly brushed her hair and, hands shaking slightly, applied makeup to her eyes and mouth. Returning to the bed, she hesitated for a second, then drew the gown over her head and handed it to the maid. "Show her up," she said. Nude, she fluffed up the pillows and pulled the sheet and coverlet to her waist.

Aden entered the room. If she was surprised at Pamela's bare breasts she didn't show it. Pamela held out her arms. "I'm so glad you've come to see me." Aden crossed the room and bent to receive her kiss. Their lips touched briefly, then Aden straightened and said, "I'm not going back to Lahore. Can you put me up for a few days?"

"Of course." She looked past the girl. "Would you mind closing the door, darling?" A moment later Pamela, standing now, said, "Let me help you with your things."

Aden slipped her jacket off and tossed it onto the window seat. Pamela unbuttoned the sleeveless blouse and pushed it from her shoulders, revealing a thin nylon brassiere that barely covered the girl's breasts and did nothing to conceal the stiff dark nipples. When it, too, lay on the floor they embraced. Strong fingers caressed Pamela's bottom. Aden backed away and stepped out of her skirt. "I thought about you all weekend," she said.

They had lived together for nearly three years. To the outside world they were "roommates," but no one was fooled. The look on Pamela's face whenever Aden was nearby gave it away. She was helplessly, hopelessly in love but she knew, despite the passion, that her love was not reciprocated. The younger woman went through the motions but, in truth, she loved only herself. When given a choice between Pamela and the other things she used – drugs, men, other women – she usually spurned Pamela.

Tears, pleading, and rage had made no impact, and Pamela had finally decided to settle for whatever Aden could give.

When she began her acting career, Aden insisted that she, too, be allowed to display herself to the camera, but she was never a success. Despite an exotic, beautiful face and voluptuous body, her narcissism doomed her to failure. She performed for herself, not the audience, and the parts became less and less until they dried up altogether, in spite of her relationship with Pamela. At the same time she began to lose control of herself. The booze and the pills and the powder had so transformed her that even the low-level gentry with whom she played scorned her. In and out of hospitals and asylums at Pamela's expense, she had begun to satisfy her needs with children that she picked up off the street. Finally at the end of her tether, Pamela had issued an ultimatum that Aden flatly rejected. A month later Pamela, alone, boarded a jetliner at Heathrow and journeyed to the New World to continue her career.

She took the letter from her purse and read it again.

> *Dear Pamela,*
>
> *I am drug-free, mostly booze-free and alone. I live in a small flat in Chelsea and do some modeling to put food on the table.*
>
> *I have managed to partially repair relations with my family – I say partially because they want me to come home and I can never do that – and I want to now at least apologize to you.*
>
> *I'm sorry. Please don't think I want anything else from you. I'm a taker, and I've*

*taken enough. You were kind to me and I
repaid you with crap.*
I'm sorry.
Aden

Finding her had been easy. Getting her to come to America had been harder, but she had agreed at last. Pamela would fly to London and they would cruise back to New York, slowly, and learn about each other again. At the last minute, business complications prevented her from making the trip, but Aden had laughed and said she would be just fine by herself. The ship left Southampton on a Friday, scheduled to arrive in New York a week later. Her name was *Victoria.*

"THE LONG and the short of it," said Tony Markham, "is that they traced those four bombs the size of a small suitcase to London where they disappeared into the great maw of a city of seven million people, many of whom don't speak English and don't give a damn about England." He stopped. "They don't believe that any foreign government is involved." He laughed. "They know more about what's going on in Cairo or North Korea than what's happening in East London."

"So they probably fell into the hands of criminals or fanatics or both," I said.

"Yes."

We were seated in the library at the Master's Lodgings once more. I looked around the richly-furnished room – cherry paneling, parquet floor, busts of Aristotle and

Homer, a giant globe in one corner and a baby grand in another – and wondered briefly if it would still be here next week. There were several objects grouped together on the far wall – a pair of curved swords, some sort of intricate tapestry and a framed antique map of Kashmir. I rose to inspect them. "What's all this?" I said.

"Parting gifts for service in the last government. I was the Special Ambassador to the former Raj but, of course, they didn't call it that."

"What did you do?"

"Spent most of my time drinking tea in Islamabad and New Delhi." He paused. "I was *supposed* to be mediating a small dispute caused by the Partition. It was useless. They had no interest in the land at issue. They are Hindus and Muslims and they hate each other. That's the bottom line."

I pointed to the map. "Which one gave you this?"

He smiled. "Pakistan, of course. You'll notice that there are no borders, no Line of Control dividing Kashmir into Indian and Pakistani provinces. It's all Pakistan."

"The future as Pakistan sees it?"

Markham nodded and handed me a glass. "The Indians disagree." He looked out the window. "The sun's shining finally. Let's walk in the garden." He pushed through the French doors, and I followed.

We moved along straight brick paths that bisected beds of flowers and shrubs framed by grass that was already turning brown. Persian ironwood trees, their orange leaves thinning to reveal slivers of loose gray bark, stood at precise intervals beside the walks. "I assume your friends at Whitehall have no actual evidence that the *Victoria* bomb was theirs?" I said.

"No."

I sipped from the too full glass of scotch barely cooled by a single cube of melting ice. "Well, I guess all this ignorance may account for their approach to the evacuation."

"How do you mean?"

"Cromwell has told everyone that the evacuation is voluntary. Dean West spoke to me about it this afternoon."

"No one will go unless the government makes them go." I nodded. "It's insane. Why take the chance?"

"Politics, I suppose."

"It's disgusting. They're risking thousands of lives so that *The Daily Telegraph* can't make fun of them." I nodded again. "We have to do something."

"Like what?"

We were quiet for several minutes. Markham broke the silence. "We have to make them *want* to go."

"How? Wellbourne would probably have us arrested if we say too much."

"Cromwell told West it was a bomb, surely?"

"Yes."

"Then we need to make that threat real."

"How?"

"We will gather the heads of the houses, a few officials from the University, and the Mayor, and whomever they choose to bring with them – somewhere." He paused. "The Sheldonian, I think. It has plenty of seats already set up, and they've fitted it with a theater screen."

I smiled. "You're going to show them a movie?"

He ignored me. "I'll take care of getting them there. I'm Master of Balliol and Duke of Aylesbury. Most of them owe me something." He paused. *"You* will explain the threat. You'll no longer be just a student, of course."

"I believe Cromwell has already seen to that. What shall I say?"

"You won't have to tell them anything that Wellbourne said, or even mention the letters. Just talk about the map and –"

"That's not going to convince anyone –"

Markham held up his hand. "Wait. Then we'll show them a film."

"What film?"

"A film of the destruction of *Victoria* and the murder of a thousand people. And we'll tell them that you were an eyewitness to the explosion, that it's very real and there's reason to believe a similar bomb has been planted here."

"There's a film?"

"Yes."

"But who –"

"The White Star people film every departure from Southampton. *Bon voyage* memories and all that. I have a copy."

"How come?"

"It was part of the government's investigation. I didn't want it to be lost." He stopped. "So I made a copy. It's horrific, of course, but that's the point."

We were silent again. "When will we have this meeting?" I said.

"I'll set it up for tomorrow at six o'clock. That way they can discuss it for themselves at dinner." He turned for the door. "I'll get started now. I have to be in London tonight."

CHAPTER TWO

KHAN STEPPED onto the worn gray boards of the platform and checked his watch by the light of the moon – six o'clock. The bells tolled the hour in different tones, the clocks of the colleges speaking to one another. His was the last train of the day. He had selected it because, contrary to his usual custom, he preferred to arrive in Oxford unremarked. The few passengers who left the train with him were claiming taxicabs or walking toward the car park. His luggage had preceded him, so he would walk to the College of the Prophet Muhammad.

He crossed the Isis at Hythe Bridge and continued east on George Street. At Magdalen Street he turned north, past a churchyard enclosed by a wrought-iron fence, to St. Giles'. He paused for a moment across from the Chancellor's residence. Somewhere inside was the evidence of Aden's shame, photographs that had cost Khan a thousand pounds a month for the past four years. The money was unimportant, but the idea that the man who lived at St. Giles' House might reveal his sister's corruption was unbearable. The threat had to be removed.

He continued up St. Giles'. At Keble Road he passed the multi-colored facade of Keble College and entered the University Parks just north of the Science Area. A few hundred meters inside the Parks, he pushed through a gate and, seconds later, stood on the pitch that was the home ground of the Oxford Cricket Club. The Pavilion was exactly the same – the chimneys, the narrow cupola, the three gables overlooking the porch – but the grounds were different. The green manicured lawn that once seemed to go on forever was now circumscribed. The sky and the horizon that had provoked the illusion were gone. A great swath of the pristine parkland had been dedicated to the vast quadrangle – with its implacable forty-foot walls, corner minarets and arched openings – of the College of the Prophet Muhammad. A hedge of thorns, its foliage blood-red in the moonlight, surrounded it.

In spite of heavy-handed prodding from the British government, the Mosque at Oxford had been controversial. Even the dons, most of whom gave eager voice to their support for all things "oppressed," were doubtful. Could a culture so certain of its beliefs and so quick to defend them fit in? In fact, the Prophet's college recalled an earlier time at Oxford, a time when Oriel and New College were dedicated to the Virgin Mary, and Worcester and Trinity were founded by Benedictine monks. The curriculum and admissions standards at the Mosque were far more rigid than those at the other colleges – a circumstance smiled upon but secretly deplored by the panjandrums at the University of Oxford – and mingling was forbidden. The ban on fraternization had been instituted by the Mosque, but it was welcomed by the other colleges because it permitted Oxford to pride itself on its tolerance without actually having to tolerate.

Suddenly, the silence was shattered by a loud, insistent voice coming from the college. It was a sound at once familiar and yet so foreign to this place – the call to prayer, the fifth and final one of the day. He waited in the Pavilion until the time for prayer was over, then rose and turned east toward the Cherwell. Entry into the Mosque would be in that direction, south and east, facing Mecca.

"WE ARE honored to have so – revered a figure as yourself to work with our cricket team," said Imam Akhem. "I myself know little about the game. Perhaps you can instruct me." He smiled.

The Imam had three geometric objects on his desk, all made of onyx – a cube, a pyramid and an orb. Khan picked up the ball and rolled it in his hands. It was the same size and heft as a cricket ball, but much harder. He looked across the desk at the old man in his ill-fitting Western clothes. "I'll do all I can to help you, Imam Akhem."

The Imam smiled again and touched the collar of his jacket. "We wear these clothes most of the time. We wear our robes when they wear theirs." Khan nodded. "I understand that you are here for more than cricket. If *I* can help *you,* please let me know."

"Thank you, sir."

Imam Akhem looked thoughtful. "The Chancellor of the University called me a few minutes ago. He said that someone has threatened Oxford with a bomb. Does that interest you, Abram Khan?"

"Yes, sir. Very much."

The old man nodded. "There's talk of an evacuation. We will not go."

"But, Imam –"

"We will not flee from the madness of the infidels. Allah will protect us."

"It may not be the infidels, Imam Akhem."

"Anyone who would do such a thing is an infidel, my son. Allah does not condone murder or wanton destruction." He paused. "Some of our brothers preach violence. We smile because, after all, they are our brothers, but we will not join them." He stopped again. "We are inevitable, Abram Khan. We don't need to kill to prevail."

The telephone rang. Akhem crossed the room and answered it. He frowned as he listened. "No. That was not our agreement. You were supposed to return today." He turned his back and listened again. "Very well. I'll give you a week." He laid the receiver down and, head bowed, returned to his desk, his visitor forgotten.

"Imam?"

Akhem raised his head, a weary smile on his face. "Our brothers are impatient, Abram Khan. Inevitable is not soon enough."

"THE DEAN instructed me to give you this, Mr. St. Cyr," the scout said as he handed over the note. I pushed my plate away and turned to look at the high table. I was seated near the east end of the room, at the middle of three strings of tables that stretched over one hundred feet to the low platform – two or three risers – where the high table was placed. Light from the moon poured through the traceried windows, supplemented by shaded double lamps on each table, and the beams and arches of the gilded hammerbeam roof, black with age, loomed over us. Portraits of the founders, Cardinal Wolsey and Henry VIII, and other notables in the history of the House of Christ, looked down at the high table, and dozens of others hung haphazardly along the dark wainscoting on the north and south walls. Wolsey and Henry were side-by-side, an irony probably lost on most of those in the hall. Intended by Wolsey as a great Catholic college, Christ Church had instead become an arm of the Church of England when his former friend and co-founder quarreled with the Pope.

I unfolded the note:

> *Mr. St. Cyr:*
> *I have requested that the high table*
> *remain after dinner to discuss the matter*
> *I spoke of today. I would appreciate it if*
> *you would join us.*
> *West*

A few minutes later I climbed the steps – there were three – and found an empty chair at the end of the table. The Dean nodded and smiled, and stood up to address his colleagues. "I had a telephone conversation with the Chancellor today," he said. "He advises that we have had another bomb threat. No specific location has been mentioned. Just *Oxford.*" He paused. "He has requested that we consider evacuating. I gather it would be only a matter of days, no more than a week." The Students at the high table, restive since the words "bomb threat" had been uttered, began to grumble. Chairs were pushed back, napkins dropped on the table.

West raised his voice slightly. "I had another conversation on the same topic just before dinner with Duke Mark – with the Master of Balliol." The signs of departure abated. "He told me that the threat is serious and he has asked me, and those of you who are – who wish to come, to gather at the Sheldonian tomorrow evening at six. He tells me that he and our friend here –" he smiled at me again "– will demonstrate the gravity of the threat." He stopped once more. "Anthony Markham is not a frivolous man. Some of us may differ with his – beliefs, but no one at this table can doubt his intellect and his dedication to this place. I will be at the Sheldonian and I hope that all of you will join me." He pushed in his chair. "We will decide after dinner tomorrow."

The Dean caught up with me on the stairs. We paused beneath the giant plaster parasols that decorated the walls and ceiling. "I look forward to your presentation," he said.

"Thank you, sir. I hope you'll be convinced."

He shook his head. "That's not necessary for me. Markham's word is more than sufficient. I'm going out of curiosity and because I want the others to attend." I nodded. "Where I will go *after* that is the question. If – if this place is destroyed, there's no place for me."

"But there are other –"

He shook his head. "No," said Dean West, "there are not."

I crossed Tom Quad and climbed my staircase, depressed by the uncertainty that Cromwell and Wellbourne had created. Oxford *had* to be evacuated. Until that was accomplished, everything else was secondary.

The scene that greeted me as I entered my rooms brought a smile to my face. A small fire had been laid and an extra bundle of wood placed beside the hearth. I approached the fireplace. There was a pale blue envelope on the mantel. Oxford's preferred method of communication had always charmed me. They had telephones, of course, but the most significant messages were still written by hand and entrusted to the informal delivery performed by porters and scouts. I picked up the envelope and read my name: "Georges." There was only one person on this side of the Atlantic who called me by my first name.

>*8:00 P.M.*
>*I'm in the Royal Suite at the Randolph.*
>*Do come.*
> *G*

I grinned. Was the Royal Suite really good enough for Guin? Probably not. I looked at my watch – it was almost ten o'clock. Was it too late to call on her? No. Was it a good idea? No again. The credits on her side of the ledger were piling up. The piper would have to be paid.

I descended the staircase and passed under the old bell tower adjacent to it. Mist from the Cherwell and the Isis lay on the ground like felled clouds. I paused as I walked through the gate. Looking east past Corpus Christi, I could just see the pinnacles of Merton's tower through the fog. I turned north on King Edward Street to the High, and took a right on Turl. A few moments later, I was again standing outside the Master's Lodgings at Balliol. I stopped there, and thought about turning back. I was sure that Markham would not approve of this dalliance, and I didn't like deceiving him.

Relations with women had been difficult since the death of my wife. The bittersweet idyll of our brief marriage and the manner of her death made any new liaison an infidelity, this one doubly disloyal because it was the sister of my friend. Markham protected himself with irony and cynicism, and Guin was spared neither, but I had seen him look at her and I knew that it mattered. Still, the self-control instilled in me by my mother apparently did not extend to Guin Markham.

I approached the Randolph Hotel. Its facade was yellow brick and stone and its four stories were topped by a high-pitched roof with gabled windows and more than a dozen chimneys. The Gothic turrets, windows and doorways lent it a mien appropriate to Oxford but, at just more than a hundred years old, it was actually one of the newer buildings in town.

I passed under the portico off Beaumont Street, entered the hotel and paused beneath the vaulted ceiling of the vestibule, crowded with tourists even at this hour. Where exactly *was* the Royal Suite? It wouldn't do to inquire. I crossed the room to the Bell Captain's stand. "Do you have a brochure that describes the rooms and suites here?" I said to the young woman behind it. She smiled, drew a colorful pamphlet from one of the slots before her and handed it to me. "Thanks." I re-crossed the lobby, noticing the mosaics on the floor, and sat down in an Empire armchair next to the fireplace.

As I leaned back and unfolded the brochure a familiar figure lumbered down the stone staircase directly in front of me – Cromwell. I turned my head and watched out of the corner of my eye as he walked past me to the door. What sort of game was Guin playing? A few seconds either way and we would have met on the stairs.

The Royal Suite was on the second floor. I took the carpeted steps two at a time. At the top I was confronted by a man behind a podium.

"May I help you, sir?"

"I – was looking for the Royal Suite."

The man looked down at his book. "Your name, please?"

I felt my face reddening. So much for discretion. "St. Cyr."

The man looked up and smiled. "Yes, sir. Lady Guinevere is expecting you. It's at the end of the hall."

I thought about leaving but decided that it was too late. As I walked down the long hallway, I considered "Lady Guinevere." Guin was obviously entitled to the "Lady," but I'd never heard it used before. And "Guinevere?" I reached the double doors and, ignoring the lighted doorbell, knocked. Who would answer? Had she brought a retinue of servants the whole twenty miles from Aylesbury?

Guin opened the door. She smiled. "Come in, darling," she said, and stood aside. I walked to the middle of the room. "Champagne?" she called.

I turned around. "Do you have any scotch?"

"Of course. How do you like it?"

"Just ice."

"Lots of ice?"

I smiled. "Yes." I sat down on a red damask sofa and watched her as she made my drink. The room was elegant, but completely outclassed by its occupant. She wore a long dressing gown, black, and her white-gold hair had been twisted into a French knot. The minimal makeup was the same and this time she wore no jewelry at all. She bent to hand me my drink, exposing the full breasts and distended nipples I had caressed with my hands and mouth only a few hours before. She sat down beside me.

We drank in silence for a moment. "I couldn't bear the thought of not seeing you today," she said finally, "so I decided to come to Oxford for a visit."

"Does Tony know you're here?"

"I've no idea. It's not a secret."

I hesitated. "What about Cromwell?"

She laughed. "No. It wouldn't make the slightest difference if he did."

"He hasn't been here?"

"No." She grinned. "Don't be jealous of poor John, darling." She put her glass down and leaned toward me, her lips at my ear, her hand reaching for the swollen flesh in my lap. "I'm soaking wet," she whispered. "Can we talk later?" Without waiting for an answer, she rose and untied the sash of her gown. She had a stunning figure. The firm breasts gave way to a narrow waist and flared hips, and her long legs were strong and trim. The golden patch of matted hair beneath her smooth belly was at the level of my eyes, and when she stepped closer I could indeed see the moisture inside her thighs. When she drew nearer still, the aroma of her sex reached my nostrils and, when she put her hands behind my head and pressed my face against her, I could taste it.

A few minutes later she knelt between my knees and, hands trembling slightly, unzipped my pants. When I was fully exposed she sat back on her haunches, her tongue moving over her open lips, and gazed at me. "Oh, God," she groaned, her breath shallow and quick, the black eyes glazing over. Resting her arms on my thighs, she bent her head.

After another few minutes, I leaned closer to her and said, "I think we should get in bed."

She lifted her head and licked the slick, swollen lips. "Fuck the bed," she said. The robe slid from her shoulders as she lay back on the thick white carpet, knees raised. "Do me here."

Later, the bedclothes still undisturbed, I prepared to leave. "Will you be at Aylesbury this weekend?" she said.

This weekend was exactly that – the end of the seven days. I would probably be very busy in Oxford. "I haven't been invited."

"I'm inviting you."

I shook my head. "I can't do that, Guin."

She stared at me, the eyes a little harder now. "If you were going to have scruples, darling, you should have thrown me out last night."

"I know."

She rose and crossed the room to the bar. I was now fully clothed, she still completely naked. She moved like a great cat, graceful and unconcerned, a lioness with one of her subjects. Turning, she gestured with her glass. "I won't give up on you just yet."

"I thought you and Cromwell were a couple?"

"John doesn't care a fig about me, not really. All he cares about is Aylesbury, and he shan't have it." She threw back the champagne and poured another. "Aylesbury will be Gerry's."

"But Gerry's *your* son. How could he be duke?"

"It's a – quirk in our genealogy."

"Tony can still marry, can't he? And have a family?"

A smile played about her lips. "Did you know that he was once engaged to be married?"

"No." She nodded, the bemused expression still on her face. "What happened?"

"She caught him in a compromising position. She was a prig about things like that and she broke it off." I turned toward the door. "Georges?" I looked back. "I know that you and my brother are very good friends, but please remember that he cares about certain – things more than friendship. Be careful." I grinned. "What's funny?"

"He said the same thing about you." I opened the door.

"Darling?"

"Yes?"

"That was good advice."

I laughed and closed the door behind me. When I reached the staircase the man behind the podium was gone. I opened the book. Mine was the only name listed for the Royal Suite. Cromwell appeared as a guest of the occupant of the University Suite at the other end of the hall. There were other names, too – I. Akhem and A. Khan. I mulled that over for a moment. Who was lodging in the University Suite?

At the bottom of the stairs I hesitated, then crossed to the registration desk. I rang the bell. A sleepy-looking young man emerged from behind a door. "Yes, sir?"

"I'm supposed to meet my cousin here, but I was held up in London. I don't want to disturb him at this hour, but I need to be sure of his room. He said he was staying in the University Suite. Is that right?"

"Oh, no, sir. Miss Smythe-King is in the University Suite."

"Who?"

"Pamela Smythe-King, sir." The clerk opened a book in front of him. "What's your cousin's name, sir? Sir?" I reached the door without looking back.

It was almost two o'clock when I emerged from the hotel. During my journey back to Christ Church, I was conscious of nothing except a great fatigue until I reached Tom Tower. "Good evening, sir," said Yates.

I shook my head. "Good morning, Yates." The short walk to my rooms also passed with no notice of my surroundings. I switched on a lamp, found the box of long matches and bent to light the fire. When the small blaze was finally going, I sat down on the edge of the bed and put my head in my hands.

I tried to force their images from my mind – Gabrielle, Guin, even Gill, were distracting me. We had gone backwards on Day Two. The evacuation that was certain yesterday was now in doubt. I had a better idea of *where* the attack might come, but had made no progress at all on the *who* or the *why*. The blue and white diagram remained a mystery. It had to mean something, but what? And what was Cromwell up to?

I rose wearily, picked up an iron bar resting next to the fireplace and stirred the fire. Lifting my eyes, I saw another envelope, this one white. I picked it up. There was no name or address. I broke the seal. The handwriting was familiar. Tears washed my face as I read.

> *My Love,*
> *I dreamed about us again last night. We were children riding across the Vale toward The Downs. The sky was white and the sun was yellow and huge, and I could see Father standing at the gate. When we arrived we had grown up and Father was gone. There was no sun and the sky was purple. You held me and told me not to be afraid, but I was.*
> *I'm still afraid. Please come to me.*
> *G*

I wiped my eyes with my sleeve and stood still for a minute, gazing into the fire. Then I carefully re-folded the note and slipped it into the envelope. The writing was that of my dead wife, Gabrielle.

I placed the envelope on the nightstand and glared at it. I would not imagine that she was alive. I had boarded the ship with her, made sure that everything was as it should be, then stood on shore and watched her die. Yes, she could have walked back down the gangway, but why would she? And if she had, why not come to me? It was four terrible years later and there had been no word. It was impossible – a hoax, a cruel joke or – or what?

CHAPTER THREE

"**DID YOU** bring this envelope up last night, Andrews?" I said.

"No, sir. It was pushed under the door. I put it on the mantel when I brought the extra kindling."

"Did you see anybody on the staircase or – or outside it that you didn't recognize? Anyone at all?"

"No, sir."

A few minutes later, I leaned into the porter's untidy cubbyhole. "You didn't see a woman pass this way last night, did you, Yates? Small, dark hair?"

Yates laughed. "Bless you, sir, it ain't come to that yet. I wouldn't be much of a porter if I was just *letting* 'em come through, would I? Mind, I don't say they ain't coming in, but they ain't coming through *this* gate." He laughed again.

"What time do the other gates close?"

"Ten o'clock, sir."

"Did anyone come through here after ten?"

"Oh, yes, sir. Dons, students, dozens of 'em. Old Tom don't ring 'em home no more, you know." Yates smiled. "And lucky for you he don't, right? You were the last one in."

I smiled, too. "Does someone actually ring the bell?"

"No, sir. He's struck with a clock hammer now, except for special occasions."

I returned to my rooms. I had to manage things better. If there *was* a bomb it was going to explode in less than five days. I couldn't let this note interfere with what I was trying to do. The most important thing was to get the people out, and I hoped that would begin at six o'clock that evening. The note could wait.

I reached for it again. The unmarked envelope was plain and cheap, the same as those used by thousands of businesses every day. The note itself, on the other hand, was written on fine linen stationery. I walked to the window and held it up to the light. There was a watermark, barely discernible and impossible to identify. I removed the bomber's letter from my coat pocket and compared them. The envelopes were identical but the quality of the bomber's stationery matched that of the envelopes.

I re-read the note. The message meant nothing to me. It almost seemed like some kind of code. *Was* it her handwriting? I thought so, but there was room for error. We had never really been apart. The longest written communication I'd ever had from her was certainly no longer than this, and I had nothing now to judge it against. There was an expert who could help me, though, and he was nearby, and he might help with something else. I had lost touch with my father-in-law, not from neglect but because I had the strong impression that Claude Soleil wanted it that way. We had not spoken in three years, not since an awkward call across the Atlantic on Gabrielle's birthday. I picked up the telephone.

An hour later I left my rooms and passed once more through Canterbury Gate. When I reached Deadman's Walk, just outside the remnants of the town's south wall, I passed between Merton College on the left and Merton Field on the right and arrived at the Botanic Garden, a collection of *flora* and other things situated within a structure that could have been built only in Oxford. Its high stone walls were interrupted by three monumental gateways – classic Roman arches with intricate carvings, keystones and columns – that contrasted sharply with the Gothic bell tower of Magdalen College that floated over it from the other side of High Street.

Gabrielle's father had retired from teaching a year after we were married, and he now spent his time at the Garden cataloguing specimens. He looked up as I approached, pushed away from the cluttered table and rose. "St. Cyr." Brushing aside my hand, he embraced me. "I'm glad you've come."

Mildly surprised, I said, "Thank you, sir. It's good to see you again."

"I've been unfair to you. I've thought about it a great deal lately. I'm not – well, and we need to talk."

"What's wrong?"

Soleil smiled. "I'm an old man. I was nearly fifty when Gabrielle was born. Old men get sick and they die." He took my arm. "Let's walk, shall we?" We passed under one of the massive stone arches and turned down the High to Magdalen Bridge. On the other side of the Cherwell, we stopped at The Plain, a triangular space once occupied by a medieval church long demolished. He pointed to a stone bench and we sat down, looking across the road to the Victoria Fountain, an octagonal stone folly capped by a clock and a weather vane. The pavement around it was packed with tour buses disgorging their passengers.

I pulled the blue and white diagram from my pocket. "I know that you weren't in the weapons business, Doctor Soleil, but I thought you might have some idea what this is."

The old man spread the diagram across his knees. After a moment he said, "I'm sorry, St. Cyr. All I can tell you is that it's probably part of an old nuclear weapon design. You knew that already, I imagine."

"Yes, sir. 'AEA' stands for Atomic Energy Authority, doesn't it?"

"Yes. And this logo designates the testing regime the weapon was intended for at Maralinga – Operation Antler."

"Operation Antler?"

Soleil nodded. "Part of a series of tests in the '60's. It was widely discussed in the scientific community – and widely condemned."

"Because they were nuclear weapons?"

"Yes, and because one of them – there were three, I believe – was rumored to have a cobalt casing."

"Meaning what?"

"I'm not a nuclear physicist, my boy. As I understand the theory, a cobalt bomb has a relatively low explosive force but produces radiation that lasts much longer than, say, uranium."

"What's the military benefit of that?"

"I have no idea."

"What happened with the test?"

"I don't really know that either, but it was said to be a failure." He looked back at the diagram. "I haven't heard a word about cobalt bombs for more than ten years." He re-folded the diagram and closed his eyes. When he opened them again, he took a deep breath and said, "I want you to know something, St. Cyr. When Gabrielle came to me before she died, she was as happy as I've ever seen her. She looked forward to meeting your family. She talked of staying over there. It – it made me realize that she *had* done the right thing to marry you."

I looked away. "Thank you, Doctor Soleil."

"She told me something else, something that gave her great joy." I looked back at him. "She was pregnant. She planned to surprise you when you joined her in Cherbourg." We sat quietly. "I should have told you long ago but I thought – what good would it do? I have finally understood that it's not up to me. You have a right to know. I'm sorry."

We were silent again, longer this time. I put the diagram away and handed him the note. "That was left in my rooms last night."

I watched as Soleil withdrew the sheet of paper from the envelope and read it. Surprise, dismay and anger all crossed his face. "Someone's playing a mean trick on you, my boy. It looks like her handwriting, but it's not. How could it be?" He pushed the paper back into the envelope and gave it to me.

"Are you certain?" He nodded.

On the walk back to the Botanic Garden, I explained the bomb threat and obtained his assurance that he would be at the theater later that evening. At the mention of Markham's name, his face clouded over. "So you're still friends?" he said. I nodded. He opened his mouth as if to say something further, but changed his mind.

After leaving him, I started back the way I had come. At Merton Field, however, I turned south and walked down the path between the Cherwell and Christ Church Meadow. Crossing the river had triggered a memory and I wanted to see if the voyage that we had taken together could still be made. One of Oxford's most famous "old boys" had discovered an underground waterway that flowed beneath the center of town. He and a friend had made the journey from Hythe Bridge to the far side of Christ Church Meadow where the stream joined the Cherwell below St. Hilda's College. A few years later, two more explorers were not so lucky – their skeletons and the punt that they had launched had been discovered floating in the Meadow after a heavy storm.

Gabrielle had dared me to do it and I agreed, though I had second thoughts when she decided to join me. At first we, too, were going to use a punt but the likelihood that I would be unable to stand up in the boat caused us to switch to a canoe. The water was narrow, swift and deep – we used the paddles more to avoid the sides of the tunnel than to propel ourselves forward. The darkness was total and the flashlight that we carried had done little to allay it. Gabrielle held up her end bravely but the relief on her face when we reached Christ Church Meadow was obvious. Later, over a cozy dinner at the Trout – an out-of-the-way pub we had claimed for our own – we calculated that the ten-minute journey had covered just less than a mile.

I climbed down from the path and walked gingerly along the bank of the shallow river. There it was, south of the fork. Scattered branches and weeds obscured the opening but the flow of the water into the Cherwell was unmistakable. I saw her again stepping from the canoe, the wet blouse clinging to her small, perfect breasts, her dark nipples jutting through the fabric. I realized that I was crying. The old wounds had been re-opened, and now there was more. My wife *and* my child, and my chance for immortality, had all been lost at the hands of these assassins, and this time they had to be stopped.

Yates called to me as I turned into the House from St. Aldate's. "This was just left for you, sir," he said, handing me another envelope with the embossed letters of the Chancellor's office on the back.

> *St. Cyr,*
> *We've had a new message. I believe*
> *it's from the terrorists. Please come at*
> *once.*
> *Cromwell*

I slipped it into my pocket and turned north, wondering what new information these very chatty terrorists had delivered this time. Instead of just blowing everything up and crowing about it later, they seemed to be playing a game.

"I'VE SENT for an expert," said John Cromwell. "He's the Caliph at the Mosque. Sometimes these people come in handy."

I looked at the note, handling it carefully. "Did this come directly to you?" I said. He nodded. "Are there others, like the letters?"

"I don't know. I've put in a call to Wellbourne."

"It's in Arabic. It's a bit advanced for me but I do recognize that word at the top."

"What does it mean?"

"Judgment Day. It's mentioned frequently in the Muslim holy book."

"You mean like trumpets sounding and mountains crumbling and that sort of thing?"

"Yes."

"That doesn't seem –" The telephone rang and he picked up the receiver. "Cromwell here." He listened for a second, nodding. "We've had a note. It's in Arabic. St. Cyr says it's something about Judgment Day."

I laid the note on his desk and walked to the window. The conversation behind me continued. "Yes. Have you anything new at your end?" I looked back. He shook his head.

"Ask him about the soldiers who were supposed to start looking for the bomb today," I said. "Are they here?"

Cromwell ignored me. "I'll have it translated shortly," he said. "Then I'll send it on." He listened once more. "Yes. I understand." He laid the receiver down.

I turned. "Are we the only one with a new note?"

"So far. Wellbourne told me to warn you again of the Official Secrets Act."

"You and Wellbourne and your official secrets are going to get a bunch of people killed." He ignored me again. "What about the troops?"

"They're not coming."

"What?"

"I said they're not coming."

"Why the hell not?"

"Apparently they don't move that fast. I'm asking for volunteers here."

"God damn it, Cromwell! What's the matter with you people?" He made no answer. "Do you really want to find this bomb? Or the bombers?" He stared at me, his face blank. "Do you?"

"Don't be absurd."

I forced myself to calm down. It *was* absurd, but Cromwell and his friends had so far refused to do anything to secure Oxford or its citizens. Why? I dropped my list on his desk. "At least have someone search these places."

He looked at it and laughed. "The Mosque?"

"Yes. That would be a start."

He shook his head. "That's so offensive, St. Cyr. You're letting Markham guide you by the nose." He paused. "It's impossible."

"Why?"

"It's just not done. It's – prejudiced. And they would never permit it."

We sat without speaking. "Was there an envelope?" I said at last. He handed me one of the now-familiar white envelopes. It was blank except for the word "Oxford" printed in block letters. There was no stamp or postmark. "Where was it?"

"It was with the rest of the afternoon post."

"Which is delivered where?"

"The box out front."

I thought for a moment. "So someone just stuck this in your mailbox?" Cromwell nodded. "I don't suppose you noticed anyone loitering outside?"

"No."

"Who else is in the house?"

"No one. It's the cook's day off."

"Why would they send this to *you?*"

He was offended. "I *am* the highest ranking official at the University."

"But the letters were sent to the Home Secretary. Why would they think this would mean anything to you?"

"I don't know. I —" We heard the rap of the brass knocker at the front door. He left the room and returned with a mild-looking middle-aged man dressed in gray trousers and a bluish tweed jacket that was too large for him. "St. Cyr," said Cromwell, "this is Imam Akhem." As we bowed to each other, Cromwell picked up the sheet of paper and thrust it at him. "Can you tell us what this says?"

Akhem drew a pair of heavy black-rimmed glasses from his breast pocket, placed them in front of his eyes and took the paper. He glanced around the room, chose a leather wingback chair beside the desk and sat down. A moment later he looked up. "Would you like for me to write it down?"

"Yes," said Cromwell, "but tell us what it says first."

"All right. At the top it says, 'Day of Judgment' or 'Day of Gathering.' The rest is a sort of summary of what will happen that day. It's similar to several passages in the Koran."

"Yes, but what does it *say?*"

"It says 'The ground will explode, fog will cover the earth for a hundred years and when the fog lifts, there will be only night. The sun will set in the West, and the Beast of the Earth will emerge.'"

"What does all that mean?" said Cromwell.

Akhem smiled. "That depends on who's reading it. It's part of our religion. It's like Revelation to Christians."

"You said it's similar to the Koran," I said. "What's different?"

"Well, the most common version is that the ground will *cave in,* not explode, and the fog will cover the *skies,* not the earth." I nodded. "The fog is said to remain for forty days rather than a hundred years."

"What's the 'Beast?'" said Cromwell.

"There are many opinions about that. The most accepted is that it's a combination of several animals – a bull, a lion, a ram and so forth. The important thing is its task – to separate the believers from the non-believers."

"Anything else?" I said.

"Yes. This note says that the sun will *set* in the West."

"The sun always sets in the west," said Cromwell.

"Yes," said Akhem, "but on Judgment Day in the Koran, the sun *rises* in the west." He paused. "And west isn't capitalized."

After Akhem had gone, Cromwell said, "What are you going to do?"

"I don't know. I'm still trying to do *your* job. Don't you think that you and Wellbourne should reconsider the evacuation? And get somebody to at least try to find the bomb?"

He pursed his lips and looked at his watch. "I have another appointment in a few minutes, St. Cyr. Keep me posted on your progress."

"Who is Pamela Smythe-King?"

"That's – that's none of your affair. Goodbye."

I picked up the translation that Akhem had provided and walked through St. Giles' House to the street. According to the clock at Carfax, it was a few minutes past four. Rather than return to my rooms, I turned onto Blue Boar Street and stopped at the Bear. Inside, I ordered a pint, found a table in a corner next to a window and sat down.

Someone had left one of the London papers on the window sill. I picked it up and glanced through it idly. The front-page story was about two mosques in East London that had been burned to the ground. Arson was suspected. The last few paragraphs were devoted to the speech that Markham was giving that day. A small headline near the bottom of page five caught my eye:

ANOTHER BOMB THREAT AT OXFORD

Apparently, the government's effort to insulate itself from blame had begun. It was a wire service story datelined London:

> *The Home Office announced today that the latest in a series of threats against the City of Oxford has been received. A Home Office official, speaking anonymously, said that "of course we take it seriously, but you can't just close down the town and the University every time one of these idiots threatens a bomb." Asked what precautions were being taken, this official said, "We have stated in the most forceful way that everyone should leave*

until this matter is cleared up. We have been in touch with the Mayor and the Chancellor's Office. We expect everyone will act in his best interest."

In response to an inquiry concerning the specific nature of the threat, he declined to provide details except to say that it included a reference to an earlier explosion on the White Star Line's Victoria several years ago. "The terrorism on Victoria has been a rich source of inspiration for these people," he said.

So there it was – a clever warning couched in such a way that no one would take it seriously. They almost seemed to *want* the people to stay. There was no mention of London or Portsmouth, probably because those threats remained undisclosed. Oxford's "voluntary" evacuation had required some acknowledgement by the government.

Another, still smaller, headline drew my attention:

SUCCESSION IN AYLESBURY

What was this about?

Officials at Parliament and in the Prime Minister's office were at a loss to explain an obscure provision in the recent Housekeeping Bill that apparently affects only the Duchy of Aylesbury. No one in the Commons seems to . . .

The story referred me to another section of the paper which, unfortunately, was missing. I would have to ask Markham what was stirring in his fiefdom.

I unfolded the "doomsday" note. It seemed to support Markham's theory about Muslim terrorists. The paper and envelope were the same as the earlier letters, and the marking pen was also similar. Anyone could have done that, of course, but the language was a Muslim tongue and the message had been adapted from the Koran. Again, that didn't mean that they were necessarily Muslims, but why bother if they were not?

The note implied that the destruction of Oxford was near, presumably at the end of the seven days declared in the earlier letter. I considered the variations that Akhem had mentioned. Obviously, the planned event was an explosion, not an earthquake, and its impact would be felt on the ground rather than in the sky. But why would the "fog" cover the earth for a hundred years instead of forty days? There was virtually no "fog" after *Victoria* exploded – the dust and debris had disappeared within minutes.

That the sun would set rather than rise in the West with a capital W was easy to understand. Few places in the world were more emblematic of Western civilization than Oxford. Some people – Markham for one – believed that the sun had *already* set in the West. Was that it? Did Muslim terrorists want to destroy the University as a sign that the West was done, that a new regime was taking its place? It was as good a reason as any. All terrorism was really an attack on the dominant culture. Was that the *why?* Did it help with the *who?* I shook my head.

My mind returned to the story about burning mosques and Markham's speech. The author of the piece obviously believed that Markham's rallies were behind the attacks though she didn't say so. The sentiments expressed in the doomsday note were so familiar – had Tony decided to use the Oxford bomber to further the cause? He had been in London when the message was delivered, but he could have arranged it before he left. I dismissed the idea. The note was no good to Markham unless it was made public, and that was very unlikely. Wellbourne and his friends would never disclose further evidence of trouble at Oxford. They might have to do something about it.

Other questions remained. Why were these warnings provided ahead of the event? *Victoria* and the church at Aylesbury had been destroyed without notice. The people on *Victoria* had been slaughtered indiscriminately. Why was Oxford given the opportunity to limit the loss of life? The dons were symbols, too. And there was something else – this latest message had been hand-delivered to a very prominent mailbox.

I wondered about Cromwell. Could Markham possibly be right about him? He had been at Aylesbury when the church was blown away. He had met with the Muslim Imam at the Randolph Hotel, along with someone named Khan and Pamela Smythe-King. Who the hell were they? I shook my head again. In any event, no further alerts regarding London or Portsmouth had been received. The focus of the attack seemed to have narrowed and, since the doomsday note required no postage, those responsible for it were already here.

The bells at Carfax told me that it was quarter to six. I crossed Broad Street and approached the gate that opened onto the curved end of the Sheldonian Theater. The theater was U-shaped and the curved end was the back of the building – the front, with its pediment and temple, looked inward toward the Divinity School. It was secured from the street by an iron fence and thirteen tall plinths, each one topped by a huge bust carved from white limestone. They were called "the Emperors," and they had stood watch at the back of the Sheldonian for three hundred years. When I first came to Oxford, though, they were missing. Faceless because of the weather and the quality of the stone, they had been removed. New heads were installed at the beginning of my second year at the University.

The Duke of Aylesbury had donated the money for the new Emperors. The old carvings, all bearded, were anonymous – no one knew whether they were supposed to be gods or philosophers or kings – and the idea had been that they remain so. Markham himself had spent considerable time with the sculptor trying to ensure that they were as near as possible to the originals. At least, that was the story.

A few days after the new Emperors were erected, Markham and I had fallen into one of our periodic arguments about religion during a protracted visit to the Eagle and Child. When my namesake married the pious Catholic woman in 1785 it had, as his mother intended, ensured that ours would be a Catholic family in a country established largely by people fleeing the Catholic Church and its not-so-distant cousin, the Church of England. Madame St. Cyr had built a chapel where she communed with her God on a daily basis. She observed all the rituals and insisted that her husband do so as well. He humored her when he was at home, which wasn't often. When children came, they were Catholics, but for generations the religious characteristics of each parent were inherited according to gender – the girls were devout, the boys were not. Those wishing to marry into the wealthy, aristocratic St. Cyr family became Catholics or looked elsewhere.

My mother, Colleen Mary Fitzpatrick St. Cyr, was a Presbyterian. Her people had come to the New World a few years before the first St. Cyr arrived. They left Ireland in 1772 intending to disembark at Halifax, but were swept south by a great storm and landed in Charleston instead. Once there, they discovered that because of their religion they were entitled to land, plus money to purchase tools, supplies and materials for building a home. After certifying that they were indeed Protestants, her ancestors had been given two hundred and fifty acres and ten pounds in gold.

Subsequent generations had expanded the family's patrimony. By the time Colleen Fitzpatrick met Arthur St. Cyr, her father was the largest landholder west of Port Royal. Given her family's history, it was unsurprising that Robert Fitzpatrick and his daughter were uncompromising Protestants with no Catholic acquaintances though, of course, they knew about the Papists who lived in the castle on St. Cyr Close.

It was almost last call and the pub was nearly empty. "I have no religion," I said.

Markham laughed. "Everyone has a god."

"That's not true. I don't." I paused. "My grandmother is a very committed Catholic. My mother is an equally serious Protestant. Between them they made my father's life hell."

"Which one was he?"

"Neither. He had no religion either. He was in the middle and so was I. And so was my sister." I stopped again. "She died because of it."

"Your sister?"

"Yes."

"What happened?"

"A few days after I was born, my grandmother had me baptized in the family chapel by a Catholic priest. My mother was still in the hospital. When she found out about it, all hell broke loose. When Adrienne was born she was determined that it not happen again, but my grandmother secretly called in a priest and carried Adrienne to the chapel herself while my mother was asleep. It was a bitterly cold night, there was no fire, and the baby was immersed in very cold water." I leaned back in my chair. "She caught pneumonia and died three days later. My father was at sea, but my mother blamed him anyway. That was basically the end of my family."

"How old were you?"

"Six."

"Did they divorce?"

I shook my head. "They wanted each other too much for that – it was like a disease. My mother moved into another house. My father visited his wife." I paused. "I lived in both places until I went off to school."

"So you blame religion for all that?"

"Yes."

"Don't you think your mother and grandmother had something to do with it?"

"Of course. But there would have been no quarrel without religion."

Markham ordered another round. "Religion's not the problem. It's the people who insist that one religion, theirs, be accepted by everyone else."

Egged on by beer, I pushed my luck and our relationship. "Like the Catholics?"

He looked at me for a moment and decided to smile. "Yes, but we weren't the only ones." He turned up his glass. "Look at Oxford. First there were Catholics, then the Church of England. Those two jockeyed around a bit. Lives were lost. The Anglicans prevailed only to be displaced by the Dissenters and Nonconformists – skeptics and agnostics and Protestants. Now we have Statism, a government-sponsored profanity with more commands and less tolerance than all the others combined. And woe be unto you if you refuse to worship at the altar of the State."

"Even at Oxford?"

"Especially at Oxford. The University's been on the dole for sixty years. My class at Balliol was the last that paid anything. Neither the students nor their parents have any investment in this place." He paused. "Whitehall calls the tune now. Devotion to the State is mandatory."

"But we no longer kill in the name of religion, do we?"

"You're not listening, St. Cyr. The State *is* our religion, and how many people have been killed in the name of the State? At least the Catholics and the Anglicans, even the Protestants, tried to build something up. The great colleges here, the University buildings, the cathedrals, were created by the old religions. All this new lot does is tear things down." He paused. "They will also be pushed aside. Sooner rather than later."

"By who?"

"There are still believers in this world, my friend. Billions of them. All over the Middle East, Asia, Africa. And they, too, wish to impose their religion on us." Markham laughed. "And we, the non-believers, are making it easy for them."

"How so?"

"We've invited them in. We subsidize them and their multiple offspring while encouraging our own people to remain childless. We prepare the ground before them. They won't have to fire a shot."

"Meaning?"

"We have a perfect example right here. You've heard about the new Muslim college, I suppose?"

"Yes."

"The University, with much government insistence, *donated* the land in University Parks. The plans call for the construction of a great mosque in addition to the other college buildings. I've seen the drawings. It will be identical to the mosque in Cordoba."

"So?"

"The Muslims reigned in Cordoba for five centuries. When the Christians took it back they built a Gothic cathedral right in the middle of the mosque." Markham paused. "The mosque here won't have a cathedral. I think the message is clear. People who believe in *something* always prevail over those who believe in *nothing.*"

Later, as we walked along Broad Street, Markham said, "Stop a moment. I want to show you something."

We paused in front of the Sheldonian gate. He pointed up, to the Emperor on his left. "Who's that?" he said.

I smiled. "I have no idea."

"It's Judas." He pointed again. "Who's that?"

"Uh, Simon?"

"No. That's Thomas. Doubting Thomas." He laughed and extended his arms. "And there's Andrew and Philip and all the rest of them. It's my private joke on these pagan bigots."

"But there were only twelve of them. Who's number thirteen?"

"That's the biggest joke of all." We moved to the last Emperor on the left. "Who do you think that is?"

I looked up. The giant head was clearly visible in the moonlight. Like all the others, it wore a beard and a fluted collar. The eyes, though, were large and more distinct, like real eyes, and the hair was parted in the middle. It reminded me of someone. "I'm not sure," I said.

"Look closer," said Markham. "Can you see the scar on his cheek?"

CHAPTER FOUR

KHAN AND the Imam walked down Mansfield Road past Balliol's playing fields and cricket pitch. At Jowett Walk they paused to admire the Scholar Tree, dedicated to some worthy from St. Catherine's College a hundred years before. Sixty feet tall with a forty-five foot crown, its creamy white flowers were over, but the mass of yellow leaves – bright in the late afternoon sun – completely obscured the thick gray branches.

As they resumed their journey, Khan said, "Are you still determined to remain, Imam Akhem?" Akhem nodded. "Why attend this meeting then?"

"The Master of Balliol invited me personally. He is my enemy, Abram, and yours, too, though you don't know it. I am always interested in what my enemy has to say."

"We've been friends for a long time."

Akhem nodded again. "Perhaps. But the Duke is a man who must have enemies. He prospers only when there is someone to hate. We are an easy target." They turned the corner at Holywell Street. "He is your friend because you, too, are a sort of aristocrat, but he will turn on you one day. He must not want for enemies."

They reached the Broad and stood looking past the Emperors at their destination. "Are we *his* enemies, Imam?"

Akhem smiled. "We do not war with men, Abram Khan. We – joust for their souls." They crossed the street and pushed through the gate.

I LOOKED out across the audience as the White Star Line production of the final voyage of *Victoria* played out on the screen in front of me. Markham had been very persuasive. The lower seats behind the columns were full and half of those in the gallery were occupied as well. They had listened to me politely and, when I called for questions, there were none. The outcome seemed to be in doubt. A few of the dons had begun to nudge one another and whisper, and several had left their seats and were now standing by the doors. The reporters in the first row had closed their notebooks. I raised my eyes to the colorful allegory painted on the ceiling. Truth, and the representatives of Religion and Learning, still drove the emissaries of Ignorance – Malice, Hatred and Envy – from the field. I hoped it would prove prophetic.

Suddenly, the brilliant flash reached my eyes again and the terrible roar filled my ears and, for an instant, I felt it all wash over me as *Victoria* exploded on the screen. The whispering stopped. The audience sat upright and those preparing to leave a minute before stood straight and still. The room was utterly silent for seconds that seemed to last much longer. Markham's voice came from behind me. "St. Cyr was there," he said. "I'm sure he would tell you that the actual horror was worse. Odds are that the same bomb has been planted here. Nothing will survive the blast." He switched the projector to rewind. "We should go. The Chancellor's Office will coordinate the evacuation."

The stunned men and women remained in their seats for a time before making for the exits. No one spoke. They seemed anxious to leave. I turned to Markham. "What do you think?"

He shrugged. "We'll know soon enough. I've asked for the canvass this evening." He looked at his watch. "The vote should be done in two or three hours."

"I had more bad news from Cromwell today. We need to talk about it."

Sweat beaded his brow. He turned away from me and coughed. "All right. What about a drink?"

We crossed Broad Street and settled once more in his library. He handed me my drink and returned to the bar for his. Watching him, I realized again that his right hand was useless. I shook my head. He wrote with his right hand. The doomsday note was impossible.

We discussed the news of the day. His speech in London had been a success. I confided the details of the note and my conversation with Soleil about the diagram. I didn't mention the letter on the white linen stationery. "So Wellbourne told the truth about the diagram," said Markham. "A page from a weapon design abandoned long ago."

"What he said was true. I'm not sure there isn't more to it than that. *Why* was it left with the map?"

"Maybe it's a dodge."

"I don't think so. They don't have to leave any clues at all. Why leave a false one?"

He nodded. "You said something about bad news and Cromwell?"

I grimaced. "He and that son-of-a-bitch Wellbourne have reneged again. The Army's not coming to look for the bomb."

"Why not?"

I shook my head. "Who knows? Cromwell *says* he's looking for volunteers."

He looked thoughtful. "I told you they'd like to see Oxford in ashes."

"I'm starting to believe you."

"We don't have the resources to look for the bomb. And we just told everybody to leave town. There's no one to help."

"I know."

We were quiet. "What's on for tomorrow?" Markham said finally.

"The critical thing is to get these people out of here. Once that begins – *if* it begins – I'll worry about the bomb again."

The iron knocker on the front door sounded and Markham left the room. He returned with a tall rangy man with close-cropped black hair. I rose as they came through the door. "A.K., this is Georges St. Cyr. St. Cyr, Abram Khan." Khan extended his hand and I took it. "Sit down, A.K., please. What about something to drink?"

"Nothing, thanks," said Khan. "What's wrong with your hand?"

"Tore some tendons. It'll be all right in a few weeks."

Khan nodded. "I've just come from your show at the Sheldonian."

"What did you think?" said Markham.

"Very impressive. I've never seen – anything like that explosion. It was terrifying."

"Will everyone go?" I said.

"Probably. I can tell you one group who's staying, though. My new house. The Mosque."

"Why?" said Markham.

Khan smiled. "I'm not entirely clear on that. It has something to do with our inevitability." Markham nodded. "I'd like to help you if I can."

"Why would you do that?" I said.

Khan stared at me. "My sister was on *Victoria.*"

We were silent. I looked at my watch. "I have to get back to the House. Tony can fill you in."

THE TWO men passed out of Balliol Hall and walked south across the Garden Quadrangle. Halfway down the quad, Markham stopped and turned around. "Look," he said. "Tell me what you see."

Abram Khan looked back. The hall, still brilliantly lit, was a mixture of the medieval, Gothic and Renaissance. Its lancet windows were flanked by heavy stone buttresses but there was also a balustrade on the east end, and a spire that was almost whimsical rising from the pitched roof. "I see a building that might be three hundred years old or maybe just a few. Like most of the buildings here."

Markham laughed. "I believe that the hall was actually constructed about a hundred years ago." He pointed to the Senior Common Room situated next to the Hall, an undoubtedly modern structure with wide rectangular windows on the first floor and narrow rectangular windows on the second. Its flat, bleak exterior, devoid of even the simplest architectural detail, contrasted sharply with the lavish design elements of the building next to it. "They're trying to ruin the architecture here, too. That monstrosity was built while I was in the service." He paused. "After I was elected Master, I intended to tear it down. There was really no opposition from the Fellows or the students. They had tired very quickly of the banal masquerading as style."

"But it's still here."

"Yes." Markham turned away. "I've decided to leave it for the time being as a – a symbol." They emerged from the library passage into the Front Quadrangle. "Are you sure you won't stop for a drink or something?"

"I don't want to get on the wrong side of the Imam. Thanks for dinner. I'll see you in a couple of days."

Markham pushed through the doors to his library. He considered Khan – why was he really here? He had encountered ISI several times during his tour in Pakistan, and he had discovered Khan's association with the intelligence service. Was he just a cricket coach or something more? Unless he had changed radically in the past few years, Khan was no zealot, but he worked for an organization that was no stranger to Muslim terrorism. Had they sent Khan to kill him? Or had he really come to avenge his sister?

He turned his mind to the evacuation. It would go forward now. He had hesitated over the film and finally decided that it was necessary. His own house had just voted to go. He had expected the decision but was surprised at the lack of opposition. Some of his Fellows always voted against him on principle alone.

AT DINNER that evening I half-expected another invitation to the high table but it wasn't forthcoming. Dean West rose before the food was served and confirmed the rumors about the evacuation. "We are meeting after dinner to decide what the college will do," he told the students seated at the tables in front of him. "If we choose to go, you must go as well. If we stay, however, you as individuals may decide to go anyway. You will be advised of our decision as soon as it is made."

Shortly before eleven, Andrews knocked on my door and reported that the House of Christ was "closed" as of midnight two days hence. "Anyone needing a place to go, or transportation," said Andrews, "should contact the Dean." Just before closing my eyes, I opened the *Victoria* file again. Someone named Aden Khan had indeed been on board that day at Southampton and, curiously, she was sharing a stateroom with Pamela Smythe-King.

I STEPPED into the corridor as the train pulled into Paddington Station. The exodus behind me had already begun. This train was full and dozens of people left back at the station in Oxford awaited the next one. Breakfast had been barely attended and, when I returned to my rooms afterward, the other students on my staircase were gone. I, too, would have to leave by tomorrow night. Christ Church would be closed and no exception had been made for me.

I reached the exit as the train came to a halt and the doors slid open. A moment later I passed under the Clock Arch and hailed a cab. "Middle Temple Lane," I said. Thirty minutes later, I climbed out of the taxi, entered the gate and walked down the narrow street that ran between the Middle and Inner Temples, two of England's four Inns of Court. The familiar brick and stone buildings loomed on either side. At Fountain Court I skirted Middle Temple Hall and crossed to the far side. Number Eleven Garden Court was the last building on the right. I walked up the steps and pushed through the door.

The young woman behind the desk was new. "My name is St. Cyr. He's expecting me." She picked up the telephone and murmured into the receiver. After a few seconds she put it down and nodded towards the stairs. When I reached the top, I crossed the landing and knocked on a door. It opened immediately.

"Hello, Fitz." We shook hands. The Supervisor of the London Office looked precisely like the English solicitor that he was. Now in his late sixties, the skin on his angular face was unwrinkled, the pure white hair and mustache perfectly manicured. He had been in charge of the London branch for ten years. "Sit down," he said. "I hoped you'd come by."

I smiled. There wasn't much that happened in Great Britain, or all of Europe for that matter, that this man didn't know. The arrival of one of his former agents, ostensibly to study again at Oxford, would not go unnoticed. "Thank you, sir."

When I began at Annapolis I was unsure what I would do. I was there because my father, and my father's father, had been there. I was interested, in the abstract, in flight school. The prospect of fighting the Navy's F-4 Phantom seemed to hold out the best prospect for one-on-one combat. After a time, though, I began to consider something else.

When we threw our hats into the air at graduation I was the only one among my classmates whose next stop was Coronado Island, California. I was instructed in munitions and demolition, all branches of the martial arts and high-altitude parachuting. At the conclusion of my training, I was recruited by the Defense Intelligence Agency and sent to its school in Arlington Hall, Virginia. The focus at DIA was analysis – the missile gap, the continuing impact of China's Cultural Revolution, turmoil in Africa – that was often unrelated to the problems at hand. I was restless. I wanted to *do* something, to test the skills that I had honed since childhood. I went to one of my father's classmates, the man who was now Chief of Naval Operations, for advice. As a result of that meeting, I found the niche that I'd been seeking.

Within the Central Intelligence Agency's Directorate of Plans was a small, self-contained unit known as the Office of Policy Coordination. This innocuous-sounding group was actually the country's most highly-trained cadre of clandestine warriors. It received product from the CIA but it operated outside the confines of CIA management. The National Security Council directive that created it defined the mission as "all activities" in defense of the United States that could be conducted so as to permit the government "to plausibly deny its responsibility." Those activities included sabotage, demolition and evacuation, economic warfare and the subversion of hostile states. Its agents, never more than twenty, were experts in all types of weaponry, assassination and the use of explosives.

The violence and death associated with my work was new. Prior to my first assignment with the Office, the disruption of a coup in Monrovia, I had never killed anything. At first, the butchery was thoughtless. I did it because I'd been trained to do it and, like a disembodied specter observing my own performance, I reveled in my ability to live while others died. The indifference to death had started to change after a few years, and my resignation from the Office had been unwelcome.

"I understand that you're helping with our little problem up at Oxford," said my former chief.

I laughed. The Official Secrets Act would not be observed in this office. "Yes, sir. And I need some help."

He nodded. "I'll tell you what I can, Fitz. Off the record, of course."

"Of course." On the chance that some part of my mission was unknown, I described everything that had occurred since my conversation with the British Ambassador. There were no interruptions. When I finished, I sat back and waited.

The man across the desk leaned forward. "I can tell you four things," he said. "First, the stolen bombs were recovered within days. All of them. Second, John Cromwell is not the buffoon he probably seems to you. He's a first-rate nuclear physicist and he was deeply involved in the weapons program. Third, the proliferation of weapons, including nuclear weapons, has increased markedly in the past few years. Even the Muslim states, one in particular, may have the capacity to produce the bombs we're talking about." He paused. "And fourth, the cobalt bomb program *was* abandoned in the '60's but not because it failed the test at Maralinga. It passed with flying colors."

We regarded each other for a moment. I took a deep breath. "So Wellbourne lied about the bombs."

"Yes."

"Why?"

"Think about it, Fitz. The British recovered the bombs and, finally recognizing the potential for mischief, destroyed them. A year later, *Victoria* was incinerated by a weapon with precisely the same characteristics. What conclusion would *you* draw?"

"That – that another country or – someone had designed and built the same bomb or –"

"Or?"

"Or – that the Brits' own design had fallen into the wrong hands."

"I believe the latter's more likely, don't you?" I nodded. "So does the British government. It's one thing for terrorists or thugs or even some rogue country to have stolen bombs. They didn't have the detonators, so the bombs were virtually useless. But *Victoria* showed that someone was capable of building the bomb *and* the detonator." He stopped. "Many bombs and many detonators, maybe. Wellbourne's story was good enough for you and Markham. They wouldn't take a chance on the truth getting out."

"Do you think that Cromwell really has something to do with this?"

"I've known John Cromwell for years. I tell you about him because he's an angry, bitter man who believes that he's been denied things he should have had. He hates Oxford and everything it stands for." He paused. "He lost the fortune his father left him, but it doesn't seem to have slowed him down."

"Was he involved with this bomb?"

"I don't think so. He worked on the nuclear side of things, but it's likely that he at least knew about it."

I remembered the conversation at Aylesbury Abbey. "I know that he's familiar with the concept."

He nodded. "He probably had access to the plans."

"If the cobalt bomb was a success, why was it abandoned?"

"I believe they decided that it had no war-making application." He stopped. "Soleil's description of it was pretty close. It's designed to create a high level of radioactivity but it's not really more – *deadly* than uranium. It just lasts longer."

"How does it work?"

"The explosive elements of a nuclear weapon are encased in ordinary metallic cobalt. When it's detonated, the cobalt becomes radioactive. The explosive force is reduced, but the fallout is increased."

"Greater range?"

"Not necessarily. The most important thing is that the radioactivity lasts much longer than an ordinary nuke."

"How long?"

"Several years. And it doesn't blow away. It just falls to the ground and lies there."

"What happened at Maralinga?"

"They tested a very small bomb encased in cobalt. There wasn't much damage and the fallout covered less than a thousand square meters, but it was virtually uninhabitable for five years."

"Was Cromwell involved?" The Supervisor nodded. "Does anybody have one of these things now?"

"Not that I know of."

"The Muslim countries you mentioned – do they have the capacity to build it?"

"One of them does – Pakistan. They've had ordinary nukes for years, and there's evidence that they are selling the technology. All it takes is money."

"So, it wouldn't be –"

"It wouldn't be the Pakistani government. That would risk total annihilation. But there are others in the Muslim world with no such scruples. In fact, they welcome that sort of thing."

The conversation drifted into other matters – mutual acquaintances, who was where, the attractive young lady at the desk downstairs. My old boss had gently urged me to think about returning to the Office and I had lied and said that I would. When Markham's name came up again, he said, "You know about his crusade against the Muslims?" I nodded. "It's dangerous. He and his friends have raised the temperature to the boiling point."

"He tells me that he feels like a stranger in his own country. And he believes that they're responsible for these threats." I paused. "Nothing you've said proves him wrong."

He nodded. "Do you know his sister?"

"Yes."

"She's a force in her own right. Many people think that she's behind Cromwell." He stopped. "She has ambitions of her own."

As I rose to leave he said, "There's another thing I should tell you. Do you remember Abram Khan? The cricketer?" I nodded. "He works for the Pakistani intelligence service. Part time, I guess you'd say. He arrived in England last Tuesday. He's in Oxford now."

I smiled. "I met him yesterday. He's volunteered to help us."

"I'd watch him carefully if I were you."

A few minutes later I again passed Middle Temple Hall but, instead of turning left to catch a cab back to Paddington, I chose the other direction and walked to the Embankment – I had two hours until the next train. When I reached the Thames I turned toward Waterloo Bridge, a few hundred yards away. Just past the bridge I veered onto Savoy Place, past an imposing brick building that served as the examinations school for the Royal College of Surgeons, and wound my way into the Art Deco elegance of the Savoy Hotel. I stopped at the entrance to the American Bar. I had never liked the room – it reminded me of the interior of a submarine decorated in pastels and cream – but Gabrielle had loved it. All special occasions in London began or ended with a couple of drinks at the American Bar.

I passed through the short passageway, crossed the room and found a seat at the low bar. A bartender appeared before me, waiting. "Plymouth martini, please," I said. "Straight up, no fruit." The drink arrived a moment later.

I considered my next step. A large part of me wanted to go home. The British government that had asked for my help was actually working against me. Wellbourne had lied about the bombs, told half-truths about an old weapons program and – seemingly interested only in the next election – undermined the effort to evacuate Oxford. The promised search for the bomb had been shrugged off. He appeared completely uninterested in the puzzle that he had asked me to solve.

I swallowed some of the cold gin and looked at my reflection in the mirror. I couldn't go. As long as it was possible that I might find the people responsible for Gabrielle's death, I would keep looking. And Markham would help me, Muslims or no Muslims. Actually, the odds in favor of Muslim terrorists had grown much shorter over the past twenty-four hours. The Arabic doomsday note and the notion that a rogue scientist might sell them a bomb certainly made it more plausible. A famous cricketer from Pakistan, now an agent for ISI, wanted to help with our investigation.

There was more reason to suspect Cromwell, too. He hated Oxford, he probably had access to plans for the bomb and he was the only one who could vouch for the delivery of the doomsday note. I considered the contrast. A band of terrorists was my traditional sort of enemy. Lacking wealth and military expertise, they pursued the age-old, rational goal of domination in a manner that enraged those accustomed to the comfortable conventions of ordinary warfare – uniforms, battlefields, the sanctity of non-combatants. Cromwell, on the other had, was a sociopath or worse. He was not seeking to protect himself or command others, he was trying to scratch a monumental itch inside his head.

The warning about Guin troubled me. Its truth was obvious. She was far more aggressive than Cromwell, and it was easy to believe that she dominated their relationship, whatever that was. If Cromwell was the bomber, then, was she pulling his strings? Why? I shook my head. It was ludicrous. She *did* have ambitions – she was certain that her son would be the next duke, and the laws of succession for Aylesbury had apparently been changed. I shook my head. Markham was the most hidebound man in all of England. It was hard to believe that he would condone such an arrangement.

I signaled the bartender for another drink. What kind of bomb was it? The map signified one version – quick, violent, all-consuming. The blue and white diagram suggested another – violent, of course, but long-lasting, more awful in its way than the other. The note left in Cromwell's mailbox had predicted a "fog" lasting a hundred years, but even one lasting only five was too terrible to contemplate.

I couldn't shake the nagging sense of unreality. In the real world, criminals and terrorists didn't tell you what they were going to do. They didn't provide maps and clues like a scavenger hunt or a search for buried treasure, and they certainly didn't give you time to get out of the way. In the real world, if there was a reason to blow Oxford up, they blew it up. I seemed caught up in a game and I didn't know the rules.

I knew what the clues meant. *What* was going to happen? An attack on the City of Oxford. *When?* In approximately three and a half days. *How?* By one of two terrible weapons. *Why?* Probably because of someone's hatred or ideology. *Who?* I had no idea. Cromwell was the next clue to consider. And another thing was unexplained – the fake letter from Gabrielle. It had arrived in one of the bomber's envelopes. Was it part of the game or not?

I looked at the neon clock over the bar. The next train to Oxford left Paddington in an hour. I was meeting Markham at six to assess the extent of the evacuation, and living arrangements for the next few days were also on the agenda. As I beckoned to the bartender and reached for my wallet, a woman sat down in the chair next to mine. I glanced at the mirror, then looked more carefully. "Hello, Fitz," she said, leaning toward me.

I inhaled her scent – roses. "Hello, Gill."

"I'VE ALREADY told you that I don't give a bloody damn about your mumbo jumbo religious bromides," said John Cromwell. He turned away from Akhem and looked at the Dean of Christ Church. "Miss Smythe-King is willing to pay you market value for Christ Church Meadow. If you won't agree to that, we'll take it anyway and you won't get half that much. Do you understand?" Dean West remained mute and still. "Do you understand?"

Pamela bit her lower lip and looked down at her lap. This was not what she had hoped for. Her effort to bring the Muslim college on board with her plans had failed dismally. Akhem's parting comment on leaving her suite was something to the effect that "the infidels in Oxford could go to hell as they chose," but his people "would not be dragged along with them." And now Cromwell was browbeating this poor old man from Christ Church. She had known John Cromwell since her Whitechapel days. Not in the professional sense – he had never shown the slightest interest in her – but Aden had captivated him, and he had been very helpful during her darkest days though his motive had proved distasteful, even to Pamela. The sensitivity he had shown back then was not on display now. "John, please, I think that –"

He turned his attention to her. "Pamela," he said in only a slightly less hostile tone, "you have to be firm with these people. They've been pottering about the streets of Oxford or – or the sands of some God-forsaken desert somewhere for too long. They need to understand that their religion and their quaint ideas about tradition and – *morality* – don't matter anymore."

Akhem rose. "You, sir, are a blasphemer and you will end as all blasphemers do." He turned for the door.

"Is that a threat?" said Cromwell.

"No. It's a conviction. Your fate is sealed." Akhem left the room.

Cromwell laughed. "Going to poke needles in his voodoo doll, I expect." He turned back to West. "You have three days. If Pamela's offer is not accepted by then we shall begin legal proceedings." Cromwell stood up. West remained in his seat. "Well?"

"What are you doing about the books?" said West.

"What?"

"The books. My Students and the Fellows at the other colleges are worried about the books."

"What books?"

"The volumes and manuscripts in the Bodleian and the other libraries. The folios and the Gutenberg and – and *Roland.* What's going to happen to them?"

Cromwell laughed. "Nothing's going to happen to them, West. This bomb scare's a hoax." He paused. "And even if it weren't, it would cost millions of pounds to move just ten per cent of them. We don't have the money. It's not in the budget."

"But –"

"And so what if they all blow up? That's what's wrong with this place. Too many books. Too much looking backwards." He gazed down at the old man. "You and your friends had better leave them alone. If I find out that you've taken even a single one, I'll have you all prosecuted for theft."

After West was gone, Pamela and Cromwell sat without speaking. He swiveled around in his chair and stared through the bay window at the back garden, intent on something at the far end. She looked around the room. Somewhere within these walls was the book she had to retrieve. She considered the gun in her purse and rejected it – for the time being.

Finally, Pamela spoke. "John, I appreciate your – help, but I'm not sure that we made any progress today."

He turned. "Yes, we did, Pamela. We're only three days away from taking over Christ Church Meadow."

"But I wanted to *convince* them, not dictate to them."

"That was never going to happen. All West cares about is his eternal landscape, and the concept of pornography is –" Cromwell smiled "– *blasphemy* to the Muslims. They force their women to cover up from head to toe." He paused. "If Akhem ever saw one of your films his head would explode."

"But –"

"Look, you want your precious college, don't you?"

"Yes, but –"

"Then you're going to have to push your way in. And there will be criticism, *lots* of criticism, along the way. People will say that you and your plans are a – a stain on Oxford." He turned away. "I wonder why you bother. It's an absurd anachronism."

"Why?"

"It has no reason for being. It should have withered away with the monarchy and the rest of the Empire."

"But – this is one of the world's great universities."

"Not for long, my dear. Not for long." He smiled. "It's past time for Oxford to realize that it's no better than the rest of this stinking world we live in." Taken aback, Pamela started to speak but he stopped her. "On the other hand," he said, smiling again, "perhaps it will all be gone in a few days. Then we can start over." He rose and looked at his watch. "I have to be somewhere shortly, Pamela. I'll let you know if I hear from West."

"Are we still on for tomorrow?"

"Of course. I'll see you at eleven."

◇◇◇

YATES HANDED me a note. "Dean West asked me to pass this along, Mr. St. Cyr."

"Thank you, Yates." I paused. "How long are you staying?"

"I'll be locking up the gates, sir. Tomorrow at midnight, the Dean said."

I nodded and stepped out onto St. Aldate's. I unfolded the note.

> *St. Cyr,*
> *Per Markham's request: 320 of 378 undergraduates are gone as are 155 of 199 graduate students. Of the 62 resident Students, 45 have left. I will speak to all that remain at dinner this evening.*
> *West*

I had already collected similar information at Pembroke and Magdalen, and had agreed to check with several of the other colleges on my way to Balliol.

I turned right on the High and looked in at Brasenose, Oriel and All Souls. The streets were deserted. Light shone from a few windows and the buildings at Radcliffe Square were lighted brilliantly, daring the unknown miscreants to do their worst. I picked up a note at University. The gate was closed and locked at St. Edmund Hall and there was no one at Queen's, either. The porters at New College and Hertford handed me folded sheets of paper and the man tending the gate at Trinity said that his tally had just been delivered to the Master of Balliol.

Markham opened the door himself. He held out his left hand. "The evacuation is a complete success," he said. "Congratulations."

"Your movie did it, not me."

"No matter." He glanced at my notes. "The average for the colleges is about eighty per cent. Queen's and Teddy Hall are completely vacant. Khan was right about the Mosque. They're all still here." We walked back to the library. "I just spoke to the Mayor. The old part of town is about sixty per cent and people are still moving out. Even North Oxford and Jericho are going." He paused. "It looks like everyone will be gone in another couple of days." He smiled. "Let's have a drink."

I nodded. "I learned something about the diagram today. We may have a bigger disaster on our hands than we thought." I recounted the history of Operation Antler. "Should we try to make it public?"

He sipped his scotch. "We don't want a panic any more than Wellbourne does. They're already leaving." He stopped. "It's a bit of a stretch, too. We *know* they have the other bombs." I shook my head. "What?"

"They *don't* have the other bombs."

"How do you mean?"

"A very reliable source tells me that those bombs were recovered and destroyed."

"Then where did the *Victoria* bomb come from?"

"My source thinks that the design for the bomb – and the detonator – has been stolen."

"By whom?"

"He doesn't know." I smiled. "But you'll be happy to hear that Cromwell *and* Muslim terrorists are possibilities."

Markham nodded. "Maybe Cromwell sold it to the terrorists. Maybe that's where he gets his money." The conversation continued over another drink. "What's next?" he said.

"I'm going to confront Cromwell. He was in a position to steal the design or he knows who was. He has access to every part of the University. He'd have no trouble hiding a bomb."

"Time grows short."

"I know. But at least no one will die if we fail." I paused. "Except the boys at the Mosque."

"Who knows? Maybe Allah will protect them." He stopped. "I'll be at Aylesbury tomorrow night. You're welcome to join us."

"Thanks, I've already accepted an invitation. Doctor Soleil called this afternoon. I'm staying with him at The Downs." I hesitated. "I'm taking another guest with me."

"Who?"

"A – young woman from Annapolis. I ran into her at the Savoy. I – I used to work for her father."

He nodded again and smiled. "You're wise to stay at The Downs. It might be a trifle crowded at Aylesbury."

She had been as determined as ever. "I'd already decided to come over here," Gill said. "Something was wrong and I was afraid. Then Dad showed me a newspaper story about a bomb and I knew that's why you were here."

"But there's nothing you can do about that."

Her eyes narrowed. "I didn't come to do anything about *that*. I don't care if the whole damned place goes up in smoke, as long as *you* don't go up with it."

I smiled. "I see. So what's your plan?"

"Plan?"

"Yes. You've made it to the Savoy Hotel. What comes next?"

"I *was* going to take the train to Oxford tomorrow, but since you're here –"

"I'm going back in a few minutes."

"Then I'll go with you."

"Then what?"

"Then – then I'll make sure that you don't do something stupid. The bomb will go off or it won't go off, and we can go home."

"Where are you going to stay?"

"With you, of course."

I shook my head. "No. You won't."

"Why not?"

"You'll be shocked to learn that I live in an all-male establishment. You couldn't get past the gate." I laughed at her expression. "Plus, I've spent the last three days trying to get people *out* of Oxford. I don't need someone moving in." I smiled. "I'll be someplace else myself starting tomorrow."

"I'll go where you go."

"Gill, it's just not –"

She laid a hand on my arm. "Don't treat me like a child. I want to be with you." She stopped. "And I *will* look after you. I promise."

I looked at her. You never know who the last girl is until one day – when you're twenty-five or thirty or even thirty-five – you discover that they've all become women, creatures with needs and motives far more complicated than your own. The open, unbearable sweetness of the child gives way to opaque layers of emotions judged necessary to survive. Gabrielle, despite her vulnerability, had always been a woman, and Guin, despite her strength, was an exemplar of the species. Gill had been a girl when we met and I suddenly, desperately, wanted her to remain one, to find a boy to please, though I knew it was already too late. I had finally convinced her to remain in London for the night. I swore that I would call her when my plans were made and I did. She would rent a car and drive up the next evening.

"I believe I can risk dinner," Markham said, breaking in on my thoughts. "Will you and your young lady do that?" He paused. "Day after tomorrow? Day Six?" I nodded. "Good. Khan will be there, and another old friend of mine."

"Who?"

He smiled. "A very lovely and successful woman named Pamela Smythe-King."

CHAPTER FIVE

MY FATHER had taught me the obvious things – how to ride and shoot, swimming and navigation. I learned the subtle skills – patience, stealth, camouflage – from my mother. When he was at sea, I lived with her at the river house. We had paddled softly across the water to Lady's Island where I followed her through marshes and pools and creeks in search of whatever animal, plant or vista she was seeking. Sometimes we would go for two or three days, fording the creeks to Cat Island or St. Helena. We carried no weapons. One summer night when I was home from school we stood rooted to the ground while a panther, who had wandered north from his native habitat, glared at us from the high branches of a loblolly pine.

When I turned thirteen she encouraged me to make those expeditions alone. Sometimes she set a task for me, sometimes not, but always she urged me to remember what I had seen, to draw a line from the prints in the sand and the scratches on the bark to the silence directly in front of me. The mastery of things that I acquired from my father helped me rise in my profession. The mastery of myself that she induced had saved my life.

It was dark when I turned north on St. Giles'. I stayed away from the light created by the streetlamps as I passed the Randolph and the Eagle and Child. I was alone, or so it seemed, and the absence of human beings made the old road an island where buildings and monuments and steeples, not trees, lined the horizon and the path. I stopped a block short of St. Giles' House and crossed to the other side of the street. A nearly full moon was uncovered by the clouds and the facade of the old house gleamed. It was wrapped in a dreadful stillness like a corpse abandoned to the worms.

I retreated into the shadows and watched. Every window on the front and side of the house, including the gables in the roof, was dark. A stone wall enclosed the house and garden, low across the front where it was topped by an iron fence. The urns on top of the pillars that were part of the fence cast shadows on the ashlar walls only a few feet away. A narrow gate opened onto a path down the side of the house to the back garden.

An hour later I crossed the road. No one had gone in or out of the house or passed me on the street. No lights had been switched on. Even if Cromwell were out for the evening, unlikely under the circumstances, surely he would have left a light on. I pushed against the garden gate – it was bolted. I pulled myself to the top of the low wall and vaulted the fence, then dropped down to the stone walk along the north side of the house.

No light showed in the back windows, and the moon disclosed a rectangular lawn bordered by gravel paths and a few trees and shrubs. A summerhouse nestled among more foliage at the far end of the garden. I climbed four steps and, after slipping on a pair of latex gloves, tried the rear door. It was locked, as were all six of the ground floor windows. A large chestnut tree grew against the corner of the house, its sturdy bare branches only inches away from one of the upstairs windows. A moment later I braced myself between the tree and the house and tried the window. It, too, was locked, so I wrapped my jacket around my fist and punched out one of the panes. I remained still, listening for an alarm or signs of life inside. Hearing nothing, I raised the sash and entered the house.

I checked the upstairs rooms quickly. No one was there and all of the windows were locked. It was the same story downstairs. The house was completely secured and deserted. Cromwell had given every indication yesterday that he would stay in Oxford at least until Day Five. This was only Day Four.

Cromwell's study was on the first floor looking out at the back garden. I turned on a lamp. The desk was bare. I shuffled through five of the six drawers – one of them contained paper and envelopes like those used by the bomber. I pushed a sample of each into my coat pocket.

The sixth drawer, the large one on the bottom right, was locked. It was a keyhole lock that could be opened with any of the old-fashioned keys typically used for antique furniture. I didn't have one of those with me, so I found a paper clip, twisted it into a new shape and inserted it in the keyhole. Seconds later the drawer was open, revealing a large leather-bound book. I opened it to the first page. Twenty minutes later I closed the book and replaced it in the drawer. I didn't bother with the lock.

I looked around. A mahogany secretary with tarnished brass pulls stood next to the door. The slots in the desk contained the usual – bills, bank statements, brokerage records, the embossed envelopes and stationery. I glanced through the financial documents. Something in the bank statements caught my eye. There were three separate deposits of one thousand pounds each made between the first and fifth of every month. What kind of investment paid out like that? I could only think of one, most likely associated with the book. I pushed the statement for September into my pocket. About to close the desk top, I noticed a bank deposit slip tucked into a checkbook – £25,000 had been added to Cromwell's account a few days earlier. Business, whatever it was, was brisk.

I went through the wide drawers at the bottom of the secretary. There was a thick roll of paper in the bottom one, bound by several rubber bands, tucked behind boxes of paper and envelopes. I unrolled the sheets and spread them on the desk. The paper was blue and the lines were white and, according to the logo in the bottom right-hand corner, the drawings were part of Operation Antler. I flipped through them. There were several different dates from June 10, 1967 to September 25, 1967, and none of them was September 1.

I returned the bundle to the secretary and decided to leave the same way that I had come. I paused outside Cromwell's bedroom, then entered it again, just to make sure. A wallet, a set of keys and some loose coins still lay on the dresser. I counted the money – it was just short of £200. One of the keys matched the locks on the doors. Wherever he was, without money or identification, it was not Cromwell who had locked the doors at St. Giles' House.

Outside again on the gravel path that ran parallel to the back of the house, I turned for the gate. A voice, tinny and distant, stopped me. I dropped to the ground. I heard other voices. They seemed to come from the summerhouse twenty yards away. After my eyes had completely adjusted to the dark, I crossed the lawn, moving in a low crouch.

The summerhouse was a miniature temple with four columns and a pediment, and its roof sported a dome like the one that capped the Camera in Radcliffe Square. There were iron benches on either side of the raised floor. The voices came from behind an almost closed door between them. I pushed the door open, allowing the moonlight to penetrate the tiny room. Cromwell, naked, lay on his left side. There was a small hole just above his right ear. Dried blood encircled the hole and a slight trickle had reached the bottom of his jaw. An empty leather camera case and a cotton robe hung from the back of the door. The voices came from a transistor radio that lay next to his head.

I felt rather than heard something behind me. I switched off the radio and added it to the cache in my pocket. Kneeling between the shrubs and the summerhouse I watched as a hooded figure climbed the back steps and entered the house. Seconds later, a light came on in the study just before the curtains were drawn across the window. I waited. After no more than a minute, the light was extinguished and the figure emerged, clutching something in both hands, and hurried toward me. I backed further into the bushes. After a few seconds inside the summerhouse, the cloaked figure crossed the lawn and disappeared around the corner of the house.

I approached the back of the house again and tried the door. It was open. I made a quick survey of the other rooms, then entered Cromwell's study. There was something in the room that wasn't there before but it evaded me. After confirming that the drawings were still in the secretary I sat down behind the desk and opened the bottom right-hand drawer. The leather book was gone.

I remained in Cromwell's chair, in the dark, considering. It was at once more and less complicated now. Cromwell would have had much to answer for had he still been able to speak. In addition to the other things that made him a suspect, the Operation Antler drawings were in the bottom drawer of his secretary and he had a ready supply of the bomber's stationery in his desk. Was his death related to the threat against Oxford? It didn't seem likely. The locked house and the book and the camera case, not to mention the small caliber weapon used to fire a bullet into his brain, argued for a different conclusion altogether.

Still, even dead Cromwell was the prime suspect. Yes, the drawings seemed a bit obvious and yes, blowing up the place in a colossal fit of pique seemed overdone, but there it was. The £25,000 argued for a slightly different, but no less culpable, scenario. Other than a shadowy band of Muslim terrorists, he was the *only* suspect and there was no longer any chance that he would disclose the location of the bomb.

I looked at my watch. If there *was* a bomb, it would explode in just less than seventy-two hours. Why not proclaim Cromwell the bomber, lament his failure to mention where the bomb was before he died, and leave Wellbourne and his friends to pick up the pieces? Because, whatever the state of the evidence in the case of the Oxford bomber, there was nothing that tied Cromwell to the death of my wife and unborn child. Indeed, the only tangible connection between *Victoria* and Oxford was a black circle and a red X on an ordinary road map.

I leaned back in the chair. My approach had been backwards from the beginning. Instead of assuming that the investigation at Oxford would lead to the *Victoria* bomber, I should have started at the other end – that was really why I had come in the first place. The current explanation for *Victoria* was terrorism. The Brits had lied about everything else. Why credit their story about *Victoria?* I started to rise and, for the second time that evening, sensed the presence of someone else. I stepped behind the drawn curtains and waited.

Peering through the narrow opening between the drapes, I watched as Abram Khan entered the room and switched on a light. After searching the secretary – he ignored the drawings – Khan sat down at the desk and began going through the drawers. There was nothing of interest in them, either. He paused for a moment, then turned for the door.

I parted the curtains. "Someone beat you to it, Khan."

He froze in the doorway. "Beat me to what?"

"The book."

"What book?"

"The book you were looking for."

He shook his head. "I don't know what you're talking about."

"Did you kill him?"

"Who?"

"Cromwell."

"Is he dead?" I nodded. "Well, good riddance, but I didn't kill him. Did you?"

I laughed. "I know who you are, Khan. Besides being a great cricketer. Why have you invited yourself to this party?"

"Because I want to find the people who murdered my sister."

I looked at him steadily. "It's been suggested that Pakistan may have something to do with these bombs, including the one on *Victoria*. What do you say to that?"

"I say let the chips fall where they may."

"What brings you to St. Giles' House?"

He sat down in the leather chair next to the desk and looked up at me. "Cromwell has some – pictures. The house seemed to be deserted and the back door was open, so I came in to look for them."

"Photographs?" He nodded. "Sensitive photographs?" He nodded again. I resumed my seat behind the desk. "I'm going to tell you about tonight, Khan, not because I trust you but because I don't see any downside. If you really want to find your sister's killers, maybe you can help."

Ten minutes later Khan said, "Is that all you could see? Someone dressed in black?"

"Yes."

"What are you going to do about it?"

"What? The book?"

"Yes."

"I don't care about the book. It has nothing to do with *Victoria*."

"How do you know?"

I paused. "Okay. To the extent that Cromwell was involved in the *Victoria* bombing, of which there is no evidence at all, then maybe the photos are relevant, but I don't see how. I'm not going to spend time worrying about it."

He nodded. "Speaking of Cromwell, where is he?"

I turned and pulled back the curtain. "He's in that little house at the back of the garden."

"What are you going to do with him?"

"I'm going to make an anonymous call to the police." I checked my watch again. "In about eight hours. I don't want to get mixed up in a police investigation and, under the circumstances, I don't think he'll be missed tonight." I paused. "If the bomb threat is real, there'll be more important things to deal with in a couple of days anyway." I rose. "It's been a long day." We left by the back door and stopped at the gate, now unlocked.

"I want to tell *you* something," said Khan. He grinned. "To demonstrate my good faith."

"Yes?"

"That note of Cromwell's isn't really Arabic – it's English."

"What are you talking about?"

"Akhem told me. The note was in Arabic script, but it's not Arabic. It's English translated into Arabic."

I considered the possibilities. "If that's right, it's one more strike against Cromwell and – and the elimination of the only plausible evidence of Muslim terrorists." He nodded. "That's pretty convenient for you, isn't it?"

"Yes, but it's the truth. You can find someone to verify it."

"I'd have to get the note back from Whitehall. Judgment Day will have come and gone long before that happens."

Khan smiled and nodded again. "Then I guess you'll have to take my word for it." We parted a moment later, one of us headed north to the new Oxford, the other south to the old.

I WAS very tired by the time I climbed to my rooms at Christ Church, but my mind was racing. I would set Oxford aside – it appeared that Cromwell was the guilty party anyway and the bomb, if there was one, would explode on schedule – and concentrate on *Victoria*. I plucked the manila folder from the mantel and dropped into one of the leather chairs.

The government's investigation had focused on the mechanics of the plot. Boiled down, it came to this: How was the bomb planted, and who was close enough to the ship to detonate it? The second proposition was not stated explicitly, presumably because of the secrecy regarding the bomb and its detonator, but the answer could be discerned from the information that was gathered. Anyone from the cruise ship terminals south past Netley Abbey to the mouth of the River Hamble, and a similar distance east and west, could have pulled the trigger. That was an unmanageable number of people on shore, not to mention those on the Water that day. Nonetheless, an effort had been made with predictable results.

The first question was likewise unanswered. There were simply too many people moving on and off the ship while she was prepared for a seven-day voyage. Logs of vendors, repairmen and employees were kept, and the names on those logs were questioned. Likewise, visitors who boarded the day the ship sailed were tracked down.

Security procedures required that everyone who boarded within twenty-four hours of sailing be accounted for. White Star personnel checked them in and checked them out so that when *Victoria* left Southampton only the crew and paid-up passengers were left on board. I shuffled through the file until I reached five closely-typed pages dedicated to those who had boarded and disembarked. The names were arranged in the order in which they stepped onto the boat – name, time of arrival, passenger affiliation and time of departure were all noted. Passports were required. The type on the pages was small and it hurt my eyes to continue, but I resolved to get through the list before I fell asleep.

The first familiar name, my own, was on page two. I almost quit at the bottom of page four when I realized that I had started to look for Gabrielle amongst those who had left the vessel but, yawning, I turned to the last page and there it was, a few lines from the top – John Cromwell. He had boarded thirty minutes before departure and left with five minutes to spare. The passenger he had come to visit was Aden Khan.

I dropped the file on the floor and leaned back in my chair. Cromwell again, and Khan's sister, a Pakistani national who supposedly died on *Victoria*. I would have to look into that. I forced myself to pick up the report and read to the end of page five. A final notation near the bottom caught my eye. The visitor's name – Barak Khan – was unfamiliar, but the passenger he had boarded *Victoria* to see was well-known to me: "Georges St. Cyr." I closed my eyes.

◇◇◇

SHE PICKED up the telephone. "Hello."

"Pamela?"

"Yes."

"Abram Khan. I need a favor. Can I come up?"

"Of course. Give me a minute to alert the little man. I'll leave the door open."

She considered how she would receive him and decided to remain as she was, in bed covered by a sheet and a sheer negligee. Never particularly interested in the money and trinkets that came her way, Pamela collected adorers. She loved her work – not the physical grubbing, but the opportunity for self-display. Each public appearance on the arm of an Earl or a Duke or a Titan of Industry enhanced her self-regard. The respect and deference accorded them, almost invariably unearned, rubbed off on her and she had come to see herself as a leveler, a woman who could make a difference. When she realized that she couldn't do it one man at a time, she looked for something else and found it in the just-beginning-to-boom pornography industry.

She had become an instant star, not because of the size of her breasts or her readiness to accommodate whatever was thrust at her, but because she was so eager to be seen. She couldn't sing or dance. Sex was her talent and she wanted to share it with everyone. That generosity of spirit had carried over into her executive career – Pamela did all that she could to make her books, magazines and videos available to every man, woman and child and, largely successful, she grew wealthy in the process.

When Khan stepped into the bedroom she sat up, allowing the sheet to slide to her waist. He remained by the door. "I'm sorry to be so early," he said, "but I need to call London and we have no phones at the Mosque."

"None at all?"

"There's one in the Imam's quarters but I didn't want to call from there. Can I use yours?" She nodded and pointed to the telephone beside her. "I'll use the one in the other room," he said, turning away. A moment later, she followed him.

He looked up as she entered the room. "Yes," he said into the receiver, "Georges St. Cyr. It's C-Y-R, I believe. Yes. Let me know what you find. I'll wait for your call." He replaced the receiver on its cradle.

"Who is Georges St. Cyr?" she said.

"He's a friend of Markham's."

"You had to call London for that?"

He smiled. "I think he's something more, and I want to know what it is."

"Oh." She glanced at the clock on the mantelpiece and crossed the room. "I'm going to order breakfast. Would you like something?"

"No, thanks."

Moments later, the telephone rang. He picked it up. "Yes? Yes." He listened, nodding. "Anything else?" He listened again. "What operations? Where in Pakistan?" He paused. "All right. Thanks." He hung up.

She opened the drapes and stood in the bright sunlight that streamed into the room so that he could see every detail of her body through the gown. "So who is Mr. St. Cyr?"

He looked at her for a long moment, his face blank. "A very, very dangerous fellow. At one time an agent for one of America's most ruthless intelligence services." He stopped. "He's supposed to be retired."

"Why does he matter to you?"

"He's working with Markham. He spoke at the evacuation meeting." He paused again. "His wife was on *Victoria.*" He walked toward her. Her breakfast, delivered a few minutes later, was left outside the door.

PAMELA COULD see the flashing lights from the Martyrs' Memorial but it wasn't until she was within a block of the house that she realized that the police cars had gathered at her destination. She still had a professional distaste for the police, but she no longer feared them, and since she had an appointment with John Cromwell she decided to keep it. The door was answered by a ruddy-faced young policeman. "Yes?"

"I'm here to see Doctor Cromwell. Is he about?"

"Who are you?"

"My name is Pamela Smythe-King. I'm meeting with Doctor Cromwell this morning. Is he here?"

"Come in, ma'am," he said. "I'll let the Chief Inspector know that you're here."

"But –"

He was gone. A moment later, an officious older man stepped into the foyer. "Miss Smythe-King?" he said. She nodded. "I'm Chief Inspector Lewis. Are you a friend of Doctor Cromwell's?"

"Yes, Inspector. I'm supposed to meet him at eleven o'clock."

Lewis shook his head. "I'm afraid you won't, Miss. Cromwell's dead."

A shiver ran through her body. The inspector was watching her closely. "What happened?" she said.

"He's been shot in the head."

"When?"

He raised his eyebrows. "Most people express shock or sorrow when someone is murdered, Miss Smythe-King." He paused. "However, to answer your question, we believe he's been dead between twelve and twenty-four hours."

She shook her head. "He was quite alive when I left him here at 3 p.m. yesterday."

"Thank you, Miss. That's helpful. How do you know Doctor Cromwell?"

"We've been friends for many years."

"Why were you here yesterday?" She explained her business in Oxford and described the meeting with West and Akhem. "Did *you* think that Akhem was threatening Cromwell?" he said.

"I took his words to mean that John was going to hell on his own, not that the Imam was planning to deliver him."

Inspector Lewis nodded. "And the other man, West, was he also unhappy with Cromwell?"

"I'm sure he was, though he didn't say so. John was threatening *him.*"

Lewis looked at her attentively. "Is there anything else you can tell me?"

"No. I don't think so."

"Are you staying in Oxford, Miss Smythe-King?"

"I'm leaving this afternoon. Are you?"

He smiled. "I'll certainly be outside the critical area if the bomb isn't found by tomorrow. Where are you going?"

"Aylesbury."

"Leave the Sergeant with an address and phone number, please. And don't go any further than Aylesbury."

Outside on the street, she turned to look at the house again. The book was gone. If the killer didn't take it, the police would. Either way, it was beyond her for the moment. She cursed her failure to act when she could.

Inside the Randolph, she crossed the lobby to the desk. The gawkers were gone – she and the clerk were the only people in the room. "Have you prepared my bill yet?" she said.

"I'm just finishing now, Miss." He handed her a message slip. "This call just came for you. From London."

She stared at the piece of paper. She wanted desperately to ignore it, but knew that she could not. "Would you place the call for me?" The clerk nodded. She picked up one of the house phones.

A moment later, a voice at the other end of the line said, "Savoy Hotel."

"Barak Khan, please."

I HUNG up the telephone. Cromwell's blackmail victims had been identified, one of them as puzzling as it was troubling. The large sum of money was a cash deposit. No one at the Office had any reason to believe that Aden Khan had not died on *Victoria*, nor was there any evidence that she ever worked for ISI. They were still checking on

Barak Khan. That left me to consider what Cromwell was doing at Southampton that day and, reluctantly, I began to think about the book.

The sexual appetites of others had never interested me unless I was personally involved. The first few pages were fairly conventional – homemade pornography, a few featuring Cromwell and another man or two. Most of the rest were also men performing the same acts on other men. I had recognized several faces, including that of Geoffrey North. Another seemed familiar – it appeared three times, always turned slightly away or a little out of focus so that a full examination of his features was impossible. When children, mostly boys, began appearing in the photographs, the book took on a more sinister significance, and I turned the pages to the end. There was plenty there to justify Cromwell's murder. Toward the back, there were two pages devoted to ordinary black-and-white pictures of a single man against a backdrop that I thought I recognized. I puzzled over them for a moment, then gave up.

As I was about to close the book, I had noticed the photo of a very beautiful woman staring straight into the camera. Her eyes were wide and her mouth and jaw were slack, and she held a little boy of seven or eight in her arms. Both of them were naked. I had seen that face, or one very much like it, before. When I made the connection, I tore the picture from the album and slipped it into my pocket.

I stared at it again. It was a female version of Abram Khan, a blonde with the same slanted blue eyes, the same high cheeks, the narrow nose and wide mouth. It might explain why Cromwell had boarded *Victoria* that day, but it told me nothing about the explosion. Or did it? At a minimum, it justified Cromwell's presence on board. Aden was on the boat and he had come to see her off. He could have boarded the vessel with a bomb the size of a small suitcase and left it anywhere, even in her cabin. But why would he do that? Did he want to kill her? She probably knew his sexual preferences. Was she blackmailing *him*? And, most importantly, was he sufficiently mad to kill a thousand people in order to destroy just one? Did Cromwell have the imagination, let alone the nerve, to do something like that, or was he really just a middle-aged English pederast who had reached the limits of his creativity with a book of dirty pictures?

I turned to the other mystery. Who was Barak Khan? Khan was a common name in India and Pakistan, but the coincidence was hard to accept. And then the idea that had been fermenting in my brain finally rose to the surface. Was I the reason that my wife and child and a thousand more were dead? Had Barak Khan, whoever he was, left a bomb on board *Victoria* under the mistaken impression that *I* was sailing that day from Southampton? I had many institutional enemies. The intelligence agencies of several countries had good reason to wish me dead. Had any of them been sufficiently vexed to risk the exposure and retaliation that might result? As North had said about Markham's Muslims, it seemed a bit of overkill, but it had to be considered.

I looked down at the deserted quad. Few, if any, of Christ Church's inmates would dine in the great hall tonight. My college was almost empty. As I watched, Dean West passed under Tom Tower and made his way slowly across the lawn. I smiled. West and Yates would be the last to go. I checked my watch – it was almost noon. I was meeting Markham in an hour and the few miles to Wolvercote would give me another chance to gauge the success of the evacuation. I hurried down the staircase and passed through Canterbury Gate. Emerging into Oriel Square, I turned north.

I paused for a few minutes when I reached the Science Area. It was a jumble of disparate structures, all built since the turn of the century, huddled together in fewer than twenty acres. The very name was emblematic of its origins. The dons had insisted that "mechanical" disciplines like chemistry and physics, devoid of any "intellectual" pretense, be segregated from the rest of the University, but Science – advancing inexorably while God retreated – now rose triumphant from its little triangle in the southwest corner of the Parks. Practical, and fully cognizant of man's inability to resist, its lights were extinguished, its adherents gone.

A little further on, however, humanity persevered. I turned east toward the Cherwell. On the far side of the Cricket Pavilion I passed into Oxford's newest quadrangle and approached a low building that stood slightly apart from the cells and other structures arranged along the walls. A huge building loomed to my right. Akhem opened the door immediately. "Mr. St. Cyr. Please enter."

"Thank you, Akhem." He opened the door wider and I passed over the threshold. He indicated an upright leather chair next to his desk. I sat down. "We have two days left. Everyone else is gone." He nodded. "I wish you'd reconsider."

He smiled and shook his head. "Thank you for your concern. I have consulted Allah. We will stay."

"Have you consulted your students?"

"They are content."

"I suppose you've heard the talk that you're staying because you know where the bomb is?" He nodded again. "Do you?"

Akhem picked up a newspaper lying on his desk and pointed to a headline near the bottom of the page. "Do you accuse your friend Markham of planting bombs?"

"He says it's war."

"He is correct. A very long war that is reaching its – conclusion."

I smiled. "You don't really believe that, do you?"

"I must."

"These things are never over. As soon as one side gains the upper hand, the pendulum begins to swing back."

"Perhaps. It is my duty to push it toward Allah."

"And those boys? What about them?"

"They will be martyrs whether they live or die. Grains of sand in an eternal landscape dedicated to Allah."

"A desert?"

He nodded. "As far as the eye can see. And beyond." I was halfway to Wolvercote before I realized that he had never answered my question.

THE TROUT Inn, built as a fisherman's cottage in the 15th century, had a gray stone facade, leaded windows and a steeply-pitched roof covered with slate. Inside were two large fireplaces, flagstone floors and exposed oak beams. Behind it, next to the rushing waters of the Isis, was a stone terrace separated from the river by a four-foot rock wall. There was a short dock with punts and canoes for rent on the other side of the wall. The weather was fine for October, and Markham had selected a table on the terrace.

We ordered food. "And bring us a bottle of the Italian Chardonnay," Markham called after the waiter. When the wine arrived, Markham poured two glasses and raised his for a left-handed toast. "Here's to success."

I lifted my glass. "If we're celebrating the evacuation, I agree with you." I swallowed my wine. "As far as the town goes, though, I'm afraid we've failed."

"Well, the people were always the most important thing."

"I guess you know that Cromwell's dead?" He nodded. "Everything points to him." I looked out over the river and shook my head.

"What about Muslim terrorists? Surely there's still a case to be made?"

"Strangely enough, there may be." I paused. "But the doomsday note has been debunked." I related the Imam's analysis. "I went through the government's dossier on *Victoria* again last night. Someone called Barak Khan was one of the last people off the ship."

"And?"

"He said he was there to wish *me* smooth sailing."

He hesitated. "And he killed all those other people to get at you?"

"Yes."

We were quiet. "I don't think that's very likely," Markham said. He poured more wine. "So you've given up on Oxford?"

"No. We still have time. I'm just looking at it from the other end."

"When are you going to Aylesbury?"

"I'm taking the four o'clock train."

He nodded. "You'll probably run into Khan and Pamela. I believe that's the train they're on."

"Are you meeting them?"

"No. I have to be in London tonight."

The food arrived. "Who is Pamela, exactly?"

"She's the most accomplished whore I've ever known. She's made millions in the pornography business." He laughed. "She wants to build a college here."

"We may need some new colleges here in a couple of days."

"Yes, and Pamela's college will be the perfect cornerstone for the new Oxford." He paused. "The old God is dead and the new gods, the fallen angels – Satan and Lucifer and the rest – will perch atop the Emperors' pedestals." He stopped again, an odd look on his face. "Instead of churches and religion, the new colleges will be endowed by sin. Hers will be the first – Lust – followed by Greed and Envy and Pride. The new Oxford will finally look just like the rest of England, and that Parliament of whores in London can rest easy at last."

I smiled and changed the subject. "Does Guin know about Cromwell?"

"Yes. I called as soon as I heard."

"Is she – upset?"

"I believe the word you're searching for is 'relieved.'"

I nodded. "Speaking of Guin, make sure you're on time

tomorrow. Drinks at 6:30, dinner at 8:00. She's planned something special. Don't be late."

"My background prevents me from ever being late."

CHAPTER SIX

I CLOSED the suitcase and looked around the room, hoping for the hundredth time that Wellbourne was right and it was all a joke. This building had been constructed before Henry quarreled with Wolsey – it was more than four hundred and fifty years old. The idea that it might be incinerated in a few hours by the hand of a dead man was repulsive. I locked the door and wished that I would be able to open it again shortly.

I turned right out of the stairwell and crossed Tom Quad to the gate. "I'll see you in a few days, Yates."

"I hope so, sir." Yates stepped outside, hand extended. I took another plain white envelope from him. "It was left for you earlier today," he said.

"Who delivered it?"

"I can't say, sir. There's no one to bring me my lunch and –" he smiled "– no one coming through the gate, so I walked over to the buttery at lunchtime and ate a hunk of cheese and some bread. It was here when I got back."

I turned the envelope over in my hands. It was blank except for my name printed in block letters. "What time was that?"

"A bit after noon, I think."

"How long were you gone?"

"Twenty – twenty-five minutes."

I nodded and slipped the envelope inside my jacket. "Has everyone gone?"

"Yes, sir. All except the Dean."

"When is he leaving?"

"I don't know, sir. He didn't say."

I nodded again. "Well, take care of yourself, Yates." I smiled. "We'll meet again – soon, I hope."

"Yes, sir. Thank you, sir."

I walked up St. Aldate's and turned left at Queen. Could this latest communication possibly be from Cromwell, commissioned before he died? And then the larger question: If not Cromwell, who?

KHAN'S EYES swept the deserted railway station. He hoped that the train would, in fact, arrive at Oxford at least one more time. He and Pamela were the only passengers waiting.

"Someone's coming," she said.

He turned. The unmistakable figure of Georges St. Cyr climbed the steps at the far end of the platform and started toward them. "It's St. Cyr," Khan said. "It's not necessary to mention his profession." She nodded.

St. Cyr stuck out his hand and Khan took it. "We're all going down to Aylesbury together, I understand," he said. Khan looked at him questioningly. "I had lunch with Markham today." He turned to Pamela.

"Pamela Smythe-King," said Khan, "this is Georges St. Cyr. He's a friend of Tony's."

She smiled and offered her hand. "Are you at the Abbey until it's over?" she said.

St. Cyr shook his head. "I'm leaving town for the bomb, but I'm staying with my father-in-law. He's about ten miles from the Abbey." He paused. "I'll see you at dinner tomorrow."

They heard the sound of an approaching train. "Well," said Pamela, "that's a relief." She drew a sheet of paper from her purse. "We change trains at the next station."

"What's that?" St. Cyr said. "Directions?"

"Yes. Tony gave them to me last week."

St. Cyr stared at her. "Did he – write them down?" She nodded. "We won't need them. I've made this trip dozens of times." He held out his hand. "May I see that?"

"Of course."

St. Cyr studied the paper as the train slowed to a stop beside them. Khan and Pamela moved toward an open door and St. Cyr followed. He pushed the paper into his pocket. They sat in an empty car for the short trip to the next platform. "When did you see Tony?" St. Cyr said.

"It was the day I arrived in England," she said. "Last Wednesday." She smiled. "He was afraid the trains might not be running."

"Because of the bomb?"

"Yes."

After a few minutes of silence, St. Cyr opened his bag and extracted a thick manila folder. He handed it to Khan. "That's the government report on *Victoria*," he said. "I thought you might find it interesting." Khan nodded. "Do you know someone named Barak Khan?"

Barak Khan? What was the inspiration for that query? He told the technical truth. "No. Who is he?"

"I don't know," said St. Cyr. "You'll see his name in the report. Maybe it'll jog your memory." He looked at Pamela. "Your name's there, too."

"Mine?"

"Yes. On the passenger list."

Pamela closed her eyes but said nothing. "Pamela was a friend of my sister's," Khan said. "She had to cancel at the last minute."

St. Cyr's face softened. He took her hand. "I was supposed to be there, too, Pamela," he said. "I'm sorry."

On the second leg of the journey, St. Cyr rose and stepped into the corridor. A minute later, he appeared in the doorway and beckoned to Khan. "Would you excuse us for a moment, Pamela?" he said. She nodded. Khan and St. Cyr walked to Markham's observation car. "I want to show you something," said St. Cyr, withdrawing an envelope from his coat pocket. "You remember the map I mentioned the other day?"

"Yes."

"Well, we have a new one." St. Cyr unfolded a road map of England. It had three black circles, and the one over Southampton Water had a red X through it. The other two circles were drawn around Aylesbury and Oxford. There were no circles for London or Portsmouth.

"Where did you get it?" said Khan.

"It was delivered to Christ Church today. The envelope and printing are the same as the letters."

"So they've decided not to bomb Portsmouth and London."

"Apparently. But why send it to me?"

"Does this let Cromwell out?"

"That's the question, isn't it? I don't know."

They stepped off the train at Aylesbury Station and St. Cyr pointed out the Bentley awaiting them. They turned in that direction and he started for the green Rover in the car park. The Bentley's chauffeur opened the doors, then called out, "Mr. St. Cyr."

St. Cyr stopped. "Yes, Edward?"

Edward walked around the car. "Her Ladyship asked me to give this to you," he said, offering a blue envelope. St. Cyr opened it and read the enclosure. After a long pause, he said, "Tell Guin – Her Ladyship – that I'll do as she asks, Edward."

"Very good, sir. Thank you."

DO YOU still keep horses, Doctor Soleil?"

"Yes. They're practically wild now. I haven't saddled either one of them in over a year."

"I'd like to borrow one this evening."

Soleil nodded. "Of course."

"Where are you going?" said Gill.

"I have an appointment at the Abbey."

She glanced at the clock on the coffee table. "At this hour?"

"Yes."

"Why not take the car?"

"It's shorter across the Vale – and quieter."

Soleil rose. "You know where everything is?" I nodded. Soleil poked at the fire. "I'll be off to bed then. I'll see you both in the morning."

After he had climbed the stairs, Gill said, "Who's your appointment?"

"Her name is Guin Markham. She's Tony's sister."

The color rose in her face. "So I've come three thousand miles to seduce you, and you're leaving me the very first night for another woman?"

"Haven't we talked about this before?"

"Yes, and I want to talk about it again."

"All right."

"What do I have to do to make you love me?"

"That's not really the question, is it?"

"What is?"

"The question you should be asking is, 'What would it be like to live with this man?'"

"I answered that one a long time ago."

I shook my head. "I don't think you gave it enough thought. I'm thirty-eight years old. I've trained all my life to be alone and, except for two short years, I *have* been alone. As a consequence, I'm also selfish – solitude breeds self-regard, I suppose. Since I was a child, the central figure in my life, with one exception, has always been me." I paused. "The exception was my wife, and there's a good chance that she was murdered because of me. It never even occurred to me that she might be hurt because of who I am." I stopped again. "You think you want me now but, believe me, you would live to regret it." I stood up. "I have to go."

She reached for my arm. "Wait." She paused. "Do you think I'm a fool? Do you think that I don't know that you're arrogant and thoughtless and, yes, selfish?" I smiled. "It's not a secret." She rose. "And I don't care. I'll tell you something else. If you could be a better man with Gabrielle, you can be better with me." She stopped again. "So go to your English lady, and enjoy yourself. I'll be here when you get back."

I watched as she left the room and crossed the foyer to the staircase. How could she possibly mean that? Shaking my head, I took the note from the blue envelope and read it again:

> *Georges,*
> *I must see you tonight after everyone's in bed. I'll make sure the gate is open. If there's a light on in the gatehouse, wait until it goes out. Use the door in my wing. Don't fail me.*
> *G*

It appeared that my English lady was about to balance her books.

The moon was full and the familiar ride across the Vale uneventful. My horse seemed pleased to have a man on her back again. I could see the gatehouse from the top of the last hill. There was no need to hurry – the light was on.

It was still lit when I passed through the gate so I dismounted and stepped inside the gatehouse to wait. It seemed to serve as a storage room – rugs and tapestries rolled up in heavy paper, paintings in plastic cases, books in wooden crates. As I opened one of the cases the overhead light, presumably operated from the main house, was extinguished. I lifted the painting and examined it in the moonlight. A minute or two later, I climbed back into the saddle and entered the alley of limes. It took me ten minutes to cover the quarter-mile between the gate and the house. Guin evidently wished to keep my visit from her guests and the sound of a horse at more than a walk might disturb them.

I stopped before reaching the courtyard and tied the horse to the last lime tree. The house was dark. I smiled. How long had it been since I last hovered outside a girl's house waiting for the other occupants to retire? Guin had a suite of rooms at the end of the west wing. I found the appropriate door, walked through a ladies' parlor and climbed the staircase. A door at the end of the hallway opened and she stepped into the corridor. She pressed against me. "Thank you," she said.

I leaned back and looked at her. The pearls were white and the robe was white as well, and her scent was the same. "What kind of perfume is that?"

"It's called Osmanthus."

"Tea olive?" She nodded. I closed my eyes for a second and remembered. Of course – Cromwell's study.

She gave me a perfunctory kiss and said, "Let me make sure that Gerry's asleep." She pushed through a door on the other side of the room. I followed her to the doorway. The low, metallic sounds of Led Zeppelin reached my ears. Guin arranged the bedclothes and bent to kiss her sleeping child. She picked up the radio, switched it off and placed it on the bedside table. We left the room. "Gerry has trouble with his hearing," she said. "He can put those little radios right next to his ear." She paused. "He must have a dozen of them."

I withdrew a radio from my pocket and handed it to her. "This must be his then."

She stared at it. "Yes," she said, finally. "Where did you find it?" I didn't answer. She slid her hands inside my jacket and pushed it from my shoulders. A moment later, naked, we fell into the bed. Her technique was more polished than ever, but the determination to make me believe that it mattered to her was missing. She had something else on her mind. I waited. "Georges?"

"Yes?"

"Thanks for picking up the radio. I've been worried sick about it." I nodded. "I – I was so intent on the camera and the photographs, and getting Gerry out of there, I just – ignored it. When I found the drawer locked I thought I would lose my mind."

We were quiet. "You have a key to Cromwell's house, I suppose?" I said.

"Yes."

"Why did you lock the doors?"

"John's cook was due that evening at six o'clock. I didn't want her to get in. I wanted it to look like he wasn't there." She stopped. "She might have discovered him somehow before I got the pictures. When I came back with a key and found the drawer unlocked and the radio gone I – I thought I was going crazy." She stopped again. "I guess you'd been there."

I nodded again. "Have you heard from the police?"

"No. I'm sure it's just a matter of time."

"Where's the book?"

She pointed to a tall wardrobe in the corner. "In the bottom drawer. Minus –"

"Minus the pictures of Gerry?"

"Yes. I've already burned them. And the film." She turned to me. "Gerry's almost deaf, and he's starting to lose his sight. And – and he's – slow for his age. The idea of that monster –" She looked away. "I want you to do something for me."

"All right."

"I want you to take me to America. And Gerry. As soon as you can."

"You can go any time you like. You don't need my help."

She shook her head. "You don't understand. I want to move there permanently. I – I want us to be married."

That was a surprise. Was this her way of ensuring my silence? I wrapped my arms around her again. "Why?"

"I'm afraid here. I need someone to help me. Someone I can count on."

"You're not afraid of anything, Guin. And I'll be glad to help you. You don't have to marry me for that."

"No. I want you bound to me. I want to be the most important person in your world." She paused. "Then I can trust you." She stopped again. "I have gobs of money of my own. We'll marry our fortunes together."

I smiled. "It sounds like a very businesslike arrangement."

"It is. It's the way we used to do things."

"What about the Abbey?"

"Tony's still young. I'll worry about that when the time comes."

I thought for a moment. "Is he back from London?"

"No. He called a few minutes ago. He's not coming back until tomorrow."

Later, as I was preparing to leave, I said, "I'm taking the book with me. There are too many people interested in it. You'll be better off without it."

During my ride back to The Downs I considered the future that she had proposed. It would be very different from my time with Gabrielle, but if I really believed what I had said to Gill, it was the best that I could hope for. In fact, Guin was the perfect woman for me – thoroughly independent, she would accept as much or as little as I could give. Love, and the effort it required, would not be an issue. I would have her affection. Her love was reserved for her child, the beautiful, flawed little boy she had killed for.

She was afraid, she said, a notion that I had dismissed, but what if it were true? Who – what – was she afraid of? The police? No. Guin was far too aristocratic to fear the law and, besides, she had a good excuse for killing Cromwell. Even if she were charged, she would probably get off. Another, unhappy thought: She was capable of murder – she had dispatched Cromwell without hesitation. Was she mixed up in the Oxford plot? Might his death expose her somehow? I rejected it again.

I stopped at the top of the hill from whence I had first viewed Gabrielle's ancient house and turned my mind to the other things I had learned that day. Most of it was minutiae that could probably be explained away, but two new developments remained. Who was Barak Khan? Was he the key to the *Victoria* bombing? Did he have anything to do with the threat against Oxford? Equally disturbing was the new map. Did it come from Cromwell? Why had it been sent? Something about it was *wrong* but I didn't know what. I had stopped thinking about the London and Portsmouth bombs long ago. I would have to call Wellbourne in the morning.

◇◇◇

THE TELEPHONE rang. "Hello?"

"Georges St. Cyr, please."

"Just a moment." Another voice came on the line. "Hello?"

"St. Cyr?"

"Yes?"

"Abram Khan. I finished the *Victoria* report last night. Is there any chance we can see that movie again?"

"Why?"

"I – don't want to say until I'm sure. Can we see it?"

St. Cyr was quiet. "Tony's in London, but – I think he left the film in the projector. I'll bet it's still there."

"Is there any reason we can't go into Oxford today?" said Khan.

"No. We have a car. Can you be ready in an hour?"

"Yes."

"All right. Meet me at the gate."

Khan stepped down the hallway and climbed to the study overlooking the Great Hall. The *Victoria* file lay open on the table. He had not actually examined the whole thing – instead, he scanned it, searching for the name that St. Cyr had mentioned. He found it in a log of visitors to the ship. The man had boarded twenty-five minutes before *Victoria* was scheduled to sail and walked back down the gangway twenty minutes later.

Khan crossed to the window and looked out at the lime trees. It was impossible to know now if his speculation was correct – there were undoubtedly thousands of men named Barak Khan who could have been in Southampton that day – but somehow it all seemed inevitable. The film would probably confirm his suspicions, but even if it didn't he planned to proceed on the assumption that he was right.

WE PARKED on The Plain and walked into town. When Pamela complained I said, "I want to see if anyone's still here. It'll be easier to spot them on foot." After crossing the Cherwell we passed Magdalen and the Botanic Garden and walked among the old colleges south of the High.

"What a beautiful old place," Gill said. "And it's so – so empty. Like a fabulous ghost town."

"Tony says that Oxford has been a ghost town for a long time," Pamela said.

We turned west on Bear Lane, then north again on St. Aldate's. Past Carfax we took Market Street – Jesus and Exeter were on the left and Lincoln and Brasenose on the right – and emerged into the splendor of Radcliffe Square. Immediately to the right was the baroque opulence of the Radcliffe Camera and, beyond that, we could see the steeple of St. Mary's Church. On the left were the Schools Quadrangle and the Divinity School, and the chapel at All Souls, built by the Archbishop of Canterbury six centuries earlier, lay straight ahead. They were all golden in the midday sun.

Gill rotated her head to take it in. "I've never seen so many wonderful buildings in one place. They're like a collection of giant wedding cakes."

As we turned north again toward the Sheldonian, Khan said, "St. Cyr?"

"Yes?"

"Someone just looked out the door of the Camera."

I frowned. "Are you sure?" He nodded. "You all go on to the theater. Make sure the film's still there. I'll join you in a few minutes." I crossed the lawn, pushed through one of the doors on the ground floor of the Camera and climbed the stairs to the library. I paused as I entered the large circular room. Light poured through the windows, those at eye level and those over the gallery, and the larger ones in the drum beneath the great wooden dome. The room was bare of furniture – the bookcases and tables and chairs were all located beneath an arcade defined by arches and massive piers engraved with pilasters – except for a single round table in the middle of the floor. A man wearing a black gown draped with a scarlet hood, his back to me, leaned over the table. "Dean West," I called.

The old man looked around, then returned his attention to the manuscript on the table. I crossed the room and stopped beside him. "Dean West?"

He turned his head. "So you've caught me out, St. Cyr."

"Yes, sir. I guess so." I stopped. "I know you don't want to go, but –"

West shook his head. "I *can't* go, St. Cyr, anymore than these books or this room or this building can go." He smiled. "But you're right. I don't want to leave, either."

THE FIRST part of the *Victoria* movie was dedicated to crowd shots of the people – passengers and well-wishers – wandering about the terminal and the dock. As the time for departure drew near, the camera was left in place overlooking the gangway, recording the backs of the people boarding the ship and the faces of those who left it. Already dreading the climax, I watched without enthusiasm.

The White Star Line had thoughtfully provided a clock showing the time remaining until departure in the lower right-hand corner of the screen. As it approached the thirty-minute mark, I began looking for Cromwell, but was unable to pick him out. Likewise, I saw no obvious Barak Khan five minutes later. I watched Abram Khan out of the corner of my eye. He appeared relaxed, no more intent on the screen than I was. Pamela's eyes were closed.

As the clock ticked down to five minutes, I became more attentive and so did Khan. Cromwell was about to depart. I scanned the faces of the people leaving the ship. "Gill. Stop the tape." The figures moving down the bridge halted in mid-stride. "Back it up a few seconds, please." The film rolled backwards. "Can you run it in slow motion?"

"I think so."

The tape began again. "All right," I called. "Stop right there." I rose and approached the screen. Khan and Pamela joined me. Pointing to a heavyset man with dark hair and a mustache, I said, "I've seen this man somewhere before." I looked at Khan. "Is this Barak Khan?"

He hesitated. "Yes."

"*Who* is Barak Khan?"

"He was my father."

"Was?"

"Yes. He was killed when I was a child." I waited. "His identity was stolen by ISI. It's a common protocol – strip the dead of their papers and use them later."

"So who is Barak Khan really?"

"His real name is – Zhev."

"Ahmad Zhev?" Khan nodded again. "Is this what you were looking for?"

"Yes."

"So the chief of the Pakistani intelligence service spent twenty minutes on *Victoria* before she sailed?"

"Apparently."

"Why?"

"I don't know." He paused. "He might have been there to see my sister."

"Why would he do that?"

"He's my – our – stepfather."

We were quiet. "Or maybe he was there for something else," I said.

"Maybe."

I looked around. "Start it up again, Gill."

A smirking Cromwell appeared at the top of the gangway. He had a large book in his hand and wore something around his neck. "Stop." I drew closer to the screen again. The book was almost certainly the one I had taken from Guin last night, but it was the camera dangling from his neck that caused the images to click into place.

Ahmad Zhev was the man in Cromwell's book, the only man with his clothes on. Cromwell had snapped his picture that day as Zhev, carrying a small suitcase, walked along the deck of the ship. The suitcase was missing when he left *Victoria* a few minutes later. Somehow Cromwell knew who he was and why he was there. What use had he made of *those* photographs? None of the blackmail checks came from Zhev.

Another mystery was also solved. Zhev had destroyed *Victoria,* and killed a thousand people, because of me. No other explanation was possible. The sheer audacity of the plot made it more believable – the ISI chief, unhappy with my interference, had decided to dispatch me personally. The other passengers provided cover for my assassination. Rational people would not believe that a thousand human beings could be murdered so that one man would die. Only terrorists, fanatics with an agenda, would commit such an act. The questions that I had entertained now seemed laughable, a product of this guilt that I had hoped to avoid. I turned to Khan. "Your stepfather tried to murder me. He failed. Does he have a new plan?"

"I don't know."

"Is he behind the Oxford threat?"

"It doesn't seem very likely, does it? What's the motive?"

"Were you sent here to kill me?"

"No. I was sent here to make sure that the British government didn't discover any Pakistani involvement."

Khan paused. "Why do you think that Zhev is the bomber?"

"That's not important now." I grimaced. "Believe me. Zhev killed your sister and my wife and all those other people because he wanted me dead."

Khan hesitated. "St. Cyr, it's – it's important that I be sure. Tell me how you know."

After a pause, I said, "All right." I explained Cromwell's camera, the suitcase and the pictures in the book.

"So you had it all along," said Khan.

I shook my head. "It's a recent acquisition."

"What are you going to do with it?"

"I'm not sure. I'll send the photos of Zhev and the tape to a friend in London."

He gazed at me steadily. "I need one of the pictures."

I nodded and slipped a photo from my pocket. "It's the only one of her," I said, handing it to him.

Khan stared at the image of his sister for a moment and tore it into pieces. "Thanks, but I need one of Zhev. With the suitcase."

I looked down at the floor, then raised my head. "All right."

"One more thing," he said.

"Yes?"

"Could you – delay sending the photos to your friend for a few days?"

I considered. "I'll give you three days."

"Thank you."

Gill had joined us. "What about Oxford?" she said.

"It was Cromwell," I said. "It's clear that he was in the middle of all this traffic in bombs. It has to be him."

"But why?" said Pamela. "He was the Chancellor, wasn't he? Why would he blow it up?"

I shook my head. I still didn't know. The *why* that I had been asking myself from the beginning remained. The evidence against Cromwell was overwhelming, but his motive was as elusive as ever.

MARKHAM LIFTED his bag from the bed and walked down the stairs. Stepping outside, he locked the door, descended another few steps and slid into the waiting cab. "Paddington," he said.

He had spent the morning at White's, reading the London papers. The people seemed to have awakened at last. Government officials all over the country were being called to account. There was violence on both sides, but that was all right – Englishmen still far outnumbered the occupiers. The tide of war was beginning to turn.

There was also much about events at Oxford, which the newspapers still portrayed – despite all evidence to the contrary – as the citadel of the aristocrats. Bomb threats, evacuations and now the murder of the Chancellor had produced a barely-disguised pleasure at Oxford's misfortune. No one actually said that the destruction of the University would be a good thing, but there was an undertone of glee, particularly in the tabloids. Even the *Times* was suggesting ways to rebuild it in a more modern, egalitarian way.

He had watched as Charles Wellbourne crossed the room. The men's clubs in London had once reflected the political beliefs of their members but, except for a few dinosaurs like him, it was no longer possible to discern any meaningful difference among parties and governments. As a result, he and Wellbourne belonged to the same clubs but they had little else in common. Still, it wouldn't hurt to find out what, if anything, the new aristocrats at Whitehall had pieced together. He rose. "Mr. Secretary?"

Wellbourne stopped and looked back. "Good morning, Your Grace."

Markham smiled and looked at his watch. "It's really past noon. Can I buy you a cup of tea. Or a drink?"

"Yes, of course. Thank you."

They passed down a short corridor to the bar. "Brandy," said Markham.

Wellbourne looked around the empty room. "I'll have a brandy, too."

"Have you learned anything about Cromwell?" Markham said.

"No. We've turned up nothing so far. The bomb and evacuation are interfering. There's a sort of – lack of purpose until the bomb is resolved."

"That's certainly understandable. Is there anything new on that front?"

"Have you heard about the new map?" Markham shook his head. "It was sent to St. Cyr. It appears they've changed their minds about Portsmouth and London." Markham raised his brows. "Their circles have been removed."

"That's good news. No one dies in London or Portsmouth, and it looks as if the evacuation in Oxford will succeed."

"Yes."

They drank in silence. "Have you heard about our show at the Sheldonian?" said Markham.

"Not the details. Some of our people were there. I'm still waiting on the report." Wellbourne looked into his glass. "I couldn't – *order* the evacuation. This entire episode is just so far-fetched –"

Markham raised his hand. "It doesn't matter now. They're going." He stopped. "Except the students at the Mosque."

Wellbourne looked at him and smiled. "That'll be a few less Muslims then, if the bomb does explode."

"Yes." He paused. "St. Cyr told me yesterday that someone named Barak Khan was looking for him on board *Victoria.* Have you heard that?"

"No. What else did he say?"

"Nothing." Markham smiled to himself. The Home Office was not curious about Barak Khan. St. Cyr's suspicions were not shared.

He put down his empty glass, but Wellbourne wasn't finished with the conversation. "Did you know that I knew your brother James?"

Surprised, Markham said, "No, I didn't." He called for the check.

"Yes, we were in school together at St. Paul's." He paused. "I – didn't know him well. He seemed like a good fellow."

Markham stood up. "He was. Thank you."

Waiting on the platform at Paddington, the image of his dead brother – provoked by Wellbourne's ill-considered recollection – reappeared in his head. James had been unhappy with the hurly-burly at Eton, and their father had finally agreed to permit him to live in London and attend St. Paul's as a day student. He was driven to school each morning and picked up in the afternoon as soon as his classes were over. He took part in none of the school's activities, and he gambled and drank and cultivated men of doubtful virtue.

When he was at Aylesbury, James refused to participate in the hunts, balls and other activities that had defined the Markham family for centuries. He took no interest in the operation of the estate and, when called upon to interact with the yeomanry, did so grudgingly and with obvious distaste. He rode badly – by the time she was six, Guin sat a horse better than he did.

As he grew older, James began to spend more and more of his time in London. He might appear at Aylesbury for a week at Christmas and another week before fall term, but his home was Belgrave Square. His habits, and his rejection of the responsibilities that would one day be his, enraged his father and they quarreled often, resulting in still more reckless behavior and fewer trips to the Abbey.

His only apparent interest at Aylesbury was Gabrielle Soleil. Inseparable as children, they corresponded frequently after James left for school and, when he was at Aylesbury, they were seldom apart. His attachment to her was deemed his only saving grace, but it was proved false when Tony encountered James locked in a rough, naked embrace with one of the grooms in the stable loft.

Fascinated and repelled at the rudeness of the assault, he was stunned when he heard the soft words and realized that James had invited it. Confused and distressed by the emotions he experienced, he had contrived to watch the same scene over and over again before James returned to London.

The sly whispers and taunting laughter of his schoolmates had been confirmed, and any alliance between James and Gabrielle was a sham designed to conceal his real desires. When James died, Markham had volunteered to break the news. She had become so hysterical, and so ill, that she was unable to attend the funeral. He had always believed that Gabrielle, naive and dazzled by her prospects, knew nothing of his brother's liaisons, an idea that she had verified during their final conversation. She had hinted at something else, too, something that raised the demons again.

CHAPTER SEVEN

ST. CYR stopped the car in front of the East Lodge Gate. "Tell Guin that Dr. Soleil wants all of you to eat dinner with us tonight," he said.

"I thought everyone was coming here," Pamela said.

"I know. We – we thought you'd like something different. It was his idea."

Khan and Pamela passed through the gate and walked slowly under the limes. When they reached the house, he said, "I'm not going in yet. Tell Guin about dinner."

Khan walked down the path to the family graveyard, considering what he would do next. The grace period granted by St. Cyr would give him time to return home before the news about Zhev was passed on. The discovery of his part in the destruction of *Victoria* would remain secret for a few more days at least. Still, Zhev would know about it, probably within the week, and it might be fatal if Khan didn't get there first.

He moved among the stones, distracted, and thought briefly about trying to assume control of the whole thing, but that would require that he deal with Georges St. Cyr and he knew that was a losing proposition. He was overmatched, and he had been on the other side too many times on the cricket pitch to believe that he could prevail. He would embrace St. Cyr and manage the rest of it as well as he could, and perhaps he would survive.

Returning to the house he entered the east wing and climbed the stairs. On the far side of the Long Gallery he opened the door to his room. He smelled her before he saw her – the expensive scent preceded the slender body stretched elegantly on the chaise next to the window – adorned by a silken pillow barely large enough to cover her belly. She turned her head and drew up a knee. The pillow fell to the floor. Swinging her legs from the chaise, she raised her arms. "I need you."

Khan had never seen any of her films, not out of religious conviction but because he required the real thing. At that moment, though, he understood why so many men and women had paid to see her. She wanted people to look at her, on the screen and on the street. The more attention she received, the more she wanted, and that eagerness for a connection with her audience drew them to her. She was grateful for the scrutiny.

He knew that she was dissatisfied with their encounter at the Randolph. He, too, had always basked in the regard of others, and he wanted her to admire him as well. As a consequence, their coupling had been delicate and polite, and the pleasure of performing that she was accustomed to was not achieved. Smiling, he moved toward her. She would brook no such disappointment this time. *This* would be a real exhibition of the art to which she had devoted her life.

He leaned over to kiss her. She turned her head. "Don't be nice to me," she said, reaching for his belt. Seconds later his pants lay on the floor. She sucked in his still swelling erection, the cupid's bow mouth pierced by his thickening shaft. Wrapping her arms around his thighs, she compelled a rhythm from his hips that, sixty seconds later, resulted in the powerful eruption that she sought. Legs weak, he tried to step back but she refused to let him go, her eyes raised to his while her mouth continued to work. His fingers tangled her hair. When she had again produced the fat, rigid flesh that she required, she fell back on the chaise and opened her legs. "Stick it in," she said. "Hurry!" She clawed at his back as he slid into the slick opening, and instantly forced him into a violent cadence that brought more explosions, this time from her. Again she rejected his effort to leave her, gripping his body with her arms and thighs and ankles, grinding against him, and again he felt the weight and the friction. They thrust themselves at each other until she quivered and jerked, over and over, and he arrived at another, less ferocious, relief.

He was finally incapable of movement. Her arms and legs were relaxed at last, but he was unable to raise himself up or even roll over. He was conscious of his inert flesh weighing on her, pressing her down, but his body refused to relieve hers. She lay beneath him, eyes closed, damp ringlets clinging to her forehead. She opened her eyes and smiled. He smiled, too, and, a moment later, fell asleep.

AS WE rounded a curve and crossed over the last wooden bridge, I caught sight of a man standing inside a circle of Waverly trees several hundred yards from the house. I slowed and pulled to the side of the road. "I'll get out here," I said to Gill. "I'll see you in a few minutes." I watched as she continued toward the house, then started up the hill.

The dark gray aspens, completely bare, guarded the burial ground like sentinels. I had avoided it since my return because she wasn't really there, and her absence obliged me to recall how she died. Now that I knew about Zhev the ache was even worse, but I owed her memory, and her father, an explanation. I would acknowledge my responsibility to both of them.

I had met Gabrielle during one of my weekends at Aylesbury Abbey. The guests were riding to hounds that day. Markham cared nothing about fox hunting, but the local hunt rode across his property as they had done for centuries and he felt it was his duty to accompany them. Likewise uninterested in watching a pack of dogs rend a fox, I begged off and rode instead in the opposite direction, across the Vale of Aylesbury. It was an easy ride. The Vale had a few gentle slopes but it was mostly flat, and a narrow path was worn over it from the Abbey. Carpets of bluebells and clumps of wildflowers relieved the various shades of green.

After ten miles or so I considered turning around but there was a particularly conspicuous hill just ahead so I decided to see what lay on the other side. At the top I looked across more of the same landscape, but there were also creeks and ponds and, a half mile away, a two-story Tudor house with a central core and two protruding gabled wings.

The horse, given his head, made his way slowly down the hill toward the house. Its fascia was faded red brick except for the attached gatehouse, gabled as well, where the bricks were white. Narrow windows of different sizes were inset into the brick in clusters of three or four and a series of heavy stone chimneys rose from the roof. Much of the building was covered in ivy and it seemed to recede into the foliage of the trees that surrounded it.

When I was within a hundred feet of the house, I noticed a woman seated on a low stool under a copse of linden trees. She wore a long white dress and a wide-brimmed white hat that tied under her chin, and she held a palette and a brush. As I watched, she daubed at the canvas before her, then laid the brush down and turned her head toward me. I slid from the saddle. She didn't move. "I hope I'm not interrupting you," I called from thirty feet away. There was no response. I drew closer. "I've just come over from Aylesbury Abbey, exploring your beautiful countryside." Her expression changed but she remained silent. "Is this your home?"

She looked up at me. Azure eyes the shape of almonds stared at me over high, prominent cheek bones. Her oval face was pale and pitch-black hair flowed past her shoulders in waves. "Yes," she said, rising. "I live here with my father. I'm Gabrielle Soleil." She extended her hand.

I towered over her. She was maybe an inch or two over five feet, and her figure was slim. The slender fingers were strong, the nails unvarnished. "Georges St. Cyr."

She smiled, showing even white teeth against a wide raspberry mouth. "You're American?" I nodded. "And you're staying at the Abbey?"

"I'm at Oxford. I'm down here for the weekend."

"Are you a teacher?"

I shook my head. "Student – older student."

"Father teaches at Oxford. Physics."

She laid the palette on the stool. Her painting of the house was almost finished. "That's very good," I said without knowing.

She wasn't fooled. "Are you studying art?"

"Um, no. English Literature."

She laughed. "It's *not* very good," she said, looking at the picture. "Two years at the Sorbonne have made me a mechanic, not an artist." She turned back to me. "I was just about to make some tea. Would you join me?"

The wooing had been short and intense – we were married two months after we met. Her English mother had been a Catholic who tried to raise Gabrielle in the Church, but when she died her daughter had drifted to the faith of her father, a Frenchman who had no real religion except his work. She had insisted on a private, civil ceremony, so one Thursday afternoon, after several bottles of champagne, we presented ourselves at the Magistrate's office on St. Aldate's, then took the train to London where we spent three euphoric days and nights at the Savoy Hotel. A month later we moved to one of the terraces in Belgravia and I took up my Navy career again. The proud recipient of a Master's degree from Christ Church, Oxford, granted during a ceremony at the Sheldonian Theater, I was even more pleased with my striking new bride. Only two things marred our happiness. The first was her almost violent antipathy for Aylesbury Abbey and its master, the second her distress at my career.

The trouble between the Soleils of The Downs and the Markhams of Aylesbury Abbey was manifest immediately.

The very first day, over tea, Gabrielle had made it clear that she would have nothing to do with Tony Markham. Her voice was so firm that I had elected to ask her father what the trouble was. After an embarrassed silence the old man had muttered something about a *"grande querrelle,"* which I took to mean one of those typically English disputes, shrouded in time, that erupt between neighbors. Her mother's family had been at The Downs on their side of the Vale even longer than the Markhams had been at the Abbey. They had probably had much to quarrel over for the past five hundred years. I pressed for further details but none were forthcoming. While Gabrielle had never insisted that I give Markham up, our friendship was obviously painful to her, so much so that I no longer accepted the invitations to the Abbey and, after Tony understood why, the invitations were no longer extended.

I had known Gabrielle for a month when, having declined a visit to Aylesbury Abbey, I ran into Markham at the train station. "So," he said, smiling, "you've decided to join us after all." I shook my head, looking past him to the road where Gabrielle waited for me in her old green Rover. Markham had followed my eyes and when he looked back his features were twisted for an instant, then smooth again. "Well," he said, "she's a lovely girl. Congratulations." The following week Tony and I had dined together as usual and watched cricket in University Parks, and no mention was made of the incident at Aylesbury Station. Gabrielle's prickliness over Markham had diminished when we moved to London. I didn't see Tony as often, and when I did I tried not to mention it.

The other problem grew worse with the move. We had been so happy with ourselves that there was little discussion of the future beyond the following day. Whenever the question of my work came up, I provided a vague description of my future post at the embassy in London. It wasn't until shortly before we were married that she pressed for more details. "I'll be the naval attaché at the embassy," I said.

"You're in the Navy?"

"Yes."

She looked stunned. "But I thought – but – you said you were studying English Literature."

I laughed. "I am. They're not mutually exclusive."

"You don't wear a uniform."

"I'm not on active duty. You'll see plenty of uniforms when we get to London."

We had moved on to other things but I knew that she was troubled, and I thought I knew why. Her father, a Huguenot, had come under the influence of a small congregation of Quakers when he came to Oxford. He had vaguely endorsed their precepts and passed them on to his daughter, but it was only the Friends' opposition to violence that had stayed with her. Now she was about to marry a man whose profession was war. She had suppressed her aversion because she loved me, but in London she was reminded of it every day and it had begun to come between us.

For my part, I agonized over the actual circumstances of my work. The job at the embassy was only a cover for the mayhem that was my actual vocation. I wasn't sure that our marriage would survive its disclosure but, returning to

London after a two-week operation in Warsaw that could have nothing to do with my duties in Grosvenor Square, I had told her the truth – almost the truth. I omitted the brutal details. She carried it around with her for several days, then brought it up after dinner one evening. "I love you, Georges," she said. "I'm not sure I would have married you if – if I had known." She paused. "The truth is I didn't want to know. When you said you were in the Navy, I could have asked. I'm not stupid or helpless, and I sensed that there was more, but I didn't want to know what it was."

"Gabrielle, I –"

She stopped me. "I didn't want to take the chance that I wouldn't marry you. So this is my fault. I'm going to put it out of my mind. We will be happy. I promise." And she had tried, but she couldn't hide the questions in her eyes or the life that seemed to leave her each time I left London. I had watched her lose her joy and her shine for more than two years – during which time I, too, was diminished – before I finally decided that she was all that mattered.

It wasn't just for her. Despite the rhetoric and reinforcement designed to overcome my humanity, I had learned that killing another member of my species was an unnatural act. A man will resist killing his fellow man at close quarters, even to the point of dying himself. Bombs and missiles, removed from the immediacy of death, made it easier. My own revulsion had set in early, and I had carried out my assignments in such a way as to curb the death that was required. Recently, the killing had been limited to self-defense. I had not reached the point where the preservation of my life was second to that of my enemy, and I suspected that I never would, a reality that gave impetus to my decision to resign from the Office.

We had planned a trip to America. She had never been in an airplane and was unhappy at the prospect, so we booked passage on *Victoria*. She decided to visit her father for a few days before the voyage and I had gone to Paddington with her. I held her close at the top of the staircase. "I'm quitting my second job," I said.

She leaned back in my arms. "What?"

"No more long, unexplained journeys. No more hush-hush meetings, or late-night phone calls. I'll be strictly nine to five at the embassy, and I might quit that, too." We had stood there, wrapped in each other's arms, long enough for her to miss her train. Finally, I dried her eyes, and we searched the board for the next one. While we waited for it, I told her about the change in my plans. "I want to see my supervisor personally. He won't be back in London until Saturday, so I can't leave with you on Friday. I'll join the ship on Saturday night in Cherbourg."

SOLEIL TURNED as I approached but said nothing. I stood before the marker, still clean amongst the weathered stones, and tried to remember her, but the only thing my agitated mind called up was an image of her face dissolving into dust as a great storm of fire and ash rose in the sky. I turned my head. "You said that Gabrielle was right to marry me," I murmured. "You were wrong." He remained silent. "She died because of me. Because of who I am." I told him about Zhev.

When I finished Soleil said, "That doesn't alter what I said to you, St. Cyr. You made her whole again. Nothing you've said changes that." He sat down on a stone bench between two thick tree trunks. "Gabrielle was badly damaged when she met you. You helped her heal."

"What was wrong with her?"

He looked away. "She made me swear that I would never tell you but she's gone and – and I think she would want you to know." He looked up at me. "For your own well-being, perhaps."

"What is it?"

"Gabrielle was engaged to be married once before. To Anthony Markham."

Stunned, I stuttered, "He never – nobody over there – ever mentioned it to me."

He nodded. "I'm not surprised. Gabrielle was very attached to Markham's brother, James. They grew up together. The Vale, The Downs, Aylesbury Abbey were all a big part of her childhood." He paused. "When he died, Tony tried to take James's place in her life. She resisted at first but he was very insistent, and eventually she accepted him." Soleil sighed. "I don't think that she ever really got over James, but the idea of becoming Duchess of Aylesbury was hard to resist."

"What happened?"

"A spectacular wedding was planned, a ceremony from the past with horses and carriages and galas that would continue for days." He closed his eyes. "When she broke their engagement he went insane. Perhaps not in the clinical sense – tantrums, threats, vandalism at the house, even here," he said, gesturing. "I finally had to send Gabrielle to Paris to get her away from him. I'm sure he was unhappy when she met you." He paused. "I'm also sure that he left that letter in your rooms."

"What?"

"Yes. A few days before James Markham died, Gabrielle began to have disturbing dreams and she got into the habit of calling on him to comfort her. She would send a note. James always came, no matter the time of day or night." He shook his head. "That note in your rooms *was* in her handwriting. It was her stationery. I'm certain she wrote it to James. His brother must have her letters."

"Why didn't you tell me that before?"

"Because I had promised not to tell you about Markham. I only decided to break that promise a moment ago."

"Why would he leave it for me like that?"

"Because he means to cause you pain."

We were silent. I finally spoke. "Why did she break the engagement?"

"She told me at the time that she caught him with another woman. In the chapel." He paused. "I was a little surprised. Markham was almost thirty years old by then and no one, not even Gabrielle, thought that he was Galahad." He stopped. "I assumed for years that it was actually catching him in the act, that *she* had been – shamed, but that wasn't it." He rose and turned for the house. I followed. "When she was here that last time I was late picking her up –" He smiled. "I ran out of petrol."

"You've never fixed the gauge?"

He shook his head. "Anyway, she told me that she ran into him at the railway station. He – cursed her, and she cursed right back, and he said something that drove her absolutely wild. She was crazy when she got to the car."

"What did he say?"

"She wouldn't tell me, but in the middle of the shouting and cursing she told him that she was pregnant." He paused. "I think she knew that would kill him. He had no wife, there was talk of some sort of sexual difficulty and an heir for the Abbey had always been at the top of his list." He stopped again. "I believe she got the reaction she was looking for."

We passed a copse of linden trees in silence and approached the house. "Did she ever tell you why she really called it off?" I said.

"Yes. During our drive to Southampton that last day."

"What was it?"

"She *did* find him with another woman. His sister."

"ABRAM," SHE whispered. His eyelids flickered. "We need to get up," Pamela said. "It's almost six o'clock." He lifted his head and stared at her. She looked into the slanted blue eyes, jolted for an instant. She had given up seeing those eyes again and, yet, here they were, gazing at her. She smiled. She was happy, too – really happy. It was years since she had felt such pleasure.

Khan rolled over and sat up on the edge of the chaise, clad only in socks, shoes and shirt. She laughed and he, looking down at himself, laughed, too. He rose and reached for his pants. She turned on her side and watched him. "What time are we leaving?" he said.

"Seven."

He nodded and dropped the pants on the bed. The shirt and socks followed and, naked, he stepped into the bathroom. When she heard the shower she rose, opened the shower door and joined him. She turned her head away from the sharp spray and laid it on his chest, her arms around his waist. "Abram?"

"Yes?"

"What are you going to do about that man? Zhev?"

"I'm going to kill him if I can. If I can't, I'll at least make sure that the British do something about him."

"Won't that be – dangerous?"

He laughed. "Oh, yes. Ahmed Zhev is a very dangerous man."

"Why not let the authorities handle it?"

"Because there's no guarantee that he'll be punished. Zhev's a powerful man in Pakistan. Politicians cut deals. I can't take the chance."

She was quiet. Then: "What about the book?"

"What about it?"

"I think there are other pictures in that book. Pictures that might hurt people." She paused. "St. Cyr doesn't need them. Would he give them to me?"

"I don't know."

"Would you ask him?"

I MET them at the door. "Welcome to The Downs." Pamela crossed the threshold. I stopped Khan and handed him an envelope.

"Thanks," he said. He drew me aside. "Pamela says there are other pictures in the –"

"Not anymore. Tell her that I've already destroyed them."

"Thanks. I will."

"Where's Guin?"

"She's not coming. Gerry's not well, and she didn't want to leave him alone."

A faint alarm went off in the back of my brain. Guin had been uppermost in my mind when I asked Soleil to host this dinner party. I was afraid for her and I didn't know why. Something about the new map, seemingly a welcome declaration that London and Portsmouth were safe, was disturbing. I went to the telephone and dialed a number. It didn't ring. I hung up and tried again. There was only silence at the other end. The warning in my head grew more pronounced. I caught Soleil's eye and beckoned to him. We met in the kitchen. "I'm going to ride over to the Abbey, Doctor Soleil. I need to talk to Guin." He nodded. "I'll be back in time for dinner."

Gill stopped me at the door. "Where are you going?"

"I have to see Guin." She frowned. "I'll be back for dinner. Help Soleil with our guests."

A half hour later I paused again at the top of the last hill. Everything looked okay. I glimpsed the house through the trees. Smoke curled from the chimneys and all the lights were on.

The gate was locked. After securing the horse, I climbed to the top and dropped down on the other side. Approaching the house, my senses became more acute and my pulse slowed. Two enormous black birds crouched, unmoving, on the parapet above the door. I stood still for a minute, then crossed the courtyard and raised the knocker. The heavy toll of iron on iron was magnified by the silence, and I felt the draft of giant wings as the great birds lifted awkwardly from the roof.

No one answered. As I reached for the knocker again, Guin opened the door herself. She wore the white gown, and the pearls around her neck were black. My heart quickened, but I continued alert. "Georges," she said. "What are you doing here?"

"Are you in charge of the door now?"

She smiled. "I saw you from the window."

"I – Is something wrong with your phone?"

She nodded. "It's been out all afternoon. The telephone service in Buckingham is the worst in England." She closed the door. "Why aren't you with your guests?"

Because something is wrong, I wanted to say. "I was worried about you."

She stepped closer and put her arms around my neck. "You're sweet. That's a feature I haven't noticed before." She kissed me. "I like it." She took my hand. "Let's sit down. I'll keep you from your friends a little while longer."

A moment later I was seated in an overstuffed armchair next to a roaring fire in the Little Hall. Guin lowered herself onto my lap. Her brother's portrait looked down at us. Unlike his younger siblings, James was dark, and the expression on his face, a smile, was unpleasant. As I stared at it, a few more tumblers fell into place. I had seen other pictures of James, in Cromwell's book. "Is there something you want to talk about," Guin said, "or can we just neck?"

I put my arms around her. The latter suggestion was inviting, but the image prompted by Soleil's revelations wouldn't allow it. "Soleil told me about Tony and Gabrielle." Her body stiffened and she shut her eyes. "He said that she found you and Tony in the chapel. Is it true?"

She rose abruptly and stood staring into the fire. "Yes."

"But it's – I don't understand. Why?"

She hesitated. "I'm sorry you know this. It's nasty and sad and – I love my brother very much, Georges. Not – not in the passionate way. The normal way." She stopped. "It began innocently. We did – things together as children and then at some point he wanted more. I knew it was wrong and I resisted, but Tony's very persuasive. It started when I was sixteen." She paused again. "Mother and Father were both dead. Tony was the master of Aylesbury Abbey and – me."

The idea that anyone was her master, even Tony, was hard to accept. "Did he force you?"

She turned to me, tears coursing down her cheeks. "No. I – I wanted to please him." She looked away again, wiping her eyes with the sleeve of her gown. "It wasn't an everyday thing. He knew it was wrong, too. But there were times when he just – needed me."

"But there were other women –"

"Yes, but it was very hard with them. Often he couldn't manage at all." She smiled wearily. "That was never a problem when he was with me." She knelt before my chair and looked up at me. "I'm probably the reason he has trouble with other women."

I nodded, recalling all the "Susans" and "Alices" who had accompanied Markham over the years. "I don't suppose that doctors were consulted?"

"No." She laid her head on my knee. I stroked her hair. "He had already been unable to – perform with Gabrielle, and when she saw us, well – I'm sure that wedded bliss seemed unlikely."

"This is evil, Guin." She clutched at my hand. "Have you ever told –"

"No!" she cried. "He's my brother and – and it's not all his fault." She stopped. "And – I can't. I won't." She sat back. "I'm going to America with you and that's enough."

I took a deep breath. Something was missing – the Guin I knew would never just submit and retreat. "What did he do when you got married?"

She bowed her head. "I was never married."

"What?"

"We made that up to – disguise something else." She stopped. "When Gabrielle broke their engagement, Tony went mad. He came to me every night for weeks. I knew what he was doing, but I couldn't stop it." She looked up. "When I got pregnant, he sent me to France to have the baby, and spread the story about my 'marriage.'" She paused. "Whenever he talks about my wedding, he's really talking about his own – which also never happened."

"So Gerry –"

"Is Tony's – our son."

We were quiet. The woman I had so admired for her poise and strength was really the victim of the vilest sort of outrage, and yet she stood by the man who had corrupted her and cherished the fruit of his corruption. I rose and scooped her up, cradling her in my arms as I resumed my seat. She buried her face in my chest. "And – we've reaped the whirlwind," she said softly.

"Gerry?"

"Yes. His illness is genetic. They don't know how long he'll live." The tears returned.

"Is it still going on?"

She tilted her head to look at me. "No. It stopped when Gerry was born." She looked away. "Will this matter to us?"

I held her closer. "No."

"Thank God." She kissed me. "Thank you."

We sat quietly again. She lifted my wrist and looked at my watch. "You need to get back to The Downs."

I nodded and, after another moment, followed her to the door. "What will he do when you tell him that you're leaving?" I said.

"I've already told him." She smiled. "Before I told you."

"When?"

"Yesterday morning."

"What did he say?"

"Nothing. He – I wasn't asking permission. He can't keep me here."

I walked under the ancient limes, my step tired and heavy. It had not been a good day. In addition to the revelations about Zhev, the woman I was going to marry had lived a far different life than I had imagined, and the man responsible for her pain was the best friend I had ever had. *Had* was the operative word – Markham had apparently resented me, or worse, for years, and the obscene treatment of his sister confirmed the end of our friendship. I felt the rage and helplessness again – rage at a man who could so degrade the sister who loved him, helplessness because I could do nothing about it. To reveal Markham's wickedness would be to hold up Guin's shame to the world and cast unwanted attention on her tragic little boy, and she would never permit it. She would hate me if I tried. Nevertheless, I would find a way to let Markham know that I knew, and that somehow, some day, a price would be paid.

As I neared the gate, I glanced inside the gatehouse packed with the family treasures. Another question crossed my mind. Frowning, I felt again for Gabrielle, standing in the doorway of the chapel watching her intended ravish his sister. *That* wouldn't happen again. Guin would be gone soon, and the chapel had been destroyed. I vaulted to the top of the gate and fell to the other side.

I leaned against the gate. *The chapel had been destroyed.* That was it. That was why my brain had been so unsettled since opening the envelope on the train. I checked my watch – eight o'clock. "Oh, God," I cried. "Oh, no." I turned back to the gate, scrambled to the top once more and hurled my body to the ground. As I straightened and started to run, a terrible eruption of light struck my eyes and a massive fireball, consuming everything in its path, raced toward me. I lifted an arm to shield my eyes as shock waves, accompanied by a roar from the mouth of Hell, lifted me from the ground and slammed me into the gate.

CHAPTER EIGHT

IT WAS a testament to that singular self-regard that I had mentioned to Gill only a day earlier that my first thought was not of Guin or Gerry or the centuries-old house, all of which had just disappeared in a cataclysm of fire and smoke. As I lay on my back a few yards outside the confines of Aylesbury Abbey, the sharp edges of the gate digging into my body, my first thought was for the precision of the bomb maker that had allowed me to survive. The bomb's range was four hundred meters and the distance from the house to the gate was the same. I had been on the periphery of the explosion. A few yards closer to the house and I would have been incinerated. The shock waves that had blown me backwards had also torn the gate from its pillars. Instead of being crushed against the iron bars, I had accompanied them to their present location beneath my aching bones.

I sat up. I was probably one big bruise beneath my clothing but, as far as I could tell, nothing was broken and there was no blood. My watch still worked – it was ten minutes past eight. I pushed myself up from the ground, still refusing to look in the direction of the house. Finally, I raised my head and let my eyes focus.

There was nothing there. The house and the trees had vanished, leaving only a substantial crater and odd piles of dirt. Dust still rose in the sky. I could see the ruins of the old monastery buildings to the left, but the manor house at Aylesbury Abbey was gone. It would have no need of the time and elements that had eroded the monks' cloister. Man and his ever more brutal capacity for destruction, Markham's outraged lament only days earlier, had rendered them immaterial. The gatehouses remained, blackened on the sides closest to the explosion, parodies of the immutability they represented only a moment before.

I felt the tears. I didn't give a damn about the house or the trees or the rest of it. A beautiful woman who was about to emerge from an unspeakable shadow had been atomized. I had liked her very much and I had allowed her to die. I *knew* that something was wrong, that something awful was about to happen, and instead of trying to find it out, I had first wallowed in guilt over another death and then badgered her about a past that she wanted to forget. Gabrielle had been beyond my reach for four years – Guin was alive only ten minutes ago. I closed my eyes and pleaded for those minutes back, but time refused to move backwards or even stand still.

I heard sirens in the distance. It would be awkward to be here when the police arrived. The horse was gone, probably halfway home by now. I crossed the road and, five minutes later, stood on top of the hill and looked back at what had been Aylesbury Abbey. A dozen automobiles, their blue and red and yellow lights flashing, milled about, undoubtedly confused by the perfect oblivion of the scene before them. I turned and started down the path that had once seemed so promising.

A half-hour later I heard the sound of horses approaching. I stepped into the feathery blackness of a thick grove of yews and waited. After recognizing the rider in the moonlight, I returned to the path and held up my hand. "Hello, Khan. Thanks for coming."

Khan pulled up. "Thank the horse," he said. I climbed into the saddle. "What happened?"

"They've blown up the Abbey. Just like *Victoria.*"

"The same bomb?"

"Yes."

"And – Guin?"

"Gone. All that's left is a hole in the ground."

Khan bowed his head. "Why would someone destroy the Abbey?"

"I was supposed to have dinner there tonight." I paused. "Have you seen your stepfather lately?"

"No."

"Where is he?"

"I don't know." He turned his head. "Don't you think it's a bit much? I mean – using a bomb like that just to kill you."

"He blew up an ocean liner and a thousand people, didn't he?" He didn't respond. "The Abbey and a few more human beings are nothing to a brute like that."

"What are you going to do?"

"I'm going to find out if Zhev is in England. After that, we'll see." I stared at him. "If you hear from him, let me know."

We turned back toward The Downs. "St. Cyr?"

"Yes?"

"Please understand something. Zhev has murdered my sister. Her death is killing my mother. A bunch of Muslim thugs that Zhev was supposedly training slaughtered my father. He's destroyed my family." Khan stopped. "But he's not a fool. These – bombs are not his style. I know you have the pictures and I accept that. I want him dead as much as you do, but –"

"But what?"

"I think you're missing something. What about the Oxford thing? I can't believe that Oxford and *Victoria* and – and now Aylesbury Abbey aren't part of the same plot." He paused. "Why would Zhev blow up Oxford?"

We rode for miles in silence. I tried to forget what had happened to Guin. I could already feel the familiar darkness closing over me, and I couldn't afford that now. I would mourn later. I needed to be able to think and to act, and the first order of business was to decide about Khan. "Before tonight," I said finally, "I thought it likely that Oxford *was* apart from the rest of it. I'm not sure about that now. I'll have to think about it some more." I stopped. "And I had almost concluded that it was a hoax, and that Markham was behind it."

We had reached the top of the last hill. The only evidence of the old Tudor house at the bottom was the light shining through the narrow windows. The moon revealed only the trees and the ivy that enveloped it. Khan pulled on the reins and I stopped, too. "Markham?" he said. "Why?"

"He hates the government and the culture, Oxford's included. And he hates – hated – Cromwell. He was a symbol of everything that Markham believes is wrong. He's worried that his country is being overtaken by an alien religion and he's fighting it." I paused. "I think he may have planned the whole thing just to embarrass Cromwell and his friends, and maybe stir up people against the Muslims."

"But if it's a hoax, how would he do all that?"

"I'm not sure. It's not Day Seven yet. He would never actually destroy Oxford. I have no idea what he may have planned." I paused. "And the bomb tonight could change everything. He has things to deal with now."

"Why do you think it's Markham?"

"Little things, mostly. Silly things."

"Such as?"

"Well, the map and diagram, for instance, warning us about what's coming. Terrorists don't do that."

"But what about the map itself? It seemed to claim credit for the *Victoria* bomb."

"I believe he just used that as a starting point, something to make the government pay attention. The circle and the X over Southampton Water would ensure that people took his game seriously."

We walked the horses slowly down the hill. "What about the diagram?" said Khan.

"I think that was aimed at Cromwell. He was part of Operation Antler. I don't know where Tony got the drawings, and I'm still not sure what they mean, if anything, but they're sitting in the bottom drawer of Cromwell's secretary right now."

"Tying Cromwell to the diagram."

"Yes."

"But – the chapel at Aylesbury was actually blown up."

I nodded. "That's a weakness in the theory, of course. It's hard to imagine that he would destroy the church just to make a point. Still, at least some of the things from the chapel have been stored in the gatehouse."

"What?"

"Yes. He told me that nothing was salvaged. The gatehouse is full of stuff that used to be there." I paused. "Which leads us to his injured hand."

"What about it?"

"He told me that it happened while he was digging through what was left of the ruins. There was nothing to dig through after the bomb. It was just scattered stones."

"Still –"

"Tony's right-handed. After the 'injury' he drove with his left hand and mixed drinks with his left hand. At lunch yesterday he toasted the evacuation with his left hand."

"And?"

"He was able to write a clear set of directions for Pamela last week. And to worry about the trains."

"The trains?"

"Yes. He told her a week ago that the trains might not be running now. That was *before* the letters with the deadline arrived at Whitehall." I stopped. "There was no reason to bother about trains before those letters were received."

We reached the stable. Khan climbed down from his horse. "How do Muslim terrorists fit in?" he said.

"The government report on *Victoria* raised the possibility, and I think he just carried on with it. The map connected the new attacks to *Victoria,* and the doomsday note, stripped of its Arabic veneer, is pure Markham."

"How do you mean?"

"It's supposed to be a Muslim threat against Oxford. What it really is, though, is a dirge for Western civilization. I've heard him express the same sentiment dozens of times. It's very unlikely that terrorists or criminals would be so – philosophical." I paused. "He would have had no trouble putting it in Cromwell's mailbox." We walked to the house. "None of this really matters anymore. It's over."

"Why?"

"Because we've had a new bomb. People are really dead. Someone has hijacked the game."

"I don't understand."

"Everyone knew about the first map – I spoke of it in great detail when we were pushing for the evacuation. It was in the papers." I paused. "I received a new map yesterday."

"Deleting the circles over London and Portsmouth."

I nodded. "Of course, there was never any real threat to London or Portsmouth. That was just more to interest the government." We stopped outside the door. "The new map disturbed me, and I couldn't figure out why." I looked away. "Until an hour ago."

"What is it?"

"There was a circle and a red X over Southampton. There were circles over Aylesbury and Oxford." I stopped. "The church at Aylesbury had already been destroyed. There should have been an X there as well if the game were still on."

"But since there was no X –"

"Aylesbury would be attacked again – for real." I closed my eyes. "And it was. The make-believe was over.

Someone, Zhev probably, has intervened. A new, more deadly game has started."

"There's more?"

"There's still a circle around Oxford."

"But that leaves us where we started. Why would Zhev care about Oxford?"

"I don't know – yet." I opened the door and let Khan walk ahead of me. I followed him across the foyer to the old armory, the room that the family had used for generations as a gathering place. We stopped just inside the doorway. Soleil, Pamela and Gill were sitting around the television set. Pamela and Soleil stared at the picture on the screen – a barren, static view of the gash in the ground that had once been Aylesbury Abbey – listening to the hushed words of a reporter trying to maintain the faux decorum always demonstrated at the beginning of a new tragedy. Gill, her head in her hands, wept quietly. No one looked around.

Khan crossed the room. "Is that the Abbey?"

Soleil turned his head. "Yes, it's been –" His eyes grew large as he caught sight of me. "St. Cyr!" he cried. "We thought that – that you –"

Gill raised her head and fell back in the chair. She closed her eyes for an instant, then opened them again. "God," she said. "Is it you?" She rose and ran across the room, hurling herself into my arms. "We thought you were dead." She pointed at the television. "They said that no one had survived the blast."

"They're right about that," I said. "I was just far enough away." I stopped. "Guin's dead. And Gerry."

"Oh, Fitz," Gill said. "I'm so sorry."

I looked at my watch. "I need to make a telephone call." I unhooked Gill's arms from around my neck and left the room. When I returned, I spoke to Khan from the doorway. "Barak Khan arrived in England last Friday. He's in London now and they think he's going to Oxford tomorrow afternoon."

"What's the plan?"

"I'll try to sleep for a few hours. Then I'm going to Oxford."

"I'll go with you," said Khan.

I shook my head. "Charles Wellbourne is a friend of yours, isn't he?" He nodded. "There's something I want you to do in London. You can join me in Oxford when you're done."

"I'm going, too," said Gill.

"No. There's no reason for you to go, and there may be another explosion. If he maintains the original schedule, we have just less than twenty-four hours. If he doesn't, well –"

"I'm going," she said.

"Gill, nothing will survive that bomb. Nothing."

"I don't care. If you're going, I'm going."

I had treated her badly. She had crossed the ocean to help me, and I had done all I could to make her regret it. "All right."

There was a sudden flurry on the television set. "Have they said anything useful?" Khan said.

Soleil shook his head. "The local police thought it was a ruptured gas line at first, but the extent of the damage let that out." He looked back at the television. "They haven't mentioned a bomb yet."

Pamela looked at me. "Was – Tony there?" she said.

"No. I think he's still in London."

"Should we try to call him?"

"I don't know. I have to sort through some things first."

"What about the servants?" she said. I didn't respond. "Who would do this? Why?" I shook my head.

"Look," said Soleil. "It's Markham." Everyone turned back to the television. Markham stood outside his doorstep at Belgrave Square. Shading his eyes from the floodlights rigged to illuminate the spectacle, he said, "I have a prepared statement." His hands trembled slightly as he donned a pair of glasses and drew a sheet of paper from his inside coat pocket. He began to read.

"A few hours ago, my sister Guin and her son Gerry were killed in a horrendous explosion at our home in Aylesbury." He looked up, blinking. "Guin was thirty-five years old. Gerry was eight." I closed my eyes. His pain, his sense of loss, was undeniable – how could he have defiled her that way? What demons drove him to such a thing, to the point of purposely making her pregnant?

Markham continued. "There were also four guests and five servants in the house at the time. I have provided their names to the authorities." He paused. "I am profoundly sorry for this loss of life."

"My God," said Pamela. "He thinks we're all dead."

"Was Khan at Aylesbury?" shouted a voice from the crowd of reporters.

Markham ignored it. "While I have not yet been to Aylesbury, I'm confident from the description given me that the explosion resulted from a very powerful bomb similar to the one that destroyed the White Star Line's *Victoria* four years ago." He stopped. "The government determined that *foreign* terrorists were likely responsible for *Victoria.* I believe that terrorists planted the bomb at Aylesbury Abbey as well, although I refuse to rule out *domestic* terrorism." Khan looked at me. "I have spoken out many times about the militant religious factions that have been allowed to flourish unchecked in this country. I believe that the attack at Aylesbury tonight was an effort to silence me." He took another piece of paper from his pocket. "This note is written in Arabic. It was received by the Chancellor of the University of Oxford three days ago." He read the translation of the doomsday note out loud. "That's a description of Judgment Day in the Muslim holy book. I believe that's what they have planned for Oxford." Markham turned back to the door.

"Have you heard from the Prime Minister?" shouted another reporter.

Markham looked around. "Yes. She called a few minutes ago." He faced the crowd again. "This is the second attack on Aylesbury Abbey in less than two weeks. The government has done nothing about it. There have been credible threats against Oxford, London and Portsmouth. I won't speak of the government's efforts in London and Portsmouth, but I can tell you that the Home Office and its hand-picked Chancellor at Oxford have done all they can to thwart an orderly evacuation there." He stopped. "A bomb is supposed to explode in Oxford tomorrow. Only the efforts of private individuals, two of whom were killed at my home this evening, made the evacuation of Oxford possible." He turned toward the door once more.

"What about Khan?" cried the voice. "Was he there?"

Markham looked back, clearly exasperated. He pursed his lips. "Yes," he said, and pushed through the door.

"I must call him," Pamela said.

"No," I said. "I need to think about this. Please wait."

The scene on the television set had shifted immediately to Downing Street, and the smooth, bland features of Charles Wellbourne appeared. "Mr. Secretary," said a man brandishing a microphone the size of a small cannon, "you've just heard the Duke's remarks concerning tonight's attack on Aylesbury Abbey. Do you have a response?"

Wellbourne smiled. "I can't comment on the bomb or the threats except to say that we've successfully turned aside attacks on London and Portsmouth, and are now concentrating our efforts on Oxford."

"Can you confirm that the great cricketer Abram Khan is among the dead?" Wellbourne shook his head. "What about the charge that you've ignored Oxford and discouraged the evacuation?"

Wellbourne smiled again. "That's nonsense. We've worked very closely with the authorities in town and at the University in support of the evacuation. Oxford is now deserted."

"What are you doing to find the bomb?"

Wellbourne stopped smiling and cleared his throat. "Well – well, we've engaged a – a specialist in these things to advise us. He recommended the evacuation."

"Who is he?"

"I'm sorry. I'm not at liberty to say."

"Have you spoken with him about the Aylesbury bomb?"

Wellbourne looked down. "No. No, I haven't."

"Why not?"

"I'm – told that he was killed in the explosion tonight."

There was a long silence. "So," said the reporter, "who's looking after Oxford?"

"I'm sorry," said Wellbourne. "I can't comment on that." He disappeared from the screen.

I turned to Pamela. "Everyone, including the bomber, must believe that we're dead. I think that gives us an advantage tomorrow. I'd like to keep it that way."

"But –"

"It's only another twenty-four hours, Pamela. Markham will survive."

She looked doubtful. "I feel like I should do something." She paused. "Can I go to Oxford with you?"

"Yes. There's something you can help with, in fact. But you have to go when I say so." A few minutes later, I closed my eyes. I wanted to sleep, but couldn't. The images of two women who had been murdered in an effort to destroy me wouldn't permit it. I forced myself to think of Zhev, but the face of another man intruded.

CHAPTER NINE

PAMELA GAZED out the window as Gill negotiated the roundabout and turned the Rover toward Oxford. She mulled her lack of obedience. She barely knew Georges St. Cyr, and what harm could it do to tell Tony that they had escaped the bomb at Aylesbury? There were more important things to worry about. She felt the weight of the gun in her purse.

As they crossed a rushing stream just above its merger with the Isis she felt the old car slow and, a moment later, they were stopped on the side of the road. St. Cyr, who had been silent since they left The Downs, said, "What's the matter? Why are you stopping?"

"I didn't do anything," said Gill. "It stopped by itself."

"Try the ignition again."

Gill twisted the key. The engine turned over and caught for a few seconds, then died. "Is it the battery?"

St. Cyr shook his head. "I suspect that we're out of gas. What's the gauge say?"

"It's full."

He laughed. "Then we're definitely out of gas. That gauge broke years ago. It shows full regardless of how far you drive." They climbed out of the car. St. Cyr checked the horizon. "No gas stations." He looked at his watch.

"Should we try to find a cab?" said Gill.

"No. I don't want anyone driving into Oxford." He hesitated. "There's another way."

The car park at the Trout was full and both sides of the road were crowded with automobiles. There was a large sign over the door:

DAY SEVEN AT THE TROUT

"Quite a crowd," St. Cyr said to the girl at the door.

"Oh, yes, sir. We've been full since we opened this morning."

"Everyone watching for the bomb?"

"Yes, sir."

"Are you still renting canoes?"

"I'll have to check."

"All right."

They watched as she disappeared into the crowded room. "Are these people really here to see Oxford blow up?" said Pamela.

"You disapprove?" he said.

"It just seems a little – ghoulish, I guess."

St. Cyr smiled. "Nothing lasts forever." He gestured toward the people. "They look for the gold among the dross. Oxford blowing up is the day's entertainment."

"But it's been here for centuries," said Gill. "All those beautiful buildings and –"

"A moment in time, Gill," he said. "And those moments grow shorter and shorter."

A few minutes later they floated on the Isis toward Oxford. Just below Wolvercote, St. Cyr maneuvered the boat east into Marlborough's channel, then south down the Oxford Canal until it terminated at Hythe Bridge. They pulled the canoe onto the bank and walked to the Camera.

Pamela was startled by the silence. The day was cool and clear and the vapors rose from Christ Church Meadow in the distance, and the shadows cast by Oxford's spires were sinister. The yew hedges, and the leaves of the ivy and creeper behind them, were still. The ancient village looked abandoned. It was as if everyone had committed suicide.

As they entered Radcliffe Square Gill pointed at two black birds perched on St. Mary's steeple. "I've never seen birds like that before," she said. "What kind are they?"

St. Cyr turned his head. "I'm not sure. They look like owls." He stared at the birds. "I think they're following me." He paused. "I want both of you to keep an eye on West. I'm afraid he'll go up with the bomb if we let him."

They joined the little band standing outside the Camera. Pamela spoke to the old man in the black robe. "It's not too late to accept my offer, Dean West."

He smiled. "Perhaps I should." He turned to St. Cyr. "We've moved most of the prominent items beyond the reach of the bomb, but there's still work to be done. When is it due to explode?"

"Just past nine o'clock, if the schedule holds." St. Cyr addressed the group. "Please understand how dangerous this is. There's no guarantee the bomb won't go off ten minutes from now. I really wish you'd all leave." No one moved. St. Cyr shook his head. "All right. I want everyone on the other side of the Cherwell no later than eight o'clock." He looked at West. "Including you, Dean West. Okay?" West nodded.

The sound of many footsteps reached them. Pamela looked north past Exeter's chapel, and watched as a wide column of boys wearing white robes entered Radcliffe Square and surrounded the Camera. Their leader separated himself from the group and approached. He nodded to St. Cyr, and bowed to Dean West. "We have come to help you," said Imam Akhem. "We await your instructions."

West stared at the Imam for a minute, a bemused expression on his face. "Thank you, Akhem," he said at last. He pointed at St. Cyr. "Our friend here says we can work until eight o'clock. Will you go then?"

"We shall return to our cells at eight o'clock."

West nodded. "Very well. Let's get started." They turned toward the Camera.

St. Cyr looked at Pamela. "Don't let him disappear."

Pamela followed West up the staircase. She looked at her watch. Barak Khan – Ahmed Zhev – would be in Oxford soon, waiting for her to bring him the book. He would be unhappy when she didn't produce it, but she no longer cared.

ABRAM KHAN looked around the windowless room. The books on the shelves gave silent testimony to the disuse for which it had been selected. A complete set of the 1932 edition of the *Encyclopedia Britannica* occupied the shelves directly in front of him, and first editions of *Gaudy*

Night and *Zuleika Dobson* – their pages uncut – had been awarded pride of place on a shelf by themselves. The only newspaper in the room, probably left by a new member who had wandered in by mistake, had ceased publication three years earlier. Only the staff at White's seemed aware of its "library" – fresh flowers rose from a cut glass vase in the center of a round table – but, judging from the dust on the tables and shelves, even their attention had waned.

The door opened. He stood up. "Charles."

Wellbourne remained in the doorway for a moment, then crossed the threshold and closed the door. He took Khan's hand in both of his and smiled. "A.K. Back from the dead. Your talents are boundless."

"No talent required. Just good timing." They sat down at a table behind a low set of shelves. "Today is Day Seven, Charles. St. Cyr has asked me to help him. He believes that the Aylesbury bomb means that a bomb at Oxford is likely as well." Wellbourne nodded. Khan withdrew an envelope from his pocket. "He spoke to you yesterday about a new map?"

"Yes."

Khan slid the envelope across the table. "He wants to know if the marking pens are the same." Wellbourne nodded, picked up the envelope and started to rise. "There's something else." He sat back down. "It's important to me that you keep it to yourself, at least for a few days." Wellbourne nodded again. "A man whose passport says that he is Barak Khan is now in England. Do you know him?"

Wellbourne hesitated. "Yes."

"And you know who he really is?"

"Yes."

Khan handed him the pictures. "That same man spent twenty minutes aboard *Victoria* just before she sailed, didn't he?" Wellbourne shuffled through the photographs. "St. Cyr and I have looked at the White Star film. Zhev is easy to spot. It's beyond belief that the British government didn't recognize the chief of ISI." Wellbourne said nothing. "Why wasn't it disclosed? Why was there no investigation?"

Wellbourne gazed at him steadily. "I don't know the answers, A.K. The investigation was over when we took office. I only heard of that film when my people reported back from the evacuation meeting. There's no copy in the government's file and no mention of it. I spoke with the White Star people this morning."

"What did they say?"

"They said that the government's representative confiscated their only copy four years ago."

"Who was that?"

"The Duke of Aylesbury."

They sat in silence. "Do you know where Zhev is now?" said Khan.

"He's in his suite at the Savoy Hotel."

Khan rose. "How long will it take you to analyze the marking pens?"

"I should have it for you sometime this evening."

I HOPED that Khan's mission to London would answer the last few questions. Wellbourne had actively interfered with the task he had asked me to perform, but I didn't know if it was politics or something else. It would be harder for him to lie to Khan.

I pulled the list from my pocket. I didn't expect to find the bomb – I had given up on that when Wellbourne's troops failed to appear – but I was still looking for the who and the why, and I had recently added a new place to the list. I walked up Catte Street to Broad and stood contemplating the Master's Lodgings. There were no lights and no sign that anyone was around. The door was locked. I couldn't reach the first floor windows and, since the Lodgings were part of a solid block of buildings that formed the south wall of Balliol's oldest quadrangle, gaining entrance from the rear would be complicated. Time was limited, so I deferred my scrutiny of Markham's quarters and turned toward University Parks. Akhem and his students were at Radcliffe Square – I would inspect the College of the Prophet Muhammad in their absence.

The prayer hall at the Prophet's college was a rectangle more than six hundred feet long and four hundred feet wide. The aisles were created by double stone arches and hundreds of pillars made of onyx, jasper and granite. It had a honeycomb dome in the center of the ceiling and dozens of gilded prayer niches. Conceding again the futility of a one-man search, I poked around for a little while and moved on to the Caliph's residence.

It was spare to the point of asceticism, and there was no place to hide anything. I rummaged through a few drawers and examined the titles in the bookcase. About to leave, I opened a closet door absently, my mind on the meeting between Khan and Wellbourne. There was nothing inside but a few clothes hanging from a rod. I pushed them aside, revealing a small brown suitcase. About to close the door, I stopped – the image of a *small suitcase* stayed with me. I smiled and looked again. It wasn't really hidden, it was just sitting there. I nudged it with my foot – it didn't move. A moment later, the suitcase lay open on Akhem's desk. I twisted a few knobs carefully and removed the top of the metal casing. I was unfamiliar with much of what the shell contained, and perplexed by its careless hiding place, but one thing appeared certain – I had stumbled on the Oxford bomb.

<>< ><>

ANTHONY MARKHAM gazed at the stone in the fading light:

JAMES ALBERT MARKHAM
1937-1955

His death was the beginning – Christmas Day, nearly twenty-five years earlier. The rituals at the Abbey and The Downs were over and the four of them – he and James, and Gabrielle, and little Guin – had taken refuge in the chapel. A strange winter thunderstorm had come up suddenly – lightning followed immediately by the sharp crack of thunder seemed to strike the ground all around them – and rain and sleet driven horizontal by the wind pelted the leaded windows. James had lighted the candles, and they built a fire in the alcove that their father used as a study.

They had perched on the pews in silence, quailed by the ferocity of the storm.

It was Gabrielle who spoke first. "Shall we be married here, James?"

James, seated next to her in the front pew, answered: "Of course, if that's what you want."

Markham recalled his surprise. That they would marry might have been patent to everyone else, but somehow it had never occurred to him. Gabrielle was not yet sixteen, and James would never be a man no matter how long he lived. The title, the Abbey and Gabrielle would be his only because of an accident of birth. James deserved none of them and would do them no honor. He would join the jaded throng in London, leaving the Abbey empty and untended and, if he managed children at all, they would be just like him. James's warped preferences and sordid associations would bring her shame, and his death had saved Gabrielle from that inevitable ignominy.

He turned from the grave and made his way to the forlorn little gatehouses where he had parked the car. There were two more stops to make – another graveyard and the post office.

An hour later he was on the Oxford Road headed southwest. On the far side of Thame he joined the London Road, now moving in a more northerly direction, to Headington. He turned the main question over in his mind. St. Cyr lived. Was he in Aylesbury or London, safely away from the coming devastation, or was he still trying to prevent it? There was really no reason for him to persevere. Oxford was empty of people and abandoned by its masters, but St. Cyr had lost Gabrielle and Guin in the run-up, and it was unlikely that he would withdraw before the end.

Although Headington was well outside the range of the threat, its streets were deserted. He thought of Guin and those long ago days before despair set in. Markham had been sixteen and Guin only twelve when their father died. A succession of relations passed through Aylesbury, and the butler and housekeeper had provided more guidance than normal, but by the time he left for Oxford he was indisputably the Duke of Aylesbury in fact as well as name. He lived in college but returned to the Abbey once a week to see that his instructions were followed. He hosted lavish house parties at Aylesbury and more intimate entertainments at Belgrave Square. He accepted memberships at the Empire Club and White's and, when he turned twenty-one, he donned the ermine and claimed the time-honored seat of Aylesbury in the House of Lords.

Guin trailed after him everywhere and, since they had only themselves, they grew close. A few days before he went up to Oxford, he enrolled her at Rye St. Antony, a Catholic school for girls in Headington. Twice a week he left his rooms at Balliol and cycled to her school, located on a high plateau less than a mile east of Magdalen Bridge, where he lunched with his little sister and advised her of his progress with whatever was at hand. She thrilled at his triumphs and dismissed his defeats. On Friday afternoons, they met at Oxford Station for the ride to Aylesbury. If they remained in Oxford, he engaged a suite at the Randolph Hotel. She was often on his arm at gaudies and boat races and bump suppers, and the myriad other social occasions that graced the Oxford calendar. At sixteen, she was a lovely girl and, when she began her sixth form year at Rye two years later, she was a beautiful woman. Many Oxonians, unaware of their family ties, exclaimed at the matching comeliness of the young couple.

By the time she left school, Guin was also mistress of Aylesbury Abbey. She dealt with the servants, planned the meals and invited the guests. Moreover, when work and politics kept Markham away, she made the decisions necessary for the operation of the estate. At first, she spoke to him before deciding, then she explained it after the decision was made and, finally, she did what she felt was needed and discussed it with him if he asked. When he gave it any thought at all, he welcomed the respite from the drudgery. Orphans, they had gained strength from each another, but the malice sown so many years before had continued to flourish unnoticed, like bittersweet nightshade in a forgotten forest. It had ripened into hatred and madness, and left him alone.

He parked the car on St. Clement's and walked across Magdalen Bridge. As a young man this place had filled him with delight, but now there was only dread. The fairy tale landscape – the towers and castles and cathedrals – was no longer sufficient to cloak what Oxford had become. As he climbed the steps to the Master's Lodgings, he glanced at his watch – seven o'clock. He and St. Cyr had just more than two hours.

Inside, he passed through the house to the library. After building a fire he noticed the unopened letter on his desk. It was identical to the others – a square brown envelope with several mauve stamps. The cancellation was a blue outline of the India Gate encircled by the words

"National Capital Territory of Delhi." He reached for the letter opener and hesitated. Each one was harder to open than the last.

The sojourn on the Asian sub-continent had come at the lowest ebb in his life, a time when the effort to subdue his demons and sustain his family seemed irrevocably lost. At the same moment, he was a stranger. The mask he wore was unknown to the people around him and he relaxed his self-imposed vigil, a decisive sin for which he was duly punished. He was still surprised at the lack of regret.

He sliced the envelope open. The script was precise but the ink was faint, as if it hurt to press down on the paper.

> *My Dear Tony,*
> *This is my last goodbye. I know because the past few days have become more perfect – I see and hear things like a child. Colors are more vivid, sounds are sharper, pain sweeter. I covet the pain now – without it, I'm nothing. I go to my god, whoever he is, with your name on my lips. Forgive me.*

He remained seated behind his desk for a long time, recalling the pleasure and panic of being himself and the man responsible for it. Shaken from his reverie by the chimes of the clock, he opened a drawer and withdrew a stack of square brown envelopes. Turning to the fireplace he dropped them – one at a time – into the flames. The mask was back in place, and evidence of another life was unwise.

◇◇◇

KHAN AWAITED me on the street. The gardens were swathed in yellow police tape, and the authorities had left a sign on the front door threatening severe consequences to anyone who entered. The doors and windows were locked again. I peered through the branches of the chestnut tree. "The window's still broken," I said. "Why don't you climb up there and let us in." A moment later we were seated once more at Cromwell's desk. The suitcase, its deadly contents disarmed, sat on the floor beside me. Khan related his conversation with Wellbourne. Leaning back in the chair, I said, "Why would Markham hide the White Star film?"

"I don't know. Why did he show it at the Sheldonian?"

I didn't answer. Instead, I opened one of the drawers and withdrew a white envelope. "This is the same type of envelope that was used for the letters and the doomsday note. Map number two came in one of these as well." I paused. "The block lettering on all of them was identical. The paper's the same, too. If the marking pens match, it proves they all came from the same place."

"That points to Cromwell again."

"That's the obvious conclusion, certainly, but it's too easy. Would Cromwell just leave this stuff lying around?" I stopped. "I received something else in one of these envelopes, something that only Markham could have. He might have planted the envelopes and stationery here. And the drawings."

"But –"

"There's another thing. I have Akhem's translation of the doomsday note." I took it from my pocket and laid it on the desk. "And yet, Tony read it verbatim on television last night. How could he have done that unless he wrote it?"

"But why would he risk it? He must know that you'd figure it out."

"He thinks I'm dead." We sat quietly. "So the question is," I said at last, "is Tony a real bomber or only a pretend one? Is the game still on or not?"

"You said last night that he would never destroy Oxford. And you can't believe that he would blow up Aylesbury Abbey and – and everything."

I nodded. "But the map that predicts the bomb at the Abbey and the one here came in one of these envelopes with the same printing as the others."

Khan rose and looked across the garden at the summerhouse framed by the sinking red sun. "Those envelopes are everywhere, and anyone could have done the printing." He paused. "I just don't believe it." He turned and pointed at the bomb. "And what about that? Markham wouldn't just stick it in a closet. Maybe he's right. Maybe Akhem's the bomber."

I shook my head. "Akhem wouldn't blow up the Mosque, and there's nothing to link him to *Victoria* or Aylesbury." I picked up the telephone and handed it to him. "Let's see what Wellbourne has to say."

Three minutes later, Khan replaced the receiver on its cradle. "The marking pens on map number two are the same as all the others." He stopped. "And Zhev is still in London."

"Do you believe that he's is capable of orchestrating this charade?" He shook his head. "If you're right, that leaves Cromwell or Markham or someone else. Cromwell's dead."

"But – he could've set it all up before he died."

"Yes, but let's consider the other alternatives. That means Tony Markham, since we have no clue about someone else."

"All right. Just because he played the game doesn't mean that he's the bomber."

"What about the film?"

"Why would he blow up the Abbey? And Guin and Gerry?"

I felt a tremendous weariness as the emotions that had blinded me for so long finally gave way. A thought that I had refused to consider – festering to one degree or another since my conversation with Soleil beside Gabrielle's tombstone – forced itself to the front of my brain. "Have you been following Markham's crusade against the Black Sheik?" He nodded. "He's already the most popular man in the country. If he manages to turn the people against the Muslims and the government, he'll be the most powerful man as well."

"So?"

"Guin and Gabrielle both knew something that might have derailed his plans."

"What?"

I shook my head. Carnal knowledge of his sister and the twisted truth about Gerry's birth would be fatal to

Markham's ambitions, and there was probably something more. Gabrielle was carrying the child that should have been his, and Guin planned to make Gerry the fourteenth duke. Their deaths seemed petty in a way, but for a man on a mission nothing was unthinkable. It was all very medieval, reminiscent of the machinations of his favorite Tudor king. "It's not important now."

"Not important?"

"Not to us."

"But – surely all this killing, whatever the reason, is a little extreme?"

"Apparently not. And the attacks doubled as evidence of the Muslim problem."

"Where would he get the bombs?"

"I think it started with Cromwell. He recognized Zhev on board *Victoria* because he had sold Zhev the plans for the bomb, just like Markham said. Markham learned about it somehow – maybe from Guin – and confronted Zhev when he was in Pakistan." I paused. "I think he threatened to expose Zhev for dealing in the stolen plans, and forced him to place the bomb on *Victoria*."

"What about the game?"

"That was for me, mainly, and it also bolstered his campaign against the Muslims."

We were quiet. "You were supposed to be in both places," he said. "Was he trying to kill you, too?"

"I don't know."

"Why warn you with the map?"

"I don't know. Just playing the game, maybe."

We sat without speaking. "It's too – fantastic," Khan said at last. "What are you going to do?"

"I'm going to pay a visit to the Master's Lodgings at Balliol."

MOONLIGHT FLOODED the landscape as I crossed the Broad and climbed the steps. I turned the knob – it was unlocked. I pushed through the door and walked down the passageway to the library. The soft light of the lamps gave the room a warm glow, and a fire popped and crackled in the fireplace. Markham sat behind his desk, a gleaming revolver on the polished wood before him. "Come in, St. Cyr. I've been expecting you."

"Oh?"

"Pamela called this morning." He smiled at my expression. "We've been close for many years, St. Cyr. She told me that the party had moved to The Downs."

"Except for Guin and Gerry."

"Yes." He picked up the gun. "Sit down."

I sat in the leather armchair next to his desk. The skin on his face was tight and full of shadows, like a skull. The mutation, or revelation, of the man I had loved was complete. "I see your hand is better." He smiled but didn't respond. "Were you trying to kill me, too?"

He rose and began to make a drink using only his left hand – he carried the revolver in his right. "Scotch and ice?"

"Yes."

He looked over his shoulder. "I don't need to search your pockets, do I?"

"No."

"Good." He handed me a glass and returned to his chair. "I approached Gabrielle when she came back from the Sorbonne. I believe that she would have relented. There are worse things than being the Duchess of Aylesbury. Then you came along." He paused. "I assumed that you were on board *Victoria*. When you survived, I made other arrangements." He smiled. "I thought I might need you but now – I don't."

"So you killed all those people?" He didn't respond. "What about Oxford, then? Why the evacuation?"

"I don't want death to overshadow what's going to happen to Oxford."

"And Guin?"

"She seduced me and spawned a weakling. She was going with you."

We sat quietly. The relentless pounding inside my head told of my personal loss but I knew that wasn't the worst of it. Sacrificing a thousand lives to kill one or two *was* terrorism and Markham was the terrorist. I decided to provoke him. "She told me that you *failed* with Gabrielle."

"That's a lie," he said calmly. "I never had the opportunity." He laid the gun on his desk. "Guin hated her. She arranged for Gabrielle to find us in the chapel."

"But how could you – she was your *sister.*"

He nodded. "Yes. And she's made my life very hard since we were children."

I gave voice to another idea taking root in my brain. "Why did you kill James?"

He stared. "I knew she would betray me." He looked away. "There's a Roman aqueduct on the far side of the church at Aylesbury. One Christmas Day, when the water was high, I pushed James through the opening and watched him drown. He screamed and cried and thrust his arms toward me. I could have pulled him out but I didn't. When the screaming stopped, I turned around and saw her."

So there was another reason for Guin to die. James's murder had made his younger brother the Duke of Aylesbury, a man now on the brink of matchless power. The older boy's sexuality – anathema to Markham, the sort of thing that epitomized the decadence he scorned – had furnished an excuse to kill him, and any suspicion that Markham himself might share it would be ruthlessly suppressed. Cavorting in public with "Susan" and "Alice" would show the world that Tony was the man he said he was. "What did she do?"

"Nothing. And she didn't say anything, either. She just stared at me with those big black eyes. She was ten."

"Did she threaten you?"

He shook his head. "She never said a word. But whenever I refused to go along with her, she just looked at me the same way and I understood." He paused. "I stopped disagreeing with her about anything until Gabrielle. She made sure my engagement blew up." He stopped again. "We were bound by blood and death, and that's the way she liked it."

"She said she was afraid. Why?"

"I told her that I would kill Gerry before he became Duke."

We were silent again. "You can't possibly get away with this."

"I think you're wrong." He glanced at the clock on the mantel. "It'll all be over in forty minutes, and they won't be looking for me."

I rose and poured more scotch. "Why do you want to destroy Oxford?"

"I'm not going to destroy Oxford. We've seeded the cobalt weapon to increase the duration of the fallout. There will be minimal destruction, and the radiation will last much longer." He paused. "The bulk of the structures, the books, all of it, will be preserved inside a cloud of poison."

"A hundred years of fog?" He nodded. "But why?"

"Oxford's just a bauble for the politicians now, a place where nothing is excellent and an ever lower level of mindless mediocrity is enforced. We need to start over." He leaned forward. "The people will be able to see it, and maybe one day they'll understand what's been lost."

Conviction had become mania. His beliefs had been rejected. He would play God and use their science to force them to reconsider. The clock chimed the half hour. "I found the bomb, Tony." He stared at me. "In Akhem's rooms."

He shook his head. "No."

"But –"

"You were mostly right about Cromwell, St. Cyr. He really was in the bomb business. He and Zhev have been partners since *Victoria*. They sold one to the Black Sheik last week." He stopped. "The Mosque is a good place to hide it, I suppose. Or maybe the sheik planned to blow it up. They don't always see eye to eye." He stopped again. "The range of the cobalt weapon is precisely the same as the others. It's been planted on the roof at Carfax. The other bomb is in the Parks."

"Two bombs?"

"Yes."

"Why?"

"Because I want to preserve Oxford and destroy the cancer that infects it."

"Why kill all those boys?"

"They will die because of their – inevitability. They could have gone with everyone else. They chose to remain." He picked up the gun.

My mind worked furiously. "So bombs are now your weapon of choice. Like Wellbourne and – Guy Fawkes." He smiled. "You've murdered Guin and Gabrielle with a coward's weapon. Why not kill me with – honor?"

He sat motionless, looking down at the desk, then lifted his eyes. "All right." He rose and crossed the room to the sabers on the wall. He took one down and tossed it to me. "I'll give your honor a chance if you'll promise me something."

"What is it?"

"Give me your word that if you survive, you will accept the consequences."

What did that mean? I hesitated. He began to grow agitated, and the ticking of the clock grew louder. "All right. You have my word."

He hefted the other saber and slipped the gun into his pocket. "If you win, you'll have a choice. The bombs are set up on a detonator and a timer. If the detonator isn't used, both weapons will explode when old Tom is finished tonight." He paused. "The detonator has two buttons. Blue for old Oxford." He smiled. "*Our* Oxford. Red for new Oxford. The selected bomb will explode after Tom's last chime and the other will be disarmed. "

"Why the two buttons?"

"I told myself that I might change my mind, but that wasn't it. I believe I hoped it would come to something like this, and you would need an incentive. You can save Oxford if you kill me."

"Where's the detonator?"

He didn't answer. Instead, he opened the doors and stepped into the garden. "There's a full moon tonight," he called. "We won't need the lights."

I weighed the saber in my hand. It was much larger and heavier than a fencing saber, and its curved blade had only a single, razor-sharp edge. Designed as a slashing weapon wielded from horseback, it was completely unsuitable for the combat we were about to begin. The only redeeming feature was its purpose – it was made to kill, and it was unlikely that both of us would live. A lust for blood, a primitive hunger that should have been purged eons ago, swept over me.

I went to the doorway. Markham stood in the middle of a brick courtyard surrounded by a boxwood hedge. Oxford's vapors swirled about his feet, and I could smell the grass and the gardens. "I'm glad we've worked this out, St. Cyr." He finished his drink and threw the glass over the hedge. "I can't lose." He raised the saber and came toward me.

The clash of the heavy blades was like a smith's hammer on his anvil. He cut across my chest. I leaped backwards but not before the saber penetrated my flesh. I felt the blood oozing down my belly. He touched me again, this time at my waist, but the blade caught only cloth. Two more light touches, on my arm and neck, drew blood. He was playing with me. I had to end it quickly or he would pick me to pieces. I thrust at his left side, a useless effort because of the saber's design. He parried it automatically and dipped his blade just as he had the last time we fought, in the Long Gallery at Aylesbury Abbey. His upper body was exposed. I slashed at his shoulder but, whether from the weight of the weapon or his superior skill, he somehow turned it aside and, in the same motion, drew his blade across my thigh. I fell to one knee as blood poured from the wound.

Markham stood for a moment, watching me as I tried to rise. He looked at his watch. "Twenty-five minutes to go, St. Cyr. It should be quite a show. I'm sorry you'll miss it." He raised the saber over his head with both hands – executioner now, fencing forgotten. As he brought it down I, too, grasped my sword with two hands and lunged toward him with all my strength. The point of the blade pierced his belly and slid into his chest like a fish hook. The saber fell from his hands and we collapsed together, his arms around my neck. Our blood mingled on the bricks and soaked into the soil beneath them.

I felt my life ebbing from the wound to my thigh. "Tony?"

He opened his eyes. "Well – done, St. Cyr."

"Where's the detonator?"

"Remember your promise."

"Tony, please. Where's the detonator?"

He smiled. "Look inside my head, St. Cyr. And choose." His eyes glazed over.

I rolled away from him and crawled to the door. Everything was gray. I glanced wildly around the library and began to pull myself toward the fireplace. The door on the other side of the room opened just before the gray turned to black. "Fitz!"

CHAPTER TEN

KHAN SAT on a narrow bench, hidden in the shadow beneath the roof of the Pavilion's porch. He watched the white-robed students, led by their Imam, pass by and disappear into the darkness of the Mosque. He pondered their belief. Their presence at the Prophet's college ensured that their visible lives accorded with his teachings, but what did they *think*? Had they feigned obedience in order to come to this place, or had Oxford caused them to doubt? Or were they like him, and Zhev, men who – because of birth or circumstance – were never required to believe and, like the few everyday Christians at Christ Church or Magdalen, paid only lip service to the creed that claimed them? Was it better to truly believe or just pretend?

Zhev was responsible for the violent death of many people and, yet, Zhev prayed at the mosques and spoke with the Imams. He wondered again if it was all a sham, if the mosques and Imams and billions of believers had been invented, not to glorify their god but to exploit their fellow man. Invented by whom? He smiled – that was always the question that troubled him most.

He stood up and turned for the steps. A shadow fell across the path and he drew back. Pamela passed within a few yards of him and walked toward the gate. Confused, he started to call out and stopped. Why was she here? After a moment he followed her.

He had lied to St. Cyr. Zhev was not in London. He was in Oxford, most likely at the Imam's quarters directly in front of him. What would he know? Would Khan still be the dutiful son, Zhev's emissary charged with keeping Pakistan's nose clean? Or was he the vengeful brother, anxious for the destruction of his sister's killer and maybe something more? He opened the door.

His questions were answered immediately. Zhev sat bolt upright on the other side of the room, a pistol pointed straight at him. Pamela stood beside him. "Abram," he called. "You're just in time. Sit down." Khan stepped into the room. Akhem was behind his desk. Khan chose a chair beside him. "I was just telling Akhem that Allah won't save him." He glanced at his watch. "In about fifteen minutes this place will be dust." He turned his head toward Pamela. "Where's the book?"

"I –"

Khan interrupted. "Are you going to die with us?"

Zhev smiled. "I have a car outside. We'll be well out of range when the bomb explodes."

"We?"

Zhev looked at Pamela. "Did you bring the book?"

"Is it true?" said Akhem. Khan nodded. Akhem rose.

"What's the matter, Akhem?" said Zhev. "Lost your faith?" There was no reply. "I can't have you running around loose. You should have gone with the infidels." Akhem turned for the door. Zhev lifted the gun and fired twice. Akhem fell back into his chair, then slumped to the floor.

"**FITZ.**" **I** opened my eyes and stared into hers. "Thank God," she whispered.

I drank from the decanter she held to my lips. "My leg —"

"I've tried to bandage it, but we need to find a doctor."

I shook my head. "What time is it?"

"Five minutes to nine."

"We have to go." I started to rise. Pain shot through me like the blade in Markham's gut, and I lost my balance and fell.

"Fitz!" she screamed. "Please!" The blood began again. I reached for the desk with both hands and pulled myself up. Her face was streaked with tears.

"We have ten minutes, Gill." I leaned against the desk and unbuttoned my shirt. "We have to stop the blood." I handed her the shirt and pointed to the fireplace. The poker lay across the hearth, the bottom half propped against the grate in the middle of the flames. "Use the poker." She stared at me. "Go on. I'll be okay." I slid along the edge of the desk and fell into a chair.

"Fitz, I don't think —"

"Gill." I looked at the clock. "You have to."

She wrapped the shirt around her hand and seconds later the room was filled with a high-pitched scream and the stench of burning flesh. She sobbed uncontrollably. Blood trickled down my outstretched leg. "Do it again."

"Fitz, please —"

"Do it again! We're going to die anyway. It doesn't matter." Still crying, she applied the poker again, and then a third time. My brain flickered from gray to black and back again. I reached for her. "Help me up." All the bells in Oxford chimed as we passed through the front door – all but one, the loudest. Using the stair rail for support, I hopped down to the sidewalk. I was sure that Markham's "head" was only a few paces away. "Come on."

I leaned on her as we crossed Broad Street. "Where are we going?" she said.

"Not far." We passed the gate at the Sheldonian and stopped in front of the last pillar on the left. I rested against the iron fence and looked up. The thirteenth Emperor seemed to smile in the moonlight. "Stand under me, Gill. Give me a boost if I need it." Using only my arms, I drew myself to the top of the fence and maneuvered my legs so that the great limestone head was in my lap. There were steel latches on either side of the skull. I loosened them. The chime of a single bell, a sound that I had heard thousands of times and barely noticed, reached my ears. I divided my brain.

One, two, three . . .

I lifted the heavy stone cap and pushed it to the ground. A black metal box rested inside the cavity. There was a blue button and a red button. I had pondered the options as Markham presented them. Get to Carfax somehow, and find the bomb? No. There wasn't time, and the other bomb would be unaffected. Abandon the field, and permit both weapons to explode? No. Too many people would die. Find the detonator and choose a button? Which button?

Ten, eleven, twelve . . .

I chose.

Fifteen, sixteen, seventeen . . .

I lifted my good leg over what remained of the giant head and fell to the ground. Gill helped me up. "Run for the canoe," I said. "There's an opening on the other side of –"

"No."

"Gill, please –"

"No." She leaned against my bare chest. "I'm not leaving you."

Twenty-five, twenty-six, twenty-seven . . .

"All right." We turned west together, Gill propping me up as I hopped and dragged my useless leg behind me. We passed Trinity and Balliol, and crossed Magdalen to George Street.

Thirty-six, thirty-seven, thirty-eight . . .

I tripped and fell at the corner of Gloucester Street and George. She picked me up again.

Fifty, fifty-one, fifty-two . . .

I stopped when we reached the bell turret at the old Boys' High School. "Gill, please. Go ahead." She shook her head. "I'll come. I promise. Find the canoe. Drag it to the other side of the bridge." She hesitated. "I'll be there. I promise." She ran toward the bridge.

Sixty-three, sixty-four, sixty-five . . .

There were still fifty yards to go. I could see her ahead of me, pulling the boat across the road.

Seventy-four, seventy-five, seventy-six . . .

I grabbed for the bow of the canoe and fell again. Struggling to rise, I searched for the opening. "There," I said, pointing. We pushed into the water. "Get in." I thrust the boat into the tunnel and followed it.

Eighty-eight, eighty-nine, ninety . . .

"Fitz! Where are –"

I rolled into the canoe. "I'm here, I'm here. It's okay." I handed her a paddle. "Try to keep us off the edges." We plunged into the pitch-black sanctuary beneath the ancient town.

One hundred, one hundred and one . . .

"Why did you send me here?" said Khan.

"You were supposed to look after my interests. I didn't realize your devotion to your depraved little sister."

Khan looked down at Akhem's body. "You think *Aden* was depraved?" Zhev didn't answer. "Who told you about me?"

"Markham. And he said that you had survived the bomb at Aylesbury."

"The Brits know about *Victoria* now," Khan said. Zhev frowned and looked at Pamela again. "*I* found the book. I delivered the photos to the Home Secretary this morning."

Zhev pointed the gun at Pamela. "Is that true?" She didn't answer. "Do *you* have them?" She shook her head. Zhev smiled. "Well, I guess I'll be leaving alone." He looked back at Khan. "It won't matter."

"Why not?"

"Too many important people are involved." Zhev laughed. "It's not the sort of thing they'll want to get out. The government would certainly fall." He paused. "After tonight the whole thing will be swept under the rug."

They sat quietly. Zhev glanced at his watch. "It's getting late," he said, and started to rise.

"What happened to my father?"

He smiled and resumed his seat. "Your mother was a very beautiful woman. Your father was a drunk and a whoremonger. She deserved better."

Khan picked up the Imam's onyx ball and rolled it in his hands. "So?"

"So I suggested that there might be extra rations and maybe a virgin or two if something happened to him." The sound of a distant bell suddenly filled the room, its notes continuing one after another, many more than necessary to toll the time. They listened carefully. "I really must be going," said Zhev. He stood up, the pistol pointed at the floor. Khan rose as well. Zhev smiled again. "I'm sorry Abram. I can't take you with me." He brought the gun up.

Pamela flung herself at Zhev. As he swung the pistol toward her, Khan's right arm whirled in a blurred vertical arc. Instinctively, he shortened his delivery – it began at his waist and ended at the top of the arc – which diminished the speed and raised the angle of the ball. The onyx orb struck Zhev squarely on the forehead and he dropped to the floor. Khan crossed the room and knelt beside him. Zhev's skull was shattered, and fragments of bone had been driven deep into the tissue behind it. Blood leaked from the wound and filled the open eyes. There was no pulse. He picked up the ball and slipped it into his pocket. He looked at her. "Are you all right?"

"Yes."

They walked outside. The bell was louder, more insistent. He closed his eyes. How many were left? Could they escape? He shook his head. He didn't know which way to go. Pamela took his arm and they walked through the gate together. The Prophet's students, still in their robes, slowly gathered around them.

Great Tom sounded the last note. When Khan understood that there would be no more, he raised his eyes and braced for the blast. A mist rose from the center of the village and a terrifying noise, like the beginning crackle of thunder many times over, reached their ears. At first the mist mingled with the vapors from the rivers but, as it enveloped the walls and the towers and the spires, it changed colors – yellow first, then red, then black. The sound changed, too. It was now an increasing, other-worldly roar, rising to a crescendo as the dark cloud climbed into the sky.

They watched as the mist rolled toward them. It slowed at Jowett Walk, and stopped altogether before South Parks Road. A billowing black blanket obscured the landscape and, suddenly, the moon appeared and made it silver. The crackle and roar had lasted only a few seconds. As the reverberations faded away, a perfect silence fell upon the bleak tableau, and the mist became tiny sparkles of dust that began to settle to the ground. Like fabulous monuments in a colossal graveyard, the spires and towers and walls emerged from the fog, seemingly untouched by the violence of a moment before. The old town – coated now in silver dust – still stood, etched into the horizon by the moonlight. "It's still there," Pamela said.

Khan shook his head. "Only the buildings, Pamela. Oxford is dead."

"But –"

"Look closer." The moon was brilliant. "Look at that tree." The Scholar Tree, its foliage glowing in the early evening light only a few hours before, was bare, and its gray bark – darker now – seemed to smolder. The naked branches – crooked, broken ladders to the sky – beseeched the heavens. "Nothing's alive. It's all gray now." Old Oxford, a sepia newsreel for ten centuries, was now a black-and-white photograph frozen in time, a place where history had stopped. The new people – unshackled from the old at last – would have their chance, encumbered only by those gray bones on the horizon. He turned away from the desolate skyline. Would new Oxford be here in a thousand years?

It was not the explosion that Khan had expected, and he was surprised that he and Pamela and the boys standing about them had been spared. Had their faith paid off? He smiled to himself. Perhaps – with someone's help. He spoke to the student beside him and they passed once more into the Prophet's college. He pointed to the Imam's rooms. "Your Imam is dead," he said, "and so is the man who killed him. Take care of their bodies. I'll notify the authorities." He looked at her. "What happened to the others?"

"I left them at the Camera."

He took her hand. The key to Zhev's car was still in the ignition. He turned in the direction of Aylesbury, anxious to know who else had survived.

I WAS floating somewhere – not on the Cherwell or the Isis, certainly not on the underground stream that had preserved my life. No, I was drifting on a cloud, delivered to a painless heaven by injections and pills that made life tolerable. I barely heard the medical jargon about infusions and infections and skin grafts, and nodded every time someone offered me more dope. It kept the darkness at bay.

A VOICE close to my ear said, "It looks like we'll have to amputate."

I opened my eyes. "The hell you will."

Khan laughed. I heard Gill's voice. "Khan, you jackass, leave him alone. He needs to rest."

"He's been resting for ten days. He needs to get off his duff."

The room came into focus. Pamela leaned over me. "How are you, St. Cyr?"

I couldn't answer for a moment. "I'm – all right, I guess." I was flat on my back. I tried to push myself up.

"No," said Gill. "Stop. Let me help you."

A moment or two later, I was sitting up. Khan put a hand on my shoulder. "How's the leg?"

I had to think about it for a few seconds. "I guess it's okay." I turned my head. "It is, isn't it?"

"Yes, as long as you do what the doctors say," said Gill. "And what I say."

Khan laughed again. "That sounds like a long convalescence to me."

"Abram, stop," said Pamela. She gave me a chaste kiss. "Thank you. I still don't understand what you did, but no one was hurt except –" She glanced at the others. "We're all still here."

"What's happened?"

Khan looked at Gill. She and Pamela left the room. "Zhev is dead," Khan said. "So are Markham and Imam Akhem."

I nodded. "What about Oxford?"

"It's drenched with radioactive dust. The radiation is so intense that, even with all the protective gear on, no one can stay more than an hour or two. There's talk of a clean-up, but that's probably just talk. They say it'll be decades before it dissipates."

"Who's being blamed?"

"Cromwell and Zhev. And the Muslims. They found a copy of map number two at the sheik's church and arrested him. There've been riots all over the country." He paused. "They've gutted the Mosque."

"What happened to Zhev and Akhem?"

Khan described the final scene at Akhem's quarters. I closed my eyes. "St. Cyr?"

"Yes?"

"Gill told them about the Emperor. They found the other bomb."

I opened my eyes. "Where was it?"

"In the Cricket Pavilion. About fifty meters from where we were standing."

I smiled. "I guess you owe me one."

"Why did you do it?"

"Do what?"

"Why did you push the blue button?"

"Come on, Khan. I knew those kids were still at the Mosque."

"You could have been killed. And Gill."

I shook my head. "I – we had plenty of time."

He smiled. "Was it Markham?" I nodded. "Did he tell you why?"

"He told me that the politicians had ruined *his* Oxford, and he said they needed to start over." I paused. "That wasn't exactly right."

"Why not?"

"The Oxford that he loved never existed. It was always a part of the world that he railed against." I looked away. "But I guess they'll have to start over now anyway."

Khan nodded. "That's what Pamela's doing."

"What?"

"Starting over. She and West are opening a school for poor kids in London."

"What about you?"

Khan grinned. "I'm going to help them. I'm also going to be a famous former cricket star. I might even come out of retirement." He paused. "I can't go back to Pakistan. My mother's already here."

He turned for the door. I closed my eyes again. "Khan?"

"Yes?"

"Did Gill tell you that she's the only reason I got out of there alive?"

"No. I figured that out by myself."

GILL CLOSED her book. "Hi."

"Hi."

"Welcome back."

"Thanks."

She laid the book down and reached for my hand. "Do you want to go home?" I nodded. "The doctors say we can go any time, but you still need lots of rest and rehabilitation."

I gestured toward my leg. "What's the story?"

"They've fixed the muscle in your thigh. The burns and infection caused more trouble. They're not sure it will ever be the same. I'm sorry." She stopped. "They don't want you to fly so I've booked staterooms on *Alexandra*. Is that okay?"

I nodded again. "Thanks for sticking around."

"I don't want your thanks. I want something else." She leaned over and kissed me. After a moment, she opened a drawer beside the bed and withdrew a large blue envelope. "This is addressed to 'His Grace, the Duke of Aylesbury,'" she said.

"What is it?"

"It's – I don't quite know how to say this. It seems that *you* are now the Duke of Aylesbury."

"What?"

She nodded. "I talked to one of the lawyers. He was very clear. All the legal niceties have been squared away. You are the fourteenth Duke of Aylesbury."

I shook my head. This, then, was the "consequence" I had promised to accept. Markham's fixation on his family extended beyond the grave. He had tried to kill me three times and yet – the paradox was hard to grasp. Gill reached into the envelope and found another, unopened, with a less ostentatious inscription: "St. Cyr." It was dated October 24 – Day Seven:

St. Cyr,

I invited you here to die. Since you are reading this, I presume that I have failed. You are alive and I am dead, a circumstance that I contemplate with mixed emotions. However, since your survival is now a reality, I embrace it wholeheartedly, not because I still love you but because you are the best man I know.

When I began the campaign to take my country back an intolerable situation – one that has governed my actions for too long – required resolution. I knew that I might die in the effort and I was without issue, and an old and honorable family faced extinction. I had already decided that Gerry would not follow me. Strength, of body and character, was necessary. My inability to produce an heir had tormented me for years, and my death would mean the end of the Markham line. I considered medical procedures but all required a woman, and I was loath to submit myself to those witch doctors in Harley Street. In truth, if I was going to die, I wanted to know that a worthy man would take my place.

So I turned to the law. I accomplished the first task, a private bill in Parliament that changed the law of inheritance for the Duchy, on my own. It took almost four years because I didn't want it to become public knowledge, but at last it was slipped into a catch-all bill passed routinely at the end of the last session. I relied on my solicitors to do the rest.

I have adopted you. The final papers were signed the day before the church at Aylesbury was destroyed. You are the fourteenth Duke and the owner of considerable real and personal property despite the loss of the Abbey. It passed to you automatically, but you are named in my will just to be sure.

I don't expect you to be willing or able to continue my work, but I believe you will respect the legacy I leave behind. There are things you might do to thwart me – renounce the title, give everything away, remain childless – but I would remind you of what you, rather than some government yob or charity hack, can do. You might, for example, endow a new college or build a great seat at Aylesbury. In any event, the line would end with the fourteenth Duke, not the thirteenth.

As you know, all of the evidence points to Cromwell as the bomber. In addition to those things you're aware of, I've arranged for proof of his various transactions with Ahmad Zhev and the Black Sheik to be forwarded to the Home

Office. I'm confident that the government will find them responsible. However, if some unworthy suspicion were to fall on me (if you suspected me, for instance), it's possible that the government might try to seize your property because of what has happened at Oxford. I have discussed this in great, but circumspect, detail with my solicitors and they assure me that everything becomes yours upon my death. Since I am dead and you are not, I must assume that I was penniless when Great Tom finished his chime. I hope so.

I didn't have time to organize anything for Guin and Gerry. I trust that you will see to it.

Markham

OUR DEPARTURE was unsettling. I kept my head down as we passed through the terminal at Southampton, and allowed Gill to guide me as I limped up the gangway. *Alexandra* was *Victoria's* sister and, despite the brevity of my visit four years earlier, I seemed to recognize every deck and passageway. The scenes of celebration around the ship were exactly the same, so I made my apologies to Gill and remained in my cabin until we weighed anchor. She intercepted the well-wishers – Pamela, Soleil and, surprisingly, Geoffrey North – and blamed the leg for my absence. After the ship was underway, I knocked on the door that connected our staterooms.

She opened it. "Can I buy you a drink?" I said.

"That would be wonderful. Shall I call the steward?"

"No. Let's find the nearest bar." She studied a diagram of the ship as I cast about for the new cane. We had both hated the metal version supplied by the doctors, and Gill had spent the day before searching for one more suitable. The antique cane she chose had a thick, extra-long rosewood shaft – nearly forty inches – and a horn and silver handle in the shape of a crouching lioness. She was very proud of it, and so was I, and I never mentioned the name of the woman who came to mind each time I picked it up.

"It looks like the closest one is on the lido deck next to the pool," she said.

"All right. Let's go." I followed her into the narrow hallway and we walked to the elevator lobby. Gill pushed the button. "Let's take the stairs," I said.

"Fitz –"

"I need the exercise, right?"

"Yes, but you've already –"

"It's just three flights. I can make it." I climbed the steps slowly, one at a time. It was painful, but pain wasn't the problem. The graft had been pronounced a success, but the thick layer of skin across my thigh resisted even the minor stretching exerted on it by the action of my knee. The challenge was to eventually stretch it as far as it could go which would dictate the range of motion that I could rely on. It was unlikely that I would fence again – fencing is particularly hard on thighs and knees – but my last match with Markham had dampened my enthusiasm anyway. All I wanted to do was regain the normal use of my leg – to walk and run and climb as I had done before. According to the doctors, it was a fifty-fifty proposition. "Let's sit at the bar," I said.

After we were settled, the bartender arrived. "What can I bring you?"

"I'll have a Brandy Alexander," said Gill.

He looked at me. "Plymouth martini, please. No ice, no olives." I looked around. Only a few sun-worshippers had taken up their positions around the pool, and we were alone at the bar. Knots of people crossed the open deck and passed through the double doors at either end, exploring the vast, floating hotel that would be their home for the next seven days. As I watched them, it occurred to me that I didn't know where we were going. "What happens after New York?"

"We'll take the train to Washington. Dad's sending someone to pick us up. He wants you to spend a few days at Buchanan House."

I had been helpless for more than three weeks, a circumstance not experienced since childhood, and it made me uncomfortable. "I don't think that's necessary, Gill. I can find my way home." She stared at me, then looked away. The pain in her eyes shamed me as I had never been shamed before. The thoughtless rejection of *her* wish – the tail end of the responsibility for me that she had assumed when she walked into Markham's library – was abominable. I squeezed her hand. "I'm sorry. I really am." She tried to smile. "I have no right to talk to you that way. Buchanan House will be fine."

She shook her head. "I want you to do what you want to do, Fitz. I love you the way you are. Don't – don't try to be someone else because you think you owe me." She paused. "I don't want that." She kissed me. "Let's just be ourselves for the next few days and see how it goes."

There were three new stones in the Markham family graveyard. No suspicion, unworthy or otherwise, had fallen on him. I searched the papers for some hint that Wellbourne was looking into the suppression of the White Star film, without result. The investigation had quickly narrowed to John Cromwell and Ahmad Zhev, and those supposedly in league with them. The sketch that Markham had left behind – an effete, cowardly government appeasing Muslim fanatics – was filled in by the opposition and the press.

A black-and-white photograph found in Cromwell's secretary, widely distributed in the newspapers, seemed to tie it all together. Dated a few days before *Victoria* exploded, it showed the Black Sheik standing on the steps at St. Giles' House. He held a suitcase that might or might not have been the same one that Zhev carried on board the ship. I was doubtful. The picture wasn't there when I searched Cromwell's office and, according to Markham, the sheik had left his bomb in Akhem's closet only a few weeks before, but the police and public immediately assumed that the sheik had bought the bomb from Cromwell and passed it on to Zhev.

The sheik and his followers had been rounded up. In addition to the map, a detonator wrapped in brown paper was found at St. Mark's Church. Cromwell's photographs of Zhev, unattributed, were produced, and the White Star film scrutinized. Scotland Yard confirmed the theft and sale of the plans for the bomb left at the Cricket Pavilion and discovered, with some difficulty due to the radiation, the damning proof in Cromwell's study — even the marking pens were found. I had unwittingly added to the evidence by leaving the sheik's bomb at St. Giles' House. The government had lost a vote of confidence and elections were scheduled to choose a new one. Politicians were scrambling to take Markham's place.

I knew that Cromwell was guilty of many things but not the bombing of *Victoria*, Aylesbury and Oxford. On the other hand, Anthony Markham, thirteenth Duke of Aylesbury, was a mass murderer who had planned to kill still more people. But what was my proof?

All of the evidence against Markham was in my head, and it was only conjecture until he confirmed it. Except for my brief discussion with Khan, I had told no one about that night. I made something up for the doctors, hand-picked by my former boss, who pretended to believe me and didn't ask again. Even Gill knew nothing beyond my wound and our visit to the Emperor, and I was certain that nothing inside *his* head would implicate Markham. The actual evidence all pointed to Cromwell and Zhev. I had presented my case to Khan at St. Giles' House, and he had refused to believe it. What luck would I have with one of Wellbourne's bureaucrats? My faith in the British government was at a very low ebb. The wound to my leg might raise the question of self-defense, but death in a duel was still murder.

Markham was dead, and so was Cromwell. Only their respective memories were at issue. Neither was worth the risk.

HARRY BROWNE lifted his eyes from a book and turned his head toward me. The effort to keep the shock from his face was unsuccessful, and his mouth gave him away. "What the hell happened to you?"

"You're a sensitive soul, Harry," I said. "I've been sick."

"From what?"

"Oh, I don't know. I hurt my leg and it got infected and so forth and so on. You know what it's like when the docs get hold of you."

"How much do you weigh?"

"About twenty pounds less than the last time you saw me." He had another question, but I stopped him. "How about a drink? Scotch and ice?" He closed his mouth and nodded. I climbed into one of the high chairs, avoiding the images in the mirrors. It was certainly better than it was, but I still had a long way to go.

Harry pushed my drink across the bar. "Someone told me that the Admiral's daughter followed you over there. Is that right?"

"Yes."

A customer at the other end of the bar required attention. When he returned, I said, "What are you reading?" He held up a dog-eared paperback about "courage" by his favorite politician. "Again?"

"He was a great writer for an amateur."

I laughed. "He didn't write that book, Harry. One of his flacks did."

"What are you talking about?" The next few minutes were spent in warm conversation about the virtues of the author, at the end of which he refused to discuss it further without "concrete evidence" of the literary fraud that I had suggested. He made me another drink. "You resigned from the Navy, didn't you?" I nodded. "What are you going to do?"

"I'm going into business for myself."

"Doing what?"

"Oh, you know. Whatever might require my unmatched expertise."

He grinned. "Where will you live?"

"We – I'm looking at places around here."

He gazed at me thoughtfully. "Did what's-her-name – Gill – come back with you?"

"Yes."

"Is she helping with the house hunt?" I nodded again. "And nursing you back to health?"

"As a matter of fact, she is."

A broad smile split his face. "You two must be getting along better than the last time I saw you."

I smiled, too. "Yes, Harry, we are. Much better."

SEEN FROM a very great distance, which was the only way it could be seen, the ancient village appeared much the same. Punts and barges still floated on the Cherwell and the Isis, and the white vapors that rose from the waters surrounding the Town still reached Merton's wall. The gray beauty of the old buildings remained though the scent of the moist meadows that once drifted through the gardens and the quadrangles and the walks was gone – the lawns and gardens were gray, too, and there were no

birds or butterflies or trees. Inside the gates, the grid established a thousand years before was unchanged though the gates themselves, and the walls that they opened, had long since disappeared. The Roman theater still stood and its Emperors stared across the Broad as they had for centuries, but the triumph depicted on its ceiling had been undone. Great Tom rose over Christ Church, silent now, as were all the bells. Carfax, of course, was gone.

Had God – after consulting His Bradshaw's – taken the 8:16 from Paddington, He might have been startled, just for an instant, that no one greeted Him as He stepped onto the worn gray boards of the platform. He was familiar with this place the way an old man remembers his boyhood and His companion, the Muse whose charge was History, knew it as well. The buildings and streets were all empty now – the bachelors, canons and dons were gone, and there were no scouts or porters to serve them had they remained. God and Clio would have to cross Magdalen Bridge to Cowley or Iffley, or even London, to relieve the solitude.

None of this mattered, though, because neither God nor His Muse made the journey. They had loved her when she was young and retained some affection for her into middle age, but the past few decades had been hard. She was a museum now, albeit one whose exhibits were closed to the public, and could only remind them of what had been. They were needed in newer, more hopeful, places. The black owls had perched on St. Mary's steeple and the sun that once remained always over the horizon had set, and Malice, Envy and Hatred prevailed.

THE END

Made in the USA
Lexington, KY
12 September 2013